Joan Fleming and The

>>> This title is part of The Murder Room, our series dedicated to making available out-of-print or hard-to-find titles by classic crime writers.

Crime fiction has always held up a mirror to society. The Victorians were fascinated by sensational murder and the emerging science of detection; now we are obsessed with the forensic detail of violent death. And no other genre has so captivated and enthralled readers.

Vast troves of classic crime writing have for a long time been unavailable to all but the most dedicated frequenters of second-hand bookshops. The advent of digital publishing means that we are now able to bring you the backlists of a huge range of titles by classic and contemporary crime writers, some of which have been out of print for decades.

From the genteel amateur private eyes of the Golden Age and the femmes fatales of pulp fiction, to the morally ambiguous hard-boiled detectives of mid twentieth-century America and their descendants who walk our twenty-first century streets, The Murder Room has it all. **>>>**

The Murder Room
Where Criminal Minds Meet

themurderroom.com

Joan Fleming (1908–1980)

Joan Fleming was one of the most original and literate crime writers of her generation. Born in Lancashire and educated at Lausanne University she became the wife of a Harley Street eye surgeon and mother of four, and was already a successful children's author before she turned to crime. She is the author of over thirty novels and won the CWA Gold Dagger in 1962 for *When I Grow Rich* and again in 1970 for *Young Man, I Think You're Dying*. *The Deeds of Dr Deadcert* was made into the 1958 film *Rx for Murder*.

Two Lovers Too Many
A Daisy-Chain for Satan
The Gallows in My Garden
The Man Who Looked Back
Polly Put the Kettle On
The Good and the Bad
He Ought To Be Shot
The Deeds of Dr Deadcert
You Can't Believe Your Eyes
Maiden's Prayer
Malice Matrimonial
Miss Bones
The Man from Nowhere
In the Red
When I Grow Rich
Death of a Sardine
The Chill and the Kill
Nothing is the Number When You Die

Midnight Hag
No Bones About It
Kill or Cure
Hell's Belle
Young Man I Think You're Dying
Screams From a Penny Dreadful
Grim Death and the Barrow Boys
Dirty Butter for Servants
Alas, Poor Father
You Won't Let Me Finnish
How to Live Dangerously
Too Late! Too Late! the Maiden Cried
To Make an Underworld
Every Inch a Lady

You Can't Believe Your Eyes

Joan Fleming

An Orion book

Copyright © Joan Fleming 1957

The right of Joan Fleming to be identified as the author of this work
has been asserted in accordance with the Copyright, Designs and
Patents Act 1988.

This edition published by
The Orion Publishing Group Ltd
Orion House
5 Upper St Martin's Lane
London WC2H 9EA

An Hachette UK company
A CIP catalogue record for this book is available from the British Library

ISBN 978 1 4719 0205 5

www.orionbooks.co.uk

Printed and bound by CPI Group (UK) Ltd, Croydon, CR0 4YY

This story is entirely imaginary. The houses, the people, the private company and the Pekinese are inventions of the author, and if any similarity to existing houses, people, company or Pekineses be detected it is purely co-incidental.

J.F.

Part One

THE SCENE is a house in Regent's Park, London; amongst stately blank-faced houses the guts of which have been removed and replaced by civil servants, No. 51, Park Row looks out across the park with kindly eyes, for it is still a home. Not, in truth, the family house for which Nash designed it but at least a house with shaded lights, crackling fires and a smell of cooking.

On the front door is a neat brass plate—Mr. Tobias Totterdell. But Mr. Totterdell is no longer a practising surgeon, he has withdrawn to the top half of the house, with his housekeeper Miss Emms and his Pekinese, Tiddly Push.

The bomb that fell many years ago on three houses in the crescent as Mr. Totterdell and his wife were walking home killed Mrs. Totterdell instantly. Mr. Totterdell was badly injured and later lost one leg and the foot of his other leg. His eyes also were damaged by blast. He has, however, succeeded in adjusting himself to these adversities. He has had a lift constructed so that he can go up and down at will. The house being but a few dozen yards from the park, he spends much time in the fresh air limping along beside the lake with his thick walking-stick and his black Pekinese; Mr. Totterdell is no trouble to anyone.

The lower maisonette is let to a married couple, Richard Rangward and his wife Annabel. They have no children and are looked after by a manservant called Edward Bolton.

1

The basement is occupied by a couple, presumed to be married, called Ormer. Edna works in a bakery in Marylebone Lane and Rudolph keeps the area steps clean, attends to the boiler and carries coal upstairs, and in return for this they live rent-free. In addition he is chauffeur to Mr. Rangward. There is nothing fancy about Rudolph, as his name might suggest. It was simply that his mother had a passion for Rudolph Valentino.

This, then, is the *mise en scène*, or what they prefer to call the set-up, that the police find when they are called in to investigate the murder that took place on the evening of 19th October.

One can almost hear the voice of the attorney-general, who begins his narrative always in a pleasant " once-upon-a-time-there-were-three-bears-the-daddy-bear-mummy-bear-and-the-baby-bear " manner.

" This, then," he might say, " was the household at No. 51, Park Row on the evening of 19th October. Mr. and Mrs. Rangward had just arrived home from a holiday spent with relatives at Estoril in Portugal. They were met at London Airport by Mr. Rangward's chauffeur, Ormer, who drove them home to Regent's Park. They arrived at about five-fifteen and had tea before changing for the evening. It had been arranged by letter that two friends should dine that evening with the Rangwards, and in due course they arrived. First came Mr. Charles Shefford. He was followed some twenty minutes later by Baron Anders Halvorsen, a Swedish gentleman. He had been to a cocktail party at the Swedish Embassy and apologised for his late arrival. These two gentlemen, members of the jury, were well known to their host and hostess. They had dined at No. 51, Park Row many times and could safely be called intimate friends of the Rangwards.

" On Baron Halvorsen's arrival the four took their places at the table. Members of the jury, if you will look at your plans you will see that the ground floor of No. 51 consists mainly of one large room running from back to front of the house. At one time, no doubt, there was a partition or double doors across the room, but at the present time it is divided simply by long velvet curtains which, I am told, are not drawn across. Thus the dining-room and drawing-room are virtually one. The rear half of the room is used as the dining-room and the small kitchenette conveniently adjoins it. At no time, after the arrival of Baron Halvorsen, did any of the party of four leave the room. Edward Bolton, the manservant, cooked the meal in the kitchenette and served it from there. Throughout the meal he was going in and out through the door at the end of the dining-room.

" The meal consisted of potted shrimps and slices of brown bread and butter, roast duckling with orange salad, fried potatoes and peas, Stilton Cheese and fruit. The wine served was a fine hock of which the deceased did not partake. His doctor will tell you that he suffered from dyspepsia and insomnia and had been advised to keep off alcohol for the time being. At the end of the meal port wine was served and the guests sat on at the table, smoking and talking. Mrs. Rangward left the table to attend to the drawing-room fire; she also turned on the electric gramophone and presently she danced with first one and then the other guest. Whichever guest was not dancing returned to the table and sat down with his host.

" Members of the jury, it is important that you realise just how the room was lighted With the serving of

3

the port, the dining-room wall-lights were turned out by the manservant as he left the room and closed the door behind him. Thus the dining-room half was illuminated only by the two candles on the table. This was the usual practice. The drawing-room half was lighted solely by the light from one standard lamp and from the fire.

" The dancing had been in progress some fifteen minutes or so. Mrs. Rangward was dancing with Baron Halvorsen and Mr. Shefford got up to change the record for them. He was doing this when there was a loud cry from Mr. Rangward. He was standing up and clutching at his throat as though in great pain. They ran to him as he fell on the ground, where he lay in what appeared to be some kind of fit. This lasted for some half-minute or so, during which time they endeavoured to loosen his tie and collar, but as they were doing so he became quite limp. Members of the jury, he was dead. . . ."

It was a distinctly cold night. A dank fog hung amongst the trees in the park, to which their shrivelled leaves still clung, though occasonally one detached itself and fell gently to the ground. Round the corner and past No. 51, there came occasionally fantastic figures clad in running-shorts and white vests, with numbers sewn on to the chests thereof. Some ran and others walked, with curiously writhing gait. They panted as they progressed, and blobs of vapour rose from their mouths into the murky air. They were not space-men but simply members of running-clubs practising running and members of walking-clubs practising walking.

Opposite No. 51 stood a tall figure whose duffel coat hung round him like a becalmed flag and under whose arm was tucked a violin case. By the light of the lamp-post, inscribed William IV, his face looked curiously worn and æsthetic. He had a lock of straight black hair hanging across his forehead and his eyes looked out from dark caves. He was a myth-like creature belonging to the fog.

There were old iron railings with spear-shaped heads along the front of the houses in Park Row and at one time there had been similar railings on the opposite side of the road, between the pavement and the gardens, where the watcher stood. Some twenty years ago he would have leaned against these railings but now there was nothing to support him. He tried to squat on the concrete post which held up the wire fence and he tried equally un-successfully to hook his foot backwards on top of the wire fence, but there was no support of any kind for him. Nevertheless he stood for a long time, staring sombrely at the house.

He saw Charles Shefford arrive and leave his old green Bentley beside the lamp-post. He saw the door of No. 51 open to admit him, with the figure of Edward Bolton silhouetted against the light.

Some twenty minutes later a taxi-cab drew up at No. 51. He saw the tall figure of the Swede standing on the pavement putting his change away in his pocket as the cab moved off. He watched him approach the door, ring the bell and be admitted.

Almost immediately afterwards he saw Mr. and Mrs. Ormer come up from the basement and walk down towards Marylebone Road arm-in-arm, bound for the Dover Castle.

For a long time the watcher stared at the closed door, upon which he could just discern the figures 51. No light showed through the thickly-curtained windows; it was like staring at a sleeping face, and as unrewarding.

The passing traffic was less frequent now that the evening had settled down after the rush-hour, the passage of the athletes became less frequent too, and finally ceased.

Miss Emms, from the top half of the house, brought down Mr. Totterdell's Pekinese, Tiddly Push. She was wearing a woollen scarf round her head and clearly found the night inclement, for she hurried down to the corner and back, dragging Tiddly Push after her on his lead, not pausing sympathetically from time to time. Had she raised her head, she would have seen the gaunt watcher, but she hurried along, head down, looking only at her "drizzle boots," which she had put on to avoid catching cold from the damp pavements.

The watcher, if he can still be called that, for there was no longer anything to watch, stood for some half-hour longer. The distant boom of the clock on Big Ben striking the hour came faintly to his ear. A nearer clock busily struck ten. He tucked his violin case more securely under his arm and turned towards Marylebone Road. He disappeared from the scene just as things started to happen.

AS RUDOLPH ORMER SAW IT (I)

IT WAS A PITY that young reporter ever got himself down into my basement, cheeky young twerp. Worming his way in, getting round Edna, dear knows she's not difficult to get round, and sitting over a cup of tea just as though he was a friend. Of course, if we'd known what was going to happen we'd have been a lot more careful but who could have told that one day we'd wake up and find ourselves a common topic, as they say, with Mrs. Rangward's photograph bang on the front page of the newspapers, and insets of Mr. Shefford and the Baron, and all kind of insinuations?

For all that the papers are so discreet, read between the lines and you'll see the nasty minds of the reporters sticking out a mile. They'll talk you into saying what they want you to say. On they go and before you know where you are, you've shot off your mouth, regardless.

Very friendly they are, all-boys-together kind of thing.

" Mr. Shefford was a frequent visitor, came often to the house, did he? "

" Oh, yes," you answer. " Several times per week."

" And Baron Halvorsen, did he come often too? "

" Ditto," you say.

" Together? Did they always come together? "

" Oh, no, definitely not," you say.

The reporter nods understandingly as he stirs his tea, and all of a sudden you see what he is getting at. " Not that there was anything wrong," you say quickly.

" Of course not," the reporter says, shocked. But you

can't help what his readers are going to think, without his *saying* anything, mind you.

Edna gave me a good big kick under the table and I closed up like a clam after that. But the reporter turned to her, all sweetness and light. " Mrs. Rangward is a very good-looking woman, isn't she? "

" So-so," Edna says with that prim look on her face which she puts on when she's trying to be discreet.

" Oh, come, Mrs. Ormer, Mrs. Rangward is a very beautiful woman, don't you agree? "

" No," says Edna, " not necessarily."

The reporter winks at me as much as to say: " Jealous." But my Edna's not like that. She's not jealous of any other woman, she's no need.

There is no doubt about it that though Edna might put on a long face, trick herself out in black (which suits her a treat), shake her head sadly and murmur about " poor dear Mr. Rangward," she's tickled pink about the whole thing. There's a sparkle in her eyes like I've not seen for many a long day. When the reporter suggested that he take our photograph, Edna and me standing arm-in-arm outside the basement door, she leapt at the idea and hurried off to tidy her hair and powder her face.

The *Evening Clarion* published that photograph. " Mr. and Mrs. Ormer," it said underneath, " who occupy the basement flat of the house in Regent's Park."

Edna looked like one of those successful film stars arriving from America to make a film at Pinewood Studios. " The only thing that's missing is the mink coat," I remarked.

" That's not the only thing missing," she snapped. " Where's the smile on *your* face? Really, Rudie, you look like a wet week in June! "

8

"You might remember the occasion for taking the photograph," I reminded her, "when all's said and done we're not a couple of wedding guests!" It was just about time someone took Edna down a peg or two, so I went on: "And have you given a thought to what this is going to mean to you?" I tapped the photograph meaningly. "Your Bert," I said when she didn't seem to catch on, "he's not going to have any trouble recognising his wife from this. He'll be along here just as soon as he's free!"

That pricked the balloon all right. She blenched, as the novelists say. "And another thing," I went on, "the police are busy with their fingerprints, and what have you, at the moment, but when they've got all that tied up they're going to start on the folk in the house. They'll want to know everything about all of us."

"Well, I've nothing to hide," she bounced back.

"Edna!" I gave her a look.

"Nothing that's any business of theirs!"

"Make no mistake," I told her. "The fact that you've got a husband doing a twelve-year stretch for armed robbery is very much their business. That's just the sort of thing that will interest them."

"That's nothing to do with me."

"Nothing to do with you! It only makes you a gangster's moll, that's all."

"Rudie," she said, "are you turning nasty?" And she began to cry.

Maybe I was turning nasty but the truth to tell I was worried about that Bert of hers. Twelve years, and that meant that, with remission, he'd be out next year sometime. We've been together now, Edna and I, for five years and I reckon she's as happy as she's ever been, a lot happier if she'd only admit it. But she's never forgotten

9

Bert. Not that she's been to visit him, or anything like that, but I can tell she often thinks about him. Women are funny creatures, I'll never understand them. Bert treated her about as badly as any man can treat a woman, deceiving her all along over what he was doing and all the rest of it, and then he gets nabbed after one of these really big mail-bag shows. The natural thing would be for Edna to divorce him and settle down steady with some decent chap like me. Marry him, I mean. But will she? Not on your life. I thought women liked " to be made an honest woman of," as they say. But not Edna. " We're living in sin," I've said time and time again. " Never mind," she says, " it suits me." Well, I suppose it will have to suit me, just so long as she remembers that she's my Edna and not Bert's Edna.

Anyway, there's a time for everything and this was no time to start talking about the Bert problem. I set about it and soon got Edna drying her eyes. Presently she looked at the photograph again.

" Well," she said at last, " this is a real life drama and no mistake. You never think of murder happening to everyday folk. You read about all these murders in the paper and somehow you never think you'll ever get mixed up in one and yet here we are." She paused for thought.

" You wouldn't call the Rangwards ordinary," I pointed out. " Far from it."

" Oh, I don't know."

" In fact," I said, " Mr. Rangward's just the sort to get himself bumped off."

" But poison! " Edna rolled the word round her mouth. " Poison," she repeated; " of all the nasty things to do, poison anyone! Who do you think did it, Rudie? "

" If you ask me," I said, " he did it himself."

" Never! "

" What makes you say that? "

Edna thought for a moment. " I don't think he did, that's all."

" But why? "

" That's not the way you'd do it, is it? In front of everybody, like that. Oh, dear me, no! Besides——"

" Yes? "

" He was much too pleased with himself. Folk that's pleased with themselves don't commit suicide."

She's shrewd, Edna. She hits the nail on the head more often than not.

" And, anyway, the police say its murder. *They* don't think it's suicide," she added.

" The police! "

" That was a nasty laugh, Rudie."

" Mark my words, my girl, the police won't find out for certain how it happened. Not in this world they won't. They're up against cleverness, not just an ordinary crook like your Bert."

I suppose I asked for the slap I got on my cheek before she slammed out.

Well, they can question me till they're black in the face, they won't find anything shady in my past. They can go along to the Mile End Road, and talk to Mum and Aunty Bess about me and they'll hear nothing but good. Of course Mum's a bit sore about Edna, she'd like me to find what she'd call " some nice girl " and settle down and have a family, but that's not the way things have worked out. Come to think of it, Edna is the one and only thing Mum's got against me. She's proud of me, is Mum, proud of the way I've got on, getting myself a goodish education

11

and so on. She's quite satisfied that being chauffeur to Mr. Rangward is a good enough life's work. She's no ambition for me. I reckon that marrying a man with brains who did himself no good with them, she's satisfied with me as I am: clever enough but not too clever. That's me, so she thinks.

And so when the police get round to me I can be as honest and frank as the best of us. Thirty-one years of age and not a blot on the horizon. I'm not ashamed that my mother keeps a second-hand clothes shop in the Mile End Road and that Aunty Bess goes out touting round the suburbs, buying cast-off things from ladies in Sutton and Kingston and bringing them back for Mum to sell in the shop. I'm not ashamed of the fact that she's got no ambition. She's got a good heart, has Mum.

I never knew my Dad and just as well. We shouldn't have got on, Dad and me. He was a journalist, wrote for one of the big dailies in his better days, but drink was his trouble. Drink in a big way. Not a pint or so of an evening at the local but bottles of brandy in his bedroom, alone. And when Mum left him, taking two-year-old me and going back to her old home, he couldn't face it and chucked himself over Vauxhall Bridge at high tide.

In spite of a secondary school education, as you might say, I've always liked motor cars best of anything and it was natural for me to take to driving army vehicles as my part of fighting a world war. R.A.S.C. for the duration; not a scratch on me and not a blemish on my record. They'll find nothing wrong there.

Then five years ambulance driver-cum-hospital orderly. And they'll find nothing wrong there neither.

And then five years with Mr. Rangward. Mind you, I wouldn't have been so keen on Mr. Rangward's job if it hadn't been for the accommodation which was offered after I'd been with him a few weeks. I'd just taken up with Edna and we had to find somewhere to live. You couldn't expect Mum and Edna to hit it off, let alone live together in the same house. So Edna and I had to get somewhere on our own and when we heard the basement was going, it looked like just the thing for us.

We've had our ups and downs, there've been the usual tiffs but on the whole it's worked all right, in spite of the difference in our ages. (" Nine years older than you, *and* she looks it," as Mum reminds me from time to time.) And so far as I'm concerned, it'll go on working all right, just so long as Edna remembers she's my girl.

Well, that's me. I'm ready for them, they can come along when they like and they'll get it all pat and they'll be clever if they find anything wrong.

It's Mr. Toby that's the life and soul of this party. Half-dead, he is, so it seems a queer thing to say. But it's true. Dead from the waist down, he's not dead from the neck up, believe me. We've had some long talks about things in general, he and I, and it's surprising how we look at things the same way. I take up his coal in the lift every morning and bring down the ashes and so forth. And then, once a week, when Miss Emms goes for her day off, I've got to take Tiddly Push out for a run. When the old boy's in a good mood, and not actually listening to some symphony orchestra concert or something of the sort, he asks me to make a pot of tea and I stay up there and have a cup with him and we talk away ten to the dozen. He's got some wonderful ideas. We talk about everything under the sun—women and money and what-it-takes-to-get-on-in-the-world and women, and so on, et cetera.

13

If it hadn't been for Mr. Toby, I reckon I'd have chucked the job long ago. I like someone who treats you like a human being, which is more than you can say for that bastard Rangward.

And Mrs. Rangward?

What do I think about her?

I think this is where we'd better start a new chapter.

*   *   *

She's a puzzle, that Mrs. Annabel Rangward, and no mistake. She's a blonde, but then so's Edna and you couldn't find two women more different. Where Edna's a buttercup blonde, Mrs. Annabel's hair's straight and heavy and looks like she never does anything to it. Edna's always going off to have a perm or a set or some-such, but Mrs. Annabel's hair just hangs simply and it's the colour of . . . that jar of honey. And she doesn't have her eyebrows plucked. like any self-respecting girl nowadays. They're dark, almost black, and they shade her eyes so that they look very big and dark too. Yes, her eyes are big and dark, chestnut brown, they are, and she looks at you with them—my word, she does! And then her face is white, not white but cream. No colour in her cheeks. Edna dabs on rouge all hours of the day and I reckon Mrs. Annabel could do with a dab of rouge but no, she leaves her face dead natural and I can't say it appeals to me. Edna, now, slashes on a great mouth before she goes out and she looks a treat, I must say. Mind you, I don't say Mrs. Annabel doesn't put on lipstick but not so's you'd notice. She's trim about the legs and feet—oh, definitely. Don't I know it! Standing holding open the door of the Jag, I make a point of watching her legs as she gets in

14

just to annoy her old man. In a short, tight skirt, they're a treat. Not that they're an improvement on my Edna's legs but Edna doesn't always bother; when she's not dressed, she slops about in her beach sandals. But Mrs. Annabel—never.

Well, there it is, she's not my cuppa, too quiet. But she's got something, definitely. More than her fair share I'd say, judging by the way the men run after her.

Company director, that's what the papers call Mr. Richard Rangward. I could tell them a thing or two about company directors, in particular this company director. God strike me pink! If there ever was a phony fish masquerading as a city magnate, it's this one. Company director!

Oh, yes, he's got all the trappings—house in Regent's Park, charming wife dressed in mink, manservant, Jaguar Mark V for every day and a Bentley for Sundays (which, by the way, he only drives himself), membership of a club in St. James's Street, membership of a posh golf club in Kent, he's even got respectable relations, or rather one respectable relation—a sister, married to a titled chap and living on the Continent. He goes to the best race meetings and gets himself into the Royal Enclosure at Ascot. He goes to Liverpool for the Grand National, to Cheltenham for the Hunt Cup, to Newmarket for the Thousand Guineas, wearing his Glen Urquhart tweed suit with his field glasses hanging over his shoulder, quite the part. It's a morning-suit and white topper for Ascot and a quiet grey flannel and a bowler hat for Goodwood, and cavalry twill trousers, shower-proof jacket and a tweed cap for Sandwich. He goes to buy a picture at Christie's in a smooth brown West of England cloth and his brown bowler. He goes to Queen Charlotte's birthday ball at

15

Grosvenor House in a tail-coat, white waistcoat, white tie.

And he comes to a sticky end in his braided dinner-jacket, trousers and a plum-coloured velvet smoking-jacket with satin revers.

Company director. . . . I could tell them a thing or two.

Confidential chauffeur, that's me. Why have a chauffeur if he's got to be so blooming confidential? Why bother? Oh, I know why. He daren't go where he goes without someone with him. He's afraid of what might happen to him. So I've got to stick around, bodyguard, that's me.

"I've every confidence in you, Ormer," he says in that phoney posh voice of his. " I know I can trust you absolutely." Oh, can you, think I? " It's lucky I don't talk in my sleep," I said once, and he turned to me with that smile of his. " You can't afford to, Ormer," he says, " you can't afford to, my man."

Company director . . .

Well, he's gone now, nice and clean and tidy. Quick and neat, it was a lot better end than he deserved and whosoever done it has done mankind a good turn, I reckon. All that's left now is for the police to get their job done quick and neat too, take themselves and their information off, go back to the Yard and file it. *Unsolved*, they can write across it, like they've written across many another.

They can make what they like of Edna's past, it won't lead them anywhere but up the garden. And they'll make nothing whatever of mine.

As for what happened on 19th October, I shall tell the truth, the whole truth and nothing but the truth. " Oh, what a tangled web we weave," as Mum often says, " when first we practise to deceive." And so it's going to

16

be the whole, plain, unvarnished truth. Something like this:

My Edna and I have lived in Mr. Totterdell's house now for somewhat over five years. Mr. Totterdell is the best of landlords. I work as chauffeur to Mr. Rangward, a company director, who occupies the ground and first floor of No. 51, together with his wife and his manservant, Eddy. So far as I know there has never been any trouble of any kind in the house. We all get on very well, considering.

Considering what?

Well, considering what a mixed lot we are.

Mr. Totterdell like he is, Miss Emms, his housekeeper, a snappy old spinster who keeps herself to herself; Eddy, a crashing queer if there ever was one, but quiet and harmless in the house; Mr. and Mrs. Rangward, a happily married couple with never a cross word between them, that I've overheard; Edna and me.

Edna and I got home from our ten days in Ostend on the 18th, knowing the Rangwards would be home the following day. Edna had a week's holiday from the bakery, and with the two week-ends she just got in ten days. She was back at work on the morning of the 19th, as usual. I hosed the area and the steps, for once, and made a good job of it. When I took up Mr. Toby's coal, I had a bit of a chat with him about how we'd enjoyed ourselves away, stayed about half an hour as there was a little job he wanted done. I went downstairs and met Eddy, he was Hoovering the landing carpet. He turned off the Hoover as I passed and I had a few words with him. Told him we'd been to the Casino in Ostend and how I'd got a theory about the zero coming up once in twenty-one times, roughly. He listened, quite interested, and told me we ought to go to Monte next time, and maybe we will.

"Everything all right?" I says.

"Yes, ta," says Eddy. "But I'm busy, as there's company to-night."

"Who is it this time?"

"Stag party, Mr. Shefford and the Baron."

"The mixture as before," says I.

Eddy winked.

It's funny when you start remembering back. You remember things which you'd never give another thought to in the ordinary way. Eddy winked, and then he said: "It'll be murder one of these days!" And I laughed. Of course he didn't mean it, it was just one of those things. The sort of remark you'd make half a dozen times a week. Meaning that Mr. Shefford would kill the Baron or the Baron would kill Mr. Shefford one of these days, seeing that they're both crazy about Mrs. Annabel. Yes, it's quite a standing joke except that it's got a bit stale. Which did she like best? There was a time last spring when I was offering to make a book and quoting the odds, just to make Edna laugh. "The Baron," I'd say, "two to one on, eh?" Edna would slap my hand and pretend to be cross.

Well, I knew I'd got to meet the boss tea-time so I got on with it, carrying the hose out through the back, I ran the Jag into the mews and started hosing her.

Edna was home for dinner with a packet of fried fish which she warmed up with some chips; she got off back to work at two and left me with the washing-up to do. Not that I mind that, mark you, Edna's a good girl and I like to help her all I can. After I'd washed up, I had a bit of a lay down and then I put on my uniform and went off to London Airport in the Jag.

The plane was dead on time and presently my two came out, with porters carrying their baggage behind and people turning to look at them, because they're quite a striking couple, Mr. Rangward, company director, and his wife. She was looking much the same, as creamy-white as ever but he had a good rich tan, been sunbathing for hours, I reckon, by the looks of him. He's a bit fussy about himself, always taking pills for this and that. He's got indigestion, or he can't sleep or he's got a cold coming on, or something of the kind, so it was not surprising I should ask him how he was after his holiday.

He was fine, he said, they'd had a splendid time and it was only when we were on the way back to town, with him beside me and her in the back, that he said he'd not been sleeping well. More often than not he takes the wheel on this kind of a run when she's with him, and I sit in the back, and no doubt he told me about his sleeplessness to excuse himself for not following this practice. We had a bit of a talk about his health in general, and I complimented him on the fine tan he'd got. Then he asked if everything was all right at home and I said yes, and that Eddy was as busy as a one-armed paperhanger, getting ready for to-night's party.

Then he said was Mr. Totterdell all right, and I said just the same as ever, and he said he hoped to have time to go up and see the old boy and tell him about the holiday. He didn't have much of a life, he said. And I said, well, I don't know, he seems as happy as a lark to me, and Mr. Rangward said, poor devil and left it at that.

There isn't any poor devil about Mr. Totterdell, all the same, but that's by the way.

What next?

Well, I got them home, took up their baggage, drove

19

the Jag round to the mews and put her away. It was round about five o'clock so I went off down Marylebone to meet Edna, she's off at five-thirty, see? I walked up and down outside the bakery, just to have a look at her when she didn't know I was looking. The bakery's lighted with that strip lighting, makes you look like a blooming corpse, and I can't say it was flattering, even to my Edna. But there she was, and she's my girl, for better or for worse.

On the dot of five-thirty she came to the window to put down the blind, she got quite a turn when she saw me looking at her.

" Rudie," she exclaimed, coming out to meet me, " you look like a ghost, what's wrong? "

" Nothing whatever," I says; " it's this light, you look like the wrong side of a plaice yourself." At which she screamed with laughter and gave me a bit of a slap. " Run off and get your coat," I says, " it's going to be a rotten cold evening by the looks of it. A smog, unless I'm much mistaken."

So we went off home and Edna got us a tasty tea of bacon and eggs, and afterwards we sat by the fire whilst I did my week's football pools and Edna manicured her finger- and toe-nails. You can hear the front-door bell quite easy down in our flat, though you can't hear much that goes on above; it's a solid old house. There's always a bit going on upstairs, we take no notice of the goings and comings. But as it happens, I do remember hearing the front-door bell and a cab moving off. Edna was just getting her coat on. I reckon it was shortly after eight o'clock we locked our basement door and went up the area steps. I did happen to notice Mr. Shefford's vintage Bentley parked under the light.

There was nothing out of the ordinary about the evening at the Dover Castle. We had intended only to pop in for a quickie, but there was a good fire burning and we hadn't been there above a few minutes before Edna's manageress from the bakery and her husband came in. That started a round of drinks which led to another and it was closing time before we could turn round. We weren't high, or anything like that, but we were quite cheerful as we walked back. Edna squeezed my arm against her side. " You're looking a lot more perky now, Rudie. I was worried about you tea-time, wondered if you were in for a bout of 'flu or anything."

There was a car I didn't recognise outside No. 51. " Hallo, more guests arrived," I remarked as we went down the steps. I didn't know it was the doctor's car then, see?

We hadn't been in more than five minutes when Eddy came down. Proper excited he was, not laughing but well nigh hysterical. " What do you know? Mr. Rangward's dead, he's dead, he's dead. . . ."

He went round and round the table, looking ever so queer, it was proper weird, sounded like a gramophone that's got stuck in one groove. " Dead, he is; he's dead, dead, he's dead. Would you believe it, dead? "

Edna gave him a sharp slap on the face. " Eddy," she snapped at him, " pull yourself together."

He sat down suddenly, breathing like one of those runners in the park.

" It's true," he said when he had enough breath.

" Here," I shoved a small glass towards him containing the whisky we keep for colds and such-like emergencies. " Here, drink this up, there's a good chap and then tell us calmly what's happened."

21

Eddy did so, wiping his mouth on the back of his hand.

" I felt his heart," he said solemnly, " when we were waiting for the doctor, there was no feeling at all, quite still. We held Mrs. Rangward's mirror to his mouth, no breath coming out of him. His face is all twisted and the colour of . . ." (he looked round helplessly) " a horrible colour. Horrible! " Eddy buried his face in his two hands and Edna and I stared at each other, Edna open-mouthed. Then Edna says a funny thing. " Who did it? " she says, just like that. " Who did it? "

Eddy didn't seem to hear for a minute or so, then he lifted his face and looked at her, surprised and dazed-like. " Who did it? " he repeated. " How should I know? "

" Well, Edna," I protested, " who says it wasn't a perfectly natural end? "

No one answered that, but presently Edna says: " He was all right when you met them at the airport, wasn't he, Rudie? "

" As far as I could see." And so we went on, talking aimlessly like that for a few minutes until suddenly the door opened and Mr. Shefford stood there.

Now Mr. Shefford usually has a cheerful face, he's always the life and soul of the party. He's the sort of bloke it makes you feel better to meet, one of these high-falutin' army types to look at but hail-fellow-well-met with everybody in spite of it. He was looking pretty pasty-faced now; he's got one of those moustaches Edna calls jolly, she says he curls it up with irons; but it wasn't jolly now, any more than a butterfly caught in the rain(as that old tune goes).

" Eddy," he says, sharp, in a parade-ground manner, " you're wanted upstairs." Eddy was off like a shot but Mr. Shefford waited a moment or two, his hand on the door knob, looking at Edna and me. He said nothing, he just looked, first at Edna and then at me and back at Edna.

" Is there anything I can do? " I says at last, jumping up.

Mr. Shefford nodded. " You'd better come up and be on duty in the hall to answer the door."

I followed him up into the hall. He turned to me and said: " There'll be another doctor coming, the police doctor." Then he lowered his voice and said: " You'll hardly believe it, Ormer, but it's murder. Cyanide."

" What! One of those quick do's? "

" Yep," he said, short and sharp; " one of those quick do's. What do you know about it? "

" Goering," I reminded him; " Field-Marshal Goering, after the Nuremberg trials, before he was due to be hanged."

He nodded slowly. " Quite right, Ormer. The same sort of job." As he walked back into the Rangwards' living-room he was stiff-legged, like he was sleep-walking. He closed the door behind him and left me alone in the hall.

I looked round me as though I'd never seen the place before. I could hear voices in the living-room, but I couldn't hear what was said. Then I heard the lift descending.

There is no doubt at all that there's a bit of a thrill in spreading bad news. I knew it was Mr. Toby coming down by the time it took for the gates to open. Once he's upstairs after his daily airing, he doesn't often come down again, but to-night he explained it, as I was helping him with the doors, by saying that he knew quite well Miss Emms hadn't attended sympathetically to Tiddly Push.

She'd gone off to bed with her hot-water bottle and Tiddly Push was far from comfortable. Mr. Toby had had to bring him down himself for what he called " a second go."

Tiddly Push is a black Peke and what a dog, I've never seen such sauce! He stood there, wagging his tail and looking as pleased as Punch. I'll swear he was having the old boy on. Mr. Toby never expects any help, he limped briskly out into the hall and made towards the front door. But I took his arm, checking him, and I told him in a low voice what had happened.

" You don't say! " Mr. Toby exclaimed as he sat down suddenly on the nearest chair. He looked quite a lot older all of a sudden, I noticed. Then there was a ring at the door bell and a loud rat-tat on the front door. I opened it for the police doctor, who got himself into the living-room, wasting no time at all. Presently the family doctor put his head out of the door. " Hi, you," he says, " the chauffuer, isn't it? Get me a sheet or something."

I got a sheet out of the linen cupboard on the landing and brought it down to him. The doctor was talking to Mr. Toby, but they shut up when I came back.

" Thanks," he said, taking it from me and going back into the living-room.

" To cover the body," Mr. Toby said quietly.

Then the door of the living-room opened and out came Mrs. Rangward. She was crying, her face was all messed up, streaming with tears. She went straight to Mr. Toby, sat herself down on the floor in front of him, put her face against his knees and cried whilst he patted the top of her head, thoughtful-like and said: " There, there! Have a good cry, Annabel."

24

Tiddly Push sat on his backside and looked at them as much as to say: " Carry on, don't mind me."

Looking back, I can see now it was no place for me, standing there gawping at them. But at a time like this you don't think of things like that. At the time you're all in it together and happenings wash over you like you're something on the seashore with the tide coming in and on and over, and either you stand up to it or you get washed away, it all depends on how strong you are.

The thing about Mr. Toby is he's a mystery. You never know, for instance, how much he can see. He wears dark glasses, so dark that you can't see his eyes at all but only your own reflection in some lights, so you don't know whether he's looking at you or not. Then there are times he gropes about like a blind man and there's other times when you think there can't be much wrong with his sight, he goes straight for the thing he wants. It's only that his hands, sometimes, look like a blind man's. He's got stacks of books in his sitting-room, but you never see him reading. He's got a secretary; a young man comes three or four times per week—writes his letters, signs cheques and he reads to Mr. Toby out of *The Financial Times* and, according to what he reads, Mr. Toby rings up his stock-broker about stocks and shares.

Then he's got his wireless. And there's his gramophone with a marvellous selection of long-playing records. He's worked out a scheme for himself with bits of paper and a punch so that he can tell from the touch which record is which.

So he's busy and happy as the day is long and you can't somehow believe that he can't see much. But I don't know. There's often I've come in and found him sitting

25

in the dark and I've switched on the light and I've wondered . . . he doesn't seem to notice no difference.

I says to him once, I says: "How much do you see? Not a lot, I guess."

"I see all I want to see," he snapped, "and sometimes that's far too much." I didn't know what to make of that, but I've never mentioned the matter again.

Sometimes I look at his face. It's got a special look: it isn't like other people's look, closed it is. A closed face. Like somebody's face when they're alone and they don't know anybody's near. Maybe I'm talking a lot of rot. It's just the way he strikes me.

I thought all that whilst I was stood in the hall, waiting for the police to ring the front-door bell.

And I didn't like the idea of them coming and finding Mrs. Rangward like that, so I began to clear my throat and cough to attract their attention.

"If the police have finished with you, my dear, I should go up to bed," he said.

"The police aren't here yet, sir," I says; "it's only the police doctor. I'm waiting to let him in."

"Take Tiddly Push out on the pavement a minute for me, there's a good chap," Mr. Totterdell said.

When I brought the little dog back into the house Mrs. Rangward had gone up to her bedroom, I presume.

"Shall you be going back into the lift, sir?"

Just then the front-door bell rang.

"No, thank you. I want to stay and see what's going on."

I didn't know what to make of that, either. I went and opened the door for the policeman.

AS MISS EMMS SAW IT (I)

I CAN SEE IT all now; I should have left No. 51 straight away after Mrs. Totterdell was killed by the bomb. I shouldn't have let my sense of duty overrule my better judgment.

But then the world has changed during the twenty years I've been in this room. I've always been housekeeper to gentlepeople and I was worried that if I left I might find myself with nobodies, and I wouldn't have liked that. I came to the Totterdells as housekeeper and I've always kept that status; anywhere else I might have sunk to working-housekeeper.

I don't like change. But then I don't like violent happenings either, for all that I was in London for the duration. I've never fancied myself as one of the characters in Mrs. Christie's books that everybody reads. And what's more, I've always said murder and such horrors don't happen to nice people, gentlefolk, like I've always been used to.

Yes, I should have left Mr. Toby to find someone else to take pity on him. As it is, I've given these last twelve years or so since she died to him, slaving and toiling away, day in, day out. And what do I get for my pains?

" Emmy," he said when I was serving his breakfast the day after Mr. and Mrs. Rangward got home from their holidays. " Emmy," he said in his sarcastic way, " we've got murder in our midst, just like one of those books you and your friends are so keen on. Practised as you are in

27

the art of detection, perhaps you will be able to shed some light on the affair."

I thought he was talking nonsense, as he often does, and I pulled back the curtains and closed the window, taking no notice.

"The place is lousy with policemen," he went on, "as you will find when you take Tiddly Push down. You won't be allowed out of their sight until you've given an account of yourself, Emmy."

I stood at the foot of the bed and looked at him.

"In fact," he chattered on, "it was all I could do to prevent them coming up last night and spoiling your beauty sleep. 'Miss Emms has nothing to do with it,' I told them. 'She knows a lot about murder, but I think you will find that she knows nothing whatever about this particular murder.'"

Even then I didn't get worried; that's one of his ways of talking to me. He amuses himself, sharpens his wits at my expense. I suppose he calls it "pulling my leg"; anyway, it amuses him and it doesn't do me any harm.

"Now," he went on, "somebody in this house has been murdered. Who is it? Come on, quick. Who?"

"It ought to be you."

"I didn't say who *ought* it to be. . . . Who is it?"

I thought he was at some kind of a game, so I humoured him. "Edna Ormer," I said, "and high time too."

"A good try," he said, nodding to himself. "Edna is the type that ends up as a torso in lover's lane. But it's not Edna . . . yet."

I hadn't time to stand about so I called Tiddly Push out of his basket beside Mr. Toby's bed and went off downstairs. I got the shock of my life when I saw the policeman in the hall.

Thinking it over it might be that Mr. Toby *intended* me to go down unprepared, to be greeted by the horrible news. At least the policeman could see for himself what a shock I got when he told me, it must have been quite plain that I knew nothing whatever about it.

What a terrible thing! " Mr. Rangward has been poisoned," I keep telling myself and yet it doesn't somehow ring true. They are such a nice couple. There must be some mistake somewhere. People like that don't get murdered, it doesn't happen. That's one of the reasons I'm interested in those detective stories Mr. Toby teases me about. You know it's all a fairy tale and that nothing like that really happens, except in the underworld. And who wants to know about the underworld? And when you're reading these books you're getting a nice comfortable feeling because you know it couldn't any of it ever happen, and particularly not to you.

And now look! At No. 51, Park Row there lies a poor gentleman dead, poisoned, so they say. Yes, I should have left here long ago and this would never have happened to me.

" If Mr. Rangward has been murdered," I said, " nobody in this house has done it. It was something he picked up abroad; in Lisbon, more likely than not. You never can tell, with those foreign places and all that foreign food."

They tell me it was one of those quick poisons, instantaneous, like I have read about often enough in detective stories. Cyanide; and generally there's someone who has worked in a manufacturing jewellers at the bottom of it. In fact, when you're reading that kind of book and you happen to see it mentioned that someone is doing that kind of work or electro-plating, or even

29

professional photography, you're pretty sure to find that person will have a lot to do with the murder. Prussic acid, cyanide, they are both favourites of the detective-story writer, and there's always a smell of bitter almonds which the young man who is working as private detective has no difficulty in spotting. I never thought cyanide could be used in real life.

" Cyanide," I repeated, staggered. " That's a different thing."

They asked me what I meant and I said that if it was cyanide it would have been administered at the time. Quite, they said, there was a little dinner-party. The guests were Mr. Shefford and Baron Halvorsen, and they looked very attentively at me when they told me that.

I'm not really interested in other people's business but one can hardly live in a house like this and not know everybody's business. And, of course, I knew those two gentlemen as well as I know the Rangwards, nearly. They are always in and out. And very nice gentlemen, they are. Always polite and courteous, Baron Halvorsen in particular, whenever he meets me on the doorstep he stands at attention to let me pass. And Mr. Shefford always has a bright remark to make about the weather or about Tiddly Push. Real gentlemen, both of them.

And Mr. Rangward was a real gentleman, if there ever was one. *Was*—here I am saying *was* already, dear me. I still can't believe it.

I will have to believe it, though, so I had better sort out my thoughts and start at the beginning.

Mrs. Totterdell was a saint on earth, if ever there was one. I came to her as housekeeper the year before the war and at that time the house was run to perfection. My room, the housekeeper's sitting-room, was on the ground floor, where Eddy's kitchenette now is. The dining-room was in the front and was used as a waiting-room for Mr. Toby's patients. The room Mr. and Mrs. Rangward now have as their bedroom was Mr. Totterdell's consulting-room, but he was out for the greater part of every day, operating in the two hospitals to which he was appointed and in the West-End nursing-homes. They kept five servants apart from me and they lived in the style I have always been used to. Even after the war began in earnest they continued to live very well. It was a terrible tragedy when Mrs. Totterdell was killed, and we all thought Mr. Toby would never recover from his injuries, but somehow or other he managed to pull round, though he never saw another patient. It was a year before he was back home from hospital, minus both his feet, most of one leg and a good deal of his eyesight. I had managed to struggle along with a skeleton staff but of course his home could never be the same after his dear wife died.

When he was back home, a physical wreck, that is the time I should have left. I should have gone to Lady Horwich, as she asked me. I can remember now the exact words of her letters: *After all your kindness to my dear mother, which I shall never forget . . . nothing we would like more, than that you come to us . . . changed circumstances but then, dear Emmy, you have always been so adaptable.*

But, no, I suppose my kind heart got the better of me. I felt I should not leave Mr. Toby; Mrs. Totterdell would have liked me to stay with him and then when Mr. Toby doubled my salary, I decided I would. We struggled along till the end of the war. I had been so much looking forward to getting back to our old ways; it was quite a shock when I heard that we never should get back to normal, that he

31

was going to have the house divided into two maisonettes.

After the alterations were done and we got the workmen out of the house, an advertisement went into the paper and it was no time at all before we had literally dozens of people coming to inspect the lower maisonette. And the rent he was asking! Where all the people who came to see it got the money from beats me. But Mr. Toby explained to me that when he had to give up his work most of his income ceased too. He had a few investments which brought him in only a small sum of money. He said the rent he would get from the bottom maisonette would be mainly what he had to live on. That was another shock. I always thought the Totterdells had plenty of this world's goods, but it seems they lived right up to the edge of their income. Foolish!

Oh, dear me, we had such vulgar people looking round the house. I said to Mr. Toby: " Surely we're going to have gentlepeople, are we not? " " Very unlikely," he replied sharply. " They don't have the money these days. No, Emmy, I am afraid you will have to put up with something less than gentlepeople under the same roof as ourselves."

But he was being needlessly depressing because not long after that we had Mr. and Mrs. Rangward. It happened that I had to show them round and I took to them straight away. They were a newly-married couple and I could see at once they were the sort of people it would be nice to have. She was very quiet, very lady-like. He was the one that fussed about the kitchen arrangements, about the hot-water system, about the decorations. She just nodded and smiled and agreed with everything he said. She was wearing a beautiful dark mink coat and she had a big diamond ring on her finger; I could see *they* had plenty of this world's goods. He was a business gentleman, we understood. They liked the place so much that I took them up then and there to see Mr. Toby.

Ever since Mr. Toby came home after the bombing he has worn those dark glasses of his. Practically black they are, and I have never seen him without them. As soon as he hears me open his bedroom door in the mornings, on go those glasses. Maybe it is that that makes me feel I shall never get to know him any better. You don't know whether he is looking at you or not and it makes you feel uncomfortable until you get used to it. At first, when he came home, I thought he was blind. In fact, I tested him by turning out the lights and leaving him in the complete darkness, one evening. I came back into the room a few minutes later and he was sitting there, just as I left him.

" Mr. Toby," I exclaimed, " you're blind! "

That was the only time in my life I have ever seen him angry. " Blind! " he shouted. " What on earth are you talking about, Emmy, you fool? " He shouted and raved at me, then, almost immediately, he was sorry and begged my pardon and called himself a " quick-tempered manner-less brute." And as I was leaving the room he said: " But do remember, Emmy, I can see as well as you can. ' There's nothing good nor bad but thinking makes it so!' " I couldn't make anything of that, but he was certainly talking a lot of nonsense because he's as blind as a bat. If only he'd admit it, he'd be a lot happier because he could get those Braille books.

Well, he interviewed Mr. and Mrs. Rangward and after they'd gone he said: " I think they'll do; they seem keen to have the place and I like nice-looking people about."

I gave him a sharp look.

33

" A very beautiful girl," he said, " and the husband's a nice-looking fellow. I think they'll do, Emmy. And they're paying the rent in advance. . . ."

A little while later, when I brought in his pudding, he said:

" That mink coat! What would you say it was worth? "

I told him, and he said: " Oh, as much as that? " And as I was going out of the room he said: " And there's no need to give me that dirty look! I've eyes in the back of my head, you know."

Yes, that's the sort of thing I have to put up with.

Well, Mr. Toby had had the maisonette decorated, after a fashion. Simple, cream colour-washed walls and so on. But they sent in decorators to do a few further " improvements "; the large bedroom was papered with a pinkish satiny paper, and the living-room with the kind of wall-paper that looks like pine panelling. And then their furniture started to arrive. I say *started* because they were furnishing from nothing and everything they sent in they had just bought. It must have cost a small fortune, with things the price they are. He was keen on pictures and he went off to a sale and bought some old paintings and when they were hanging they looked like his ancestors, with lights over them, very aristocratic. And the furniture was good, too. And there were fitted carpets all over and we knew only too well what those cost.

Mrs. Rangward did not seem particularly interested in the furnishings and that did surprise me. She left it all to him and he went around carrying scraps of velvet and carpet, talking about what would be the best colour for curtains and so on. Not the sort of thing you would expect a man to be interested in but, as Mr. Toby is so fond of saying, "It takes all sorts to make a world." And I watched the progress downstairs with interest; not, as I have said, that other people's affairs interest me at all, but the Rangwards, in a way, *were* my affair.

It was not till a month or two after they had signed the lease that they finally moved in. Within a day or two of their moving in they engaged Edward Bolton as man-servant.

I have never been able to make head nor tail of Eddy, as they call him. I have had some experience of men-servants and I must say I've never met anyone like Eddy. But as time has gone on he has proved his worth. He is a fine cook, we know, because sometimes a good smell rises to us from the ground floor. (Mr. Toby always makes the same joke: "That's a very good smell," he says; "fetch me a piece of bread and butter to have with it, Emmy.")

He's not bad at housework, either. I've seen him down on his knees polishing the furniture and he never seems the least bit put out that I have seen him. He seems to like his work.

Shortly after the Rangwards came to No. 51 the old man who lived in the basement and did the boiler-stoking for the house left. Mr. Rangward told Mr. Toby he had got a new chauffeur who was looking for accommodation. So Ormer and Mrs. Ormer moved into the basement where they have been ever since.

It has been nice for Mr. Toby, having the Rangwards. At first he took little notice of them, but gradually they became more friendly.

Mrs. Rangward, as it turned out, is interested in music and that was a link with Mr. Toby. He asked her up to listen to his new gramophone records and that led to her

35

coming up again. And finally hardly a day passed but what she came up and sat with him for a time. Sometimes she'd come up for elevenses, sitting on the floor in front of the fire, drinking a cup of coffee and listening to the gramophone. Sometimes she would come up at tea-time. And then the husband took to coming up, not so often, but once or twice a week, before dinner usually. Sometimes he would bring up a bottle of sherry and other times Mr. Toby would supply the sherry. He'd stay half an hour or so and they would chat about this and that, the latest news, and the world situation and Mr. Rangward's health. Oh, yes, Mr. Rangward is—was, I should say— surprisingly fussy about his health. Always on about the latest cure for cancer or something of the kind. A gloomy subject, to be sure, but Mr. Toby, having been a surgeon at the top of his profession, was always pleased to talk about such horrors. They'd have long discussions about surgery and Mr. Toby has a store of incidents left over from his professional days.

Yes, looking back now I can see what a lot the Rangwards have done for Mr. Toby. He's a different person now from what he was when they first came. Not that Mr. Toby lacks for friends, I've never seen anyone get so many cards at Christmas as he does, three or four hundred, and most of them with some kind message in the sender's own writing. But all these old friends don't bother much about him, they rarely take the trouble to come and see him or to ring up, for all they are so full of "kind remembrances"; the Rangwards' company has done wonders for Mr. Toby.

And another thing: Mrs. Rangward always seemed to like classical music, the kind of tunes Mr. Toby likes listening to, Beethoven and such. Well, after they'd been in the maisonette about a year she had a birthday and what should Mr. Rangward give his wife but a grand piano. Not long after it arrived I saw Mr. Toby leaning over the banisters one morning.

" Listen," he said, and I listened.

Mrs. Rangward was playing and I must say I was surprised. She was playing what they call swing and singing to it. She has one of those low husky voices that they set so much store by on the radio, and the accompaniment was good, even I could hear that; flashy but clever.

" Did you ever! " I exclaimed. " Talented! "

It wasn't long after that Mr. Toby took to going downstairs and listening to Mrs. Rangward by the hour. I noticed he didn't often go down when Mr. Rangward was at home, and when I remarked on that, he said I was getting very sharp in my old age, one of those remarks I can't make head nor tail of.

There have been times, too, when Mr. Toby and she have gone off to an afternoon's concert in the week-day, when Mr. Rangward is at business. They have taken a taxi-cab and been there and back before Mr. Rangward has got home.

Not, mind you, that Mr. Rangward is the jealous type; far from it, to judge by the other men that hang around the place. Any jealous husband would have sent them packing. Besides, Mrs. Rangward is not the type of woman to make her husband jealous, not my idea of one, anyway. She's quiet, serious, with those great eyes of hers looking at you mournfully. You never hear her scream with laughter, like that Edna downstairs, for instance; she's never excited or the worse for drink; she's never in a hurry; she walks about as though she were in a dream.

37

I can even find it in my heart to sympathise with Mr. Rangward. He is fully alive, enjoys every minute of his life, except when he's got indigestion or can't sleep.

There I go! I must try and remember that the poor man is dead!

Yes, I have never thought about it before but, with things as they are, you have to think and it seems to me now that Mrs. Rangward is selfish, the type that accepts everything and does nothing in return. Useless, in a way.

She has her breakfast in bed and then, after Mr. Rangward has gone to business she goes around in her dressing-gown, a pink silk affair; she drifts about from room to room, smoking. Then presently you can hear her at the piano. . . . What Eddy thinks about her really beats me; you can hear him banging around with his Hoover whilst she's playing, taking no notice of anything. But he must think!

Still, I mustn't be critical, she's always very nice to me and any little thing I do for her she's grateful. And for that matter so is Mr. Rangward; and generous too. How could anyone want to murder such a nice gentleman?

Police all over the place and Mr. Totterdell and I have come in for our share of questions. Not that there was anything we could tell them that was of any interest to them. When they'd asked me a lot of questions that were not getting them anywhere, I ventured to tell them that there must be some mistake. It couldn't have been murder, I said. It was an accident of some sort, Mr. Rangward took the poison accidentally.

The inspector was very polite, listened to me with some attention. And then he explained that the poison that was taken could not have been used by accident. It was cyanide put up in a well-known form, a small glass capsule about three-quarters of an inch long; this broken, the poison inside causes death almost instantaneously.

It reminded me of something. Lady Horwich's old uncle had a heart condition they called angina pectoris, he had capsules of amyl nitrite he always carried about with him and when he started an attack he broke one into his handkerchief and inhaled. I asked the inspector if the cyanide capsules were somewhat similar and he said just exactly the same in appearance and it would be clear to me that nobody would swallow one accidentally, as I suggested, or, if they did, it would have no effect but pass straight through the body. To be effective it would have to be broken on the tongue.

The inspector went on to tell me that the police were well aware of the existence of these capsules; they originated in Germany and before the war were in the possession of many people who lived in dread of a violent and painful end.

" Having told you all that, Miss Emms," the inspector said, " do you still think it is not murder? "

I thought about it for a minute or so whilst he watched me. It could have been suicide, but I never thought it was. But then, nor did I think it could be murder.

" It seems impossible," I said.

" I quite agree," he said (oh, so smooth!); " but nevertheless, the impossible has happened."

Sorry as I was about Mr. Rangward I couldn't help feeling excited, quite a thrill it was.

" Well, then," I said, " it must have been one of the two gentlemen who were here for dinner."

"That is a sweeping remark, Miss Emms. Do you mean it seriously? "

39

Did I? I knew it couldn't be anybody in the house and I said as much. He asked me what made me so confident and I said I knew everybody in the house, we'd lived under the same roof for five years now and you couldn't help knowing people you were in such close contact with. " There isn't a murderer amongst us," I said finally.

" You might just as well say a germ doesn't exist, simply because you can't see it," he said irritably, and I fear he was thinking I was a fool. He went on to ask me if I was prepared to substantiate my remark about the two gentlemen who had come to dinner. Slander, he said, did not enter into it on an occasion like this. I could say what I liked, it would go ho farther.

I hadn't really seriously thought that either Baron Halvorsen or Mr. Shefford was the guilty party, but since it seemed that *someone* had done it, it was more likely to be one of them than anyone in the house. And then I said something which possibly gave me more of a surprise than it gave the inspector.

" They're both in love with her," I said, and I could feel my face going all hot.

The inspector cleared his throat. " With whom? "

" With—with Mrs. Rangward," I stammered. It seemed now as clear to me as the nose on my face.

The inspector didn't seem surprised at all. " You think that would be a good reason for—er—causing Mr. Rangward's death, Miss Emms? "

" Oh, he was possessive," I found myself saying. Now, was that quite fair? He seemed to let Mrs. Rangward do much as she pleased. " No," I said, almost arguing with myself, " he *was* possessive, he loved his pictures and his silver and his china and his two cars—and his wife. They were all his . . . kind of thing . . ." I ended lamely.

" And so you think that one of the two friends killed
Mr. Rangward because he had what they had not? "
Put like that, it did sound a bit far-fetched, but I said
that was what I supposed I meant, though he was rather
putting words into my mouth.

" Either you mean that or you don't, Miss Emms," he
said sharply, and I hurriedly said I did.

" Well, then," he went on, " which of the two would
you think the more likely to do it? "

" I wonder," I repeated and I was wondering hard.

Of course, of the two it would be more likely to be the
foreigner. I thought about Baron Halvorsen. There was
something nice about him, boyish, I would call him.
But I've seen him going away from No. 51 looking as
miserable as sin.

Now Mr. Shefford, he's all froth and bubble. " Old
boy . . . this," and " How's tricks? " and " Hallo,
gorgeous! " Full of beans and not to be taken seriously at
all. And yet there was that day when I was standing on
the front doorstep. I was using that new plastic handbag
and somehow or other my latch-key had got itself lost in
a fold of the lining. I was fumbling about when suddenly
the door burst open and Mr. Shefford rushed out, nearly
knocking me flying. His mouth was smeared with lipstick;
he was white and angry. He slammed the door of his car
and drove off in a fury. Whether he saw me or not I do
not know, but he took no notice. I slipped inside, and
there was Mrs. Rangward standing in the hall with her
arms hanging down by her side. She looked half-asleep,
those heavy eyelids of hers half-closed. " Hallo, Emmy,"
was all she said.

The inspector was looking at me all the time.

" Well ? "

41

" I was just wondering."

" Wondering! This is no time for wondering. Do some real thinking, if you please." Which I thought was rather rude, I must say.

" I don't know why you should bother about my opinion, Inspector," I said stiffly.

" Everyone's opinion is important in a case like this," he returned, a little less irritably.

But I began to think I had said quite enough, if not too much.

" I can't say, I really can't say."

This interview with the inspector took place in the dining-room which is at the top of the house. The dining-room, kitchen and my bedroom are at the top, Mr. Toby's sitting-room is on the floor below, the big room in front overlooking the park. His bedroom is adjoining it, at the back, next door to the bathroom. These three rooms are virtually the same as when Mr. and Mrs. Totterdell lived in the whole house. He uses the same bathroom and very luxurious it is, fitted out with the best that money could buy in those old days when he had money. There is a large cupboard across the corner, with mirror-doors, and that cupboard has not been turned out this last twenty years. It contains the accumulation of all those years and though I have, once or twice, mentioned turning it out at spring-cleaning time, Mr. Toby has always said to leave it alone. The bottom shelves contain some of the instruments he used to use in the old days kept in their cases; there's beautifully-made silver saws and such-like, and knives so sharp that they'd cut a hair in midair. It's my guess that sometimes, when nobody is around, Mr. Toby takes out these old instruments and handles them,

42

polishing them and brooding over them about old times. The upper shelves are covered, literally, with dozens of bottles, jars and boxes of all shapes and sizes containing goodness knows what. Some of them have Latin inscriptions written on but the labels are yellow with age.

" Goodness knows why you keep all that old junk," I said once. " If they're medicines, they'd all be stale by now. Let me give the whole cupboard a going-over."

But no. The fact is, he doesn't like anything changed. His sight is so bad he likes to have everything left where it is so that he can lay a hand on it. Any new medicines and toilet requisites he gets are pushed into the front of the cupboard, and there isn't room for much more. Well, anyway . . . after the inspector had left me and gone down in the lift, I went to see what Mr. Toby was up to. He was standing in the bathroom, fiddling away in that cupboard. " Well, Emmy, how did you get on with the inspector? "

" So-so," I said cautiously.

" You didn't drop any bricks, I hope? "

That's just part of his way of talking. He doesn't mean it seriously. " What on earth are you looking for? " I asked him.

" A small flattish oblong tin, about an inch wide and an inch and a half long."

" What's inside? "

" Tiddly Push's worm pill," he said.

" What, Tiddly Push has just been wormed! "

He didn't answer.

" Oh, surely," I said. " Let that poor animal alone."

" I have no doubt Tiddly Push would agree with you, Emmy."

His hands were roving over the things in the cupboard

with the astonishing dexterity he always shows. Neat-handed isn't the word for Mr. Toby, he hardly ever knocks anything over. " Tell me," he went on, " your eyes are better than mine, Emmy, can you see a flattish metal box? "

" Several." I picked out six or seven of various shapes and sizes and he handled each one. He shook his head. " Isn't there any other? " I stood on tiptoe to see better. " Nothing," I said. " Funny. Are you sure there isn't another, Emmy? On any of the shelves? It's got a label with Latin writing on the lid. See it? " Just to satisfy him I got a footstool and stood on it to see better.

" There is no other tin like you describe," I told him. I looked down at Tiddly Push who was, as usual, showing the greatest interest in what we were doing. " You don't want another worm pill, love, do you? " I never enjoyed the three-monthly worming of the Pekinese. Since Ormer took to coming up and taking out the dog I've let him do the job of worming. You have to stick the pill right down the dog's throat with two fingers and more often that not he heaves it back and you have to start again. I don't like it at all, but Ormer doesn't mind doing it.

" I should have thought you'd got something more on your mind than a worm pill for your dog," I said a trifle sharply.

He shut the cupboard door. " Very peculiar indeed," he remarked.

It's funny, Mr. Toby and I never have much to say to each other and yet he and Ormer talk away ten to the dozen. Ormer brings up the coals and takes down the rubbish and more often than not he stops and has a chat with Mr. Toby. What they have to talk about dear knows, I've no time to stop and listen. On my days out

I know for a fact Ormer stays and has tea with Mr. Toby.
Mr. Toby is getting on now, somewhere between sixty and
seventy he is, I'm sure, though he has never told me his
age. He'd have liked a son, that I do know, and I think
he fancies himself talking to Ormer like a father to his son.
Ormer has a nice way with him, good manners, and a
respectful air about him when he's with Mr. Toby. He's
kind, too. It was he who thought of giving Mr. Toby's
walking-stick a coat of white paint. He said nothing to
Mr. Toby but one time, when Mr. Toby spent a day or
two in bed with a chill, he took the stick and painted it
white, leaving the handle plain. Whether Mr. Toby
noticed it or not, he's never said a word, but it has relieved
my mind. If I lean out of the front-room window I can
watch Mr. Toby when he goes out for his walk. He never
goes down Marylebone way, unless there's someone with
him; he turns left and limps along Park Row until he
comes to the corner where you cross over the road and
into the park. There he stops, on the edge of the pavement; Tiddly Push, on a lead, sits down beside him as
though he was prepared to sit there a lifetime. Before the
walking-stick was painted I used to be scared out of my
wits that he would get run over, thinking the traffic was
stopping for him, and slipping in front of a car. But now
I feel a lot happier because as soon as the motorist sees
the white stick he stops and more often than not he shouts
to Mr. Toby to cross, and once on the island the same
thing happens with the traffic coming the other way. For
all they say about the carelessness of motorists, I think
they're always very nice about the blind. Not that it's a
busy road, there's no buses or lorries along it, only private
cars in the park, but its been a big comfort to me since
Ormer painted the stick. Yes, Ormer's a good lad, the

45

only thing that's wrong with him is that awful Edna of his, years older than he is, too.

"I want you a minute, Emmy," Mr. Toby said when we'd finished with the bathroom cupboard. "In here." He beckoned me into the sitting-room and shut the door carefully before he sat down.

"Now, have you thought about the inquest? Any of us may be called upon to give evidence." He wasn't looking at me. "Come closer," he said suddenly; "I can't feel your presence at that distance. Stand there." I was only a couple of feet away from him. "I'd like to know what's in your mind, Emmy."

I felt hostile at first, who wouldn't? And then I thought that maybe there was some sense in what he was trying to convey.

"You've got to make up your mind what you're going to say *before* you go into the witness-box, Miss Emms, so that you don't get confused and flustered and make a bad impression. It isn't a question of being untruthful, you're on oath and you've got to tell the whole truth and nothing but the truth. But the witness-box is no place to start speculating or, as you might put it, *wondering* and ' now that I come to think about it,' sort of thing."

It was uncanny. I wondered for a moment if he had been listening at the door when the inspector and I were talking, but that sort of thing is quite below Mr. Toby. But he had hit the nail on the head and I was glad he couldn't see how my face went red.

"They put words into your mouth, and thoughts into your head that you've never had there before," I said.

"That's just what you mustn't let them do," he answered, banging his hand down on the arm of his chair. "You aren't without imagination altogether, stimulate it

46

a bit and you'd be off. Let me give you a word of advice, don't let yourself be led up the garden, keep your mind strictly on *facts*. Picture the household as it was the day the Rangwards left for their holiday in Portugal, could you by any possible stretch of imagination see, a really foul murder (and poisoning is the worst kind of murder) taking place in this household? No, of course you couldn't. Well, keep your mind on those lines and you'll be all right."

" The difference is," I couldn't help pointing out, " that the murder has taken place. As the inspector said, the impossible *has* happened."

" And you are wiser, after the event, you mean? "

" Yes."

" Well, just be as a little child, a babe unborn, the innocent one that you were *before* it happened."

I shuffled about, a little uneasily. I wish I could have undone the talk with that wretched inspector.

" You know the way things are going, don't you, Emmy? "

When I didn't say anything he went on: " Mrs. Rangward is going to be suspect Number One."

If that wasn't enough to make anyone shriek I don't know what is. I must have let out a small cry of surprise and shock.

" Yes," he said, " that's startled you. But that's the way their minds are working, believe me."

47

AS EDNA SAW IT

You DIDN'T NEED to look twice to see that my lady Rangward was in the family way. It wasn't that she'd begun to lose her shape but she had that look about her; I can't describe it, I'm no great hand at description, but it was the same sort of look a cat has when it's like that, kind of thick-set and contented with a blank look in its eyes.

She's got what it takes, that woman. The likes of me go struggling on, reading the woman's magazines and doing the things they tell us to, all to attract men, to keep our looks, our shape, our hair; it's a lifelong struggle.

And there's the likes of her. No need for her to make an effort. She's like that woman in the Greek legend they talk about on the wireless sometimes; Circe or whatever her name was, the one who lured men to their doom. I often wondered what it was Circe had that I hadn't got and since I've known Mrs. Rangward I know she's got it and I haven't, though I still can't exactly say what it is. You can't see Circe bothering herself about Pan-Cake Make-Up and Mirror-Sheer nylons, you can't even see her worrying herself about her waist measurements (nor her bust measurements for that matter). Wrinkles didn't trouble her either, women like that don't get wrinkles because they don't worry. I reckon they don't think much, and it's thinking and worrying that gives you wrinkles, my word it is, and all the creams in the world won't help them.

Look at that silly bitch upstairs now (it sounds like I'm

jealous, and so I am) her face is as smooth as an egg, but there isn't as much behind the shell as you get in an egg. Dopy. Half-asleep. She feels instead of thinking and that's why she's so marvellously good with the piano, she *feels* it, she doesn't *think* it. She's got nothing to worry about.

Phew, may the Lord forgive me for being a cat! But, talking about the Lord, it's a shame the way some of us start off life with everything that's necessary so's we've no need to make an effort to get what we want out of life (example: the Rangward female), and the rest of us have to sweat and plan and use our loaves and get our faces and our foreheads wrinkled and lined in the struggle to get and keep what we want in this world.

Take me and Rudie now, for example. For all that he's been so faithful these five years, I'm not sure of him and I never shall be; it's that passionate type you've to watch. I reckon it will be all right so long as I can give like for like (return passion for passion, as Auntie Meg puts it in her correspondence in the magazine *Ladies Only*), but once I start to cool off, as like as not Rudie will be away after another blonde. It's then I may be glad of my poor old Bert, in my old age. Bert's a criminal (sounds funny, but there's no denying it), still he's a faithful old so-and-so, and he's not much bothered with passion. Time may come when I'll be glad to fall back on old Bert. Anyway, in the meantime I've got to keep Rudie guessing, and I won't be so daft as to divorce Bert and marry Rudie, I'd be laying up for myself a packet of trouble that way. Marriage wouldn't hold Rudie if once he took it into his head to go after someone else, and that's a fact.

Well, here we are right bang in the middle of one of those real-life dramas " fraught with human emotions," as they say in the *Sunday Cordial*; right in the middle of a slap-up murder, with the quality involved right up to the neck.

And nobody but me seems to have spotted that the heroine of this real-life drama is in the family way. It must be my nasty mind. I wonder if Miss Emms has a clue? She's a self-centred old thing and I doubt that she even knows the facts of life; too interested in herself to see what's going on in front of her nose.

One thing—I'm certain as my name's Edna that Mr. Rangward isn't the father of that child-to-be. Supercilious blighter! I can almost hear him: " Going to have a baby? Oh, Annabel, how clumsy!" Yes, I can see him too, looking down his nose, trying to look the gentleman. Maybe that is why she murdered him.

Come to think of it, maybe she's cleverer than she looks. They don't hang a pregnant woman; the judge gets all soppy about them too. If she gets as far as the dock at the Old Bailey, there won't be a dry eye in court. The barristers and the lawyers will all but fall over backwards, they'll be that sorry for her. At the end of her trial she'll be acquitted and she'll be helped into that dark mink coat of hers by the wardresses and she'll go down the marble steps and out—into the arms of—which? Mr. Charles Shefford? Or the Baron?

Upon my word I don't know which I'd choose but as likely as not she'll choose the one that is the father of her child-to-be.

I've often wondered where she was off to on those afternoons she goes out on her own. There's many a time, when I've finished my dinner and hurry off up the area steps to get back to the shop for two-fifteen, I see she's had her lunch, as they call it, and is off out. I've followed her down to the Marylebone Road many a time. Of course, there's times she goes out with old Mr. Toby, then they take a taxi to the Festival Hall or some such. But other times she goes off quickly, as though she had some appointment. It's not the hairdresser, because she never goes there; and it's not shopping, she's not interested in shopping; and it's not to meet a woman friend, because there never was anyone had less women friends, she hasn't one that I know of. But she's off to meet someone, I'll swear it. She has that look about her. The Baron or Mr. Shefford? We're back to the same old question.

You couldn't find two people more different than the Baron and Mr. Shefford. Mr. Shefford, Charles, they call him, is the army type, ex-Guards, playboy of the smart world. Goodness knows what he does with himself all day long; apart from smart race meetings and golf with Mr. Rangward on occasional week-ends. He's a bit on the old side to be the Deb's Delight, but that's the type he is. His old father's got a flat in Albany (not *the* Albany, you miss out *the* if you're in the know), and Mr. Charles lives with him there; if you ask me he's waiting for the old boy to pop off. Until then he's not in a position to marry, that's my guess. Gets all his love-making on the side, as you might say. He's been hanging around Mrs. Rangward as long as I've known them and I guess that kind of affair suits him down to the ground.

And did I mention it? He's ever so handsome.

Then the Baron. He's handsome, too, but in a different way. He's tall, well over six foot and plenty of fair hair that tries to be curly but he smooths it down hard. Thin as a lath, pale as a piece of pastry; he's got glamour. He looks like he could easily get hurt, so young looking and, at times, he looks like he's going to burst out crying. I do sound sloppy; but I can see that if I had that much of the mother in me I'd fall for him.

The Baron hasn't known the Rangwards above a year now. It's surprising what a lot Rudie picks up from scraps he overhears when he's driving. He tells me the Baron has a wife and three children in Sweden; he's divorced, though I don't know who divorced whom, but he's no playboy. He's not one to take things lightly, or I'm very much mistaken. He's tense, lives on his nerves, I should say.

Now Rudie and I were having a bit of a chin wag after this murder and Rudie threw it off lightly that Mr. Rangward possibly killed himself; and I couldn't agree less and when Rudie asked me to explain, I couldn't. I could not put my finger on exactly why I was sure he didn't and I still can't. But I can say this with equal certainty, if Mr. Rangward is the sort that does *not* commit suicide, the Baron definitely *is*. He's dead serious, takes everything at its face value and nothing with a pinch of salt. Uncertain of himself, too.

Dear me, I seem to be doing a lot of laying down the law about some things that you wouldn't think I'd know much about. But then, you can't live in the same house as people and not know a lot about them, if you are interested in folk, which I am. Miss Emms might, she prides herself on " minding her own business " and that's one thing I've never been able to do and never shall. Yes, I'm nosy and that is part of not being a lady, like Miss Emms says she is.

The Baron is one of the nobs in the Swedish Embassy and as that's only a step or two down Portland Place it doesn't take him long to get here. So he's often turning up between six and seven o'clock. Mr. Rangward is generous with drinks. Eddy keeps in the living-room what Mr. Rangward calls the "grog-tray" with bottles of everything you need for cocktails. Sometimes Mr. Rangward brings a business friend back, Dr. Trench often calls, and once or twice a week the Baron and Mr. Shefford are there; cocktail time you're certain to find some entertaining going on upstairs. They go out to cocktail parties, movies, night-clubs and so on; but Mr. Rangward hardly ever keeps Rudie working at night, they go in a taxi-cab.

Eddy comes down of an evening, when they're out, and sits with us. Now there's a talker for you. He's a scream, is Eddy.

And what a one for gossip!

Well, that's the outfit. Where was I, now?

Oh, yes. Rudie says I've got to think things over carefully, getting everything straight in my mind about what exactly happened from our point of view, so there's no hesitating and stammering when it comes to giving evidence in the police court.

The first we heard of it was when Rudie and I got back from the Dover Castle. I'd just put on the kettle for a cup of tea and got myself out of those high-heeled shoes when in comes Eddy with the terrible news, very upset. Mr. Rangward had died sudden, at dinner. He was laying up there in the dining-room after some sort of fit, a horrible colour; dead.

Before I could stop myself, out it popped; I could have kicked myself, especially as there didn't seem any rhyme nor reason for saying it. "Who did it?" I said—that's me all over!

We were getting Eddy pulled together when in comes

Mr. Shefford, looking like death itself, and sharply tells Eddy he's wanted upstairs.

Mr. Shefford stood in the doorway staring at us as though he'd seen a ghost and then he and Rudie went off upstairs.

Short of going upstairs too and seeing what it was all about there was nothing for me to do but make a cup of tea, which I did. I made that tea last as long as I could and then I had to go upstairs, human nature being what it is, I couldn't have stayed down there alone, not knowing anything, a minute longer.

There was Rudie and Eddy standing by the front door, talking in low voices. Mr. Toby was sitting in a chair against the wall, Tiddly Push was laying on the floor with his head on Mr. Toby's foot. His eyes were wide open, though, roving round, watching everything. Mr. Toby's head was cocked on one side, his face wearing that listening look.

Rudie beckoned me over. " It's murder, Edna."

' Who says? " I gasped.

" The doctor."

" Go on," I says, " a doctor wouldn't throw that off! "

" It was Dr. Trench they phoned for," Eddy told me; " you've seen him often. He came into the room and sniffed, looked round, looked down at Mr. Rangward lying there and then he said: ' What's this, murder? ' Then he got down on his knees and examined the body. He said: ' My God, this *is* murder! ' He didn't say it again, it was only he was taken by surprise and it came out. He hasn't hardly said another word. And now the police doctor's in there with them."

" It was that smell," Rudie declared with a shudder. " Smelt it as soon as I put my head inside the door, I did.

That must be cyanide, I thought, though I never smelt it before, and I never want to again, ta."

Eddy looked as though he was going to be sick, or faint, or something.

" I was washing up," he began, his voice high, and shrill.

" Sh—sh! We aren't accusing you of anything."

" I cooked the meal and served it. It will be—I served the cyanide, next."

" Nobody's said that yet," Rudie reminded him sharply.

" Mr. Rangward didn't drink anything with dinner, see? " Eddy continued; " but he'd helped himself to a little port. He's bothered with indigestion again, says he can't sleep for it and Dr. Trench advised him to go gently on the alcohol, not that he has ever been much of a drinker. Not like some we have here! " Eddy swallowed nervously. " I left them, like I always do. Lights off, table cleared except for the candles, the fruit plates (those Rockingham ones Mr. Rangward's so fussy about), and the port glasses and that hobnail decanter I've always got to be so careful with. Mr. Rangward always likes things left like that before I clear out. It suits me because I can wash up and go up to bed and they can take as long as they like over port."

" Go on, man," Rudie said impatiently.

" That's all there is to it," Eddy ended. " That's all. I don't know nothing more than that. I heard a shout and a crash, like someone falling down, and I thought: ' There goes Mr. Shefford, fooling about! ' But in a minute or two someone shouts: ' Eddy! ' and the shock I got when I went into the room and saw Mr. Rangward lying there! "

Just then one of the living-room doors opened and people came out into the hall.

There seemed a lot of talk going on, and through the open door of the living-room I could just see Mr. Rangward's body lying down beside the table, covered with a sheet. Mr. Shefford seemed to be in a temper about something and the Baron's hair was ruffled like he'd been through a hedge backwards. There was five or six people I'd never seen before; plain-clothes detectives, police doctor—the lot. It seems with all these radio cars around the police can whistle up detectives and reinforcements and what-have-you in a matter of seconds. They don't leave nothing to chance nowadays; they're on to the scene of the crime in a jiffy, before even the body starts to cool off. Though, in spite of all that, it seems to me they're no more clever at detecting who done it than ever they were.

Perhaps it's a good job, though, to be on the spot quick after a crime, then they can see people before they've had time to—to put on their new faces after the shock, time to recover themselves.

Who looks guilty? I thought. I looked round. Everyone, bar the policemen, looked upset. But there was nobody, except Tiddly Push the black Peke, who seemed faintly amused, looked like they'd done it.

The police looked important; one of them, the inspector, I take it, said he wanted to have a talk with each of us separately, and asked where he could do it. Mrs. Rangward wasn't there. Mr. Toby said she'd gone up to her room, and wasn't it rather late to talk to people at this time of night? The policeman ignored that and looked at Eddy, who pulled himself together enough to suggest that he take the inspector up to Mr. Rangward's dressing-room for the interviews. The inspector said right, and he'd start with Eddy. So off they went upstairs. One of the other detectives, Lord Muck wasn't it, waved his hand and dismissed us all.

Nobody wanted to go, of course, we all wanted to stand huddled round saying " Fancy! " or something of the kind.

" Who are *you*? " Lord Muck asked me, and the same to Mr. Toby. I said nothing but Mr. Toby answered: " Nobody, my dear sir; I merely own the house. I'd like to look at the scene of the disaster, if I may."

" Nobody's allowed in there," Lord Muck said sharply, but Mr. Toby got up and limped to the door of the living-room and past the bobby in uniform standing there at attention in the presence of death, and he stopped still in the middle of the room. It was then anyone could see the old boy was blind, for all he protests he isn't. He stopped there and he didn't look towards the body or anything. He was like a dog with his muzzle lifted, sniffing.

Well, then (talking about dogs), Tiddly Push followed him in and, it was rather shocking really, that awful little black dog went up to the corpse, where it lay under the sheet and started being ever so playful, tugging away at the sheet, growling a bit in the silly way he does.

The bobby stared down at him as though he didn't know whether to burst out laughing or not. He looked round quick to see if anybody else was laughing (nobody was, of course; I, for one, was shocked).

There was the *Evening Standard* opened out, lying on the floor beside the table. One of the police, a plain-clothes man this, jumped forward. " Don't touch that." He gave the Peke a push with his foot, not exactly a kick, but a shove. Tiddly Push isn't used to being treated like that, he didn't snap, or anything, he's not that kind of a dog, but he drew back, very hurt. He sat down on his haunches and looked up at the detective as much as to say: " Who do you think you are pushing, my man? " A regular aristocrat, is Tiddly Push, lion-dog of Peking, as Mr. Toby called him sometimes.

Die, I thought I'd laugh. But I didn't have much time to struggle with the hysterical laughter I could feel coming; that blue-dressed busybody came bustling in. " Brown," he ordered, very stern, " this room must be cleared. Are we going to have a square dance round the corpse, or what? " Bad taste that, I thought, what if there had been any relatives present? " I want nobody in here at all," he shouted.

Mr. Toby bent down, clicking his fingers, and Tiddly Push walked to him and he picked him up under his arm and limped out, not touching anything as he went because he hadn't a hand to spare, what with his stick and the Peke, but straight out he walked, the way he had come in. If I'd been his daughter, I'd have been proud of the old man, and I do believe I was proud of him as it was.

I knew what Eddy meant about the smell. Regular spooky smell there was; if ever in my life I smell that smell again, and please God I shan't, I shall recognise it at once and that scene will come back to me. I'll see the old man standing there, head up, his face wearing that secret look, Tiddly Push sitting there and looking up at the detective with a regular haughty air and the rest of us, Eddy and Rudie and me cowering just inside the doorway, behind Mr. Toby, staring, like people do when there's been a nasty street accident.

Then we were back in the hall; the living-room door

was shut and the bobby stood against it with his back to
it. I couldn't help thinking; there, under that sheet, was
lying Mr. Rangward, a corpse, something you wanted to
get away from, something horrible, something that made
you sick. The smell of the good meal, and the smell of
Mrs. Rangward's perfume and the cigarette smoke may
still have been there, but there was the stronger smell, that
I shall never forget. That was the end of him, and yet,
somehow, I couldn't feel sorry for him.

Baron Halvorsen was walking up and down, he kept
running his hand through his hair, and he looked regular
haggard.

Mr. Shefford was leaning against the wall, his hands
in his pockets; he was sulky, looking down at his feet and
thoroughly upset. Both the gentlemen were wearing
dinner-jackets. Mr. Shefford is a bit short and stocky,
the athletic type; the Baron is tall, as I've said, and
slim as a drain-pipe. They took no notice of each other
whatever.

There was a bustle amongst the police, orders being
given and so on, and some of them went off. Dr. Trench
and the police doctor seemed to have gone, though I
hadn't noticed them going. Now there was only all of us,
the bobby and a young plain-clothes man left. Talk about
awkward silence!

Then Eddy came downstairs. " Your turn, Edna," he
says.

Rudie went over to Mr. Toby. " Why don't you go up
to your room? I'll go with you," I heard him murmur;
" they can send up when they want you."

So I tottered upstairs, tottered is the word, my knees
were knocking together. But it was all right, really, all
he wanted was to get my name, my age (goodness knows

for why) how long I'd been there, and what I'd heard during the evening. It wasn't long before I was back down in my own living-room.

Not long after this Rudie came down. He'd looked pale before, upstairs. In fact, now that I come to think of it he'd looked rotten all evening, had Rudie. Now he looked thoroughly upset. I gave him tea, quick.

He fiddled with his teaspoon. " What's wrong, Rudie Ormer? " I says. " Out with it and quick about it."

" Oh, Edna," he says and sighs. " Oh, it's nothing whatever."

" Don't you kid me, my lad."

I sat down again beside the table, crossed my arms and looked at him. He shifted about a bit and presently it came out. Can't keep anything from me, Rudie can't. He's ever so young, really; makes me feel my age, not half, sometimes, for all he tries to kid himself he's the master.

" Cyanide," he whispered so that I had to lean forward to hear what exactly it was he said. " Call it prussic acid, if you like. Same sort of thing. Cyanide of potassium, if you want to dress it up posh. Same thing Field-Marshal Goering used."

" Well, so what? " I said. " You keep harping on Field-Marshal Goering, what is he to you? "

" Don't try to be funny, Edna," he croaked; " there is a time and place to be funny and this isn't either."

I could see he was really upset. I put my hand on his. It didn't seem he could get the words out easy but presently, as I waited quietly, out they came. " There was one capsule of that poison in this house. I saw it only this very day. This morning, it was in a little tin box wrapped in a small, fold of cotton-wool, inside some silk strands with another dab of cotton-wool on top to keep it from rattling about." He was as white as a sheet. He wanted Tiddly Push wormed to-day. Said he'd been waiting for me to come back to do it. I thought we hadn't a pill, but if he'd wait till later on I'd get one at Boot's like I usually do. He said Tiddly Push had been starved all day yesterday in preparation. He thought he'd got the odd pill in a small tin, had it some time, he said. Told me to go into the bathroom and take a look in the cupboard. Which I did. I could only find one small tin box with one capsule in it and it didn't look like a worm pill to me. I brought it back to him in the living-room."

" Yes, what then? "

" ' Is it this? ' I asked, and I read out what was written in Latin on the label."

" He nearly jumped out of his chair. ' My God,' he exclaimed, ' do you want to poison Tiddly Push? ' ' For crying out loud,' I exclaimed, ' what do you want to keep poison in the bathroom cupboard for? ' ' I didn't know it was there,' he said; ' upon my word! It has been there quite some time. It had better not go back there, dangerous! ' "

" What did you do with it? "

" I put it down quick, like I'd been bitten. ' Now that I come to think about it,' Mr. Toby said, ' I believe that worm pill is in my bureau drawer, the little top one? See it? ' I found it easy and, seeing that Tiddly Push had been starved in readiness, I took him into the bathroom, in case he was sick, and put it down his throat then and there, and, come to think about it, that is probably why Mr. Toby came down later in the evening to take the Peke out once again."

61

" Crikey! " I said, it is a common expression, but it wasn't the time to bother about that.

Rudie was quiet at breakfast, I asked him if he'd still got that capsule on his mind and he said, Yes, not half, he hadn't. And I said, Well, what are we going to do about it, and Rudie said, Yes, what? Then he says: " Look, Edna," he says, " there's things you know nothing about and I don't want you to know, see? Nothing that affects you and me but . . ." He ruffled his hair and looked thoroughly put out. " It's like this, you've had a lot of bother. I mean, your life with Bert was not all song and dance, I reckon. I wanted things to be different between you and me. Edna . . . you've had a good five years with me, haven't you? "

He looked so earnest and worried I didn't smile, but took him quite serious. " I have, Rudie, I have."

" I've not wanted to trouble you with anything I guessed was not quite above board. So long as Mr. Rangward paid regular and we was comfortably housed, I reckon that was all we need bother about."

" What are you going to tell me? "

" Nothing very much; I'm only working up to saying that it's not all that surprising Mr. Rangward got himself bumped off. Edna . . ." Bless me, Rudie looked really pained. " Don't," he begged; " don't ask me to tell you any more about that. Ignorance is bliss and I particularly don't want us to be in the know about anything when the police come round, see? The thing is—I'm worried sick lest it was Mr. Toby played the fool."

" Played the fool? "

" Gave him that capsule. Killed him."

" Why should he? He's a dear old man."

" Never mind why," Rudie sounded real cross. " Did he, that's the point? Nobody knows about that capsule but him and me, and last night when I took him up to his room I did it on purpose. I wanted to see where the tin containing the capsule was. I'd put it down, that's all I remember. I put it down, and could I find it? Not a trace of that blasted tin anywhere. Of course with Mr. Toby there I couldn't get down on my knees and crawl around looking for it, but I did everything short of it whilst Mr. Toby was fixing a drink for us both. And another thing that worries me ... Mr. Toby and I, we're just like that. ..." Rudie clasped his hands together with fingers interlaced to show me just how close he was to Mr. Toby. " We're friends, him and me, there's nothing we can't say to each other. But last night "—Rudie shook his head—" there was something very wrong. He hardly spoke a word to me, nor I to him, for that matter. We sat and drank a whisky and soda each, and we didn't talk over the crime, same as you and me would have, or as I would have with Mr. Toby in the ordinary way. He seemed regular upset."

" So would you be upset if that had happened in your house. And come to think about it, you and I could be a lot more upset than we are, Rudie Ormer. You're out of a job from now on, and we'll have to turn out of here, lock, stock and barrel."

" There's things worry me a lot more than that. Don't you see, Edna? "

" I see what you've got on your mind," I said slowly; " but I reckon whatever Mr. Toby did is no business of ours."

" Yes," Rudie nodded. " That's the right line to take up."

So that was how it was. We agreed that we would put the whole question of that capsule right out of our heads, as best we could. I was glad Rudie had told me, when you share a secret, it's less of a strain, you're a long way towards getting it off your mind. We each had another cup of tea and by the time Rudie had drunk it he looked a lot more cheerful.

" I'm glad I've got all that off my chest," he said, " maybe there's nothing at all in it; maybe there is a perfectly simple explanation for the whole affair. After all, Mr. Toby has had that capsule by him for a long time. Maybe it was a coincidence that, the same day I get to know about it, Mr. Rangward should die of that self-same poison."

He tried to keep his voice cheerful and confident but when he came to the last part of what he had to say I could tell he felt none too bright about it.

I'm not much of a believer in coincidences myself. I know that they do happen sometimes, but not such a crashing one as that.

Rudie jumped to his feet. " Well, old girl, ten to nine. Murder or no murder you'll have to get off to work; you're the bread-winner from now on, I reckon, and I'm a kept man." He gave me a smacking kiss which led to a harder and a longer one. . . . When I left him and ran up the area steps, he was smiling and looking nearly himself again.

AS CHARLES SHEFFORD SAW IT

PERHAPS IT MAY shed some light on this curious situation if I go back to the beginning of my friendship with the Rangwards; it is a five-year story, but there is a fragment of pre-history which has suddenly become startlingly relevant. Or has it?

It was that damn' silly girl; I don't remember her name, but she was the mistress of a maharajah and, when he tired of her, she took one of his private planes and crashed herself and it off Land's End. Yes, if I can't remember her name, I can remember what she looked like; quite a floosie. It was she who took me to the Two Lovely Black Eyes.

She and I went along there after one of the parties given by H.R.H. (as she called him), and our reason for going there was probably a geographical one, because the maharajah lived somewhere in the wilds off Queen's Gate and the Two Lovely Black Eyes was one of those South Kensington night-clubs which seem to flourish in spite of their situation. This particular one, I remember, was in a building which had formerly been a Methodist chapel. The Methodists had taken themselves off to a better place of worship and the chapel had been de-consecrated, I suppose, and given over to the worship of mammon. There was a kind of macabre gloom about it which was their speciality. There was no electric light; they must have spent a fortune on candles. You could get, I remember, grills—sausages, kidneys, chops, steaks. The food was cooked over a charcoal brazier which was fitted up at the important end of the chapel, where the padre used to do his stuff. The charcoal fire gave out a warm glow and there was a good smell; yes, it was altogether not a bad place at all while it lasted.

There was quite a good piece of dancing-space, no band, but a pianist. Yes, this is where we come to the point, the pianist. She was one of the main attractions of the place, now that I come to think about it. She was one of those quiet, creamy dames you can never quite forget. She might well have been the inspiration for the silly name of the place, Two Lovely Black Eyes, though in fact her eyes were not black but a really brown brown, like a horse-chestnut and that first night I saw her she was wearing a golden satin evening-dress about the same colour as her hair. Her movements were slow and dreamy and she gave me a queer distaste for the floosie I was with, who, all at once, seemed to be jerky and shallow. However, I took said floosie in my arms and we sloped around the dance floor and every time I passed the piano I tried to catch her eye. Nothing doing. After Floosie had put up with it for a bit, she pressed my arm, and said: " I wouldn't bother, she's Virtue itself; somewhere, I dare say, she's got a pack of kids, and a husband waiting up for her back home. Maybe the husband comes to meet her, to see she comes to no harm on the way."

That seemed to me a good deal harder to believe when presently the pianist broke into song. Maybe she was an ordinary crooner, the type, slightly dated now, that you might find in any suburban dance band. I suppose my standards of taste have always been a little low (the old man has told me so repeatedly), but her singing gave me delightful shivers down my spine. That was over five years ago now, and, what do you know? It still does.

The song, I remember, " I've got that dame right under my skin," a theme, no doubt, open to hypnotic suggestion, and curiously prophetic.

The floosie was having a beast of an evening, looking at the back of my head, and, to make up for it, I filled her up with pink champagne and before long she became quite silly; her head kept slipping on to my shoulder. There was nothing for it but to see her home to her flat, or wherever she lived.

The doorman got us a cab and, as we wavered out to it, I imagined I could feel those great brown eyes following me with a sadly reproachful look.

I confess that the idea of taking the floosie out to supper after the party had been to continue the evening perhaps until the arrival of the milk, but all I seemed to want to do now was to pack her safely in at her own front door and say " Good night." I gave her such a hurried valedictory kiss that, I feel now, it was almost an insult. I left her waving gently in the non-existent breeze, like a reed in the dawn wind. That was the last I saw of her until her photograph appeared on the front pages of the popular press.

After dinner the next evening I began to get restless. No, I thought, it can't be that! But it was! Come eleven o'clock I was sitting in a cab, outward bound for the night life of South Ken. But I didn't get anywhere with the lovely pianist, nowhere. She took no notice of me whatever, not a sidelong glance, not the trace of a smile, nothing.

It was quite a small problem.

The next day was Friday and I was driving westward for a week-end's pheasant shooting at Pendlehead. Back from there, Monday wasn't a good evening, I gave

Tuesday a miss, Wednesday I had another date and Thursday saw me, once again, hell-bent for S.W.5.

I had the surprise of my life waiting for me; I thought I had the technique of the approach shot worked out to nicety, but I didn't know a thing, believe me.

I sat alone in a corner, a bottle in front of me. There is nearly always a man on his own in a night-club, a man you wonder about. Who is he? What is he doing here, by himself? And rarely do you find out. It is always someone who looks a fish out of water, someone with an expressionless face, sitting alone, quietly drinking.

The pianist was not there when I arrived and, for a moment, my heart was in my mouth, but a word with the waiter soon reassured me, she had gone to the Ladies. So I sat and felt slightly amused with myself, for once I was that lone man in the night-club. I wondered if I looked as inscrutable as they do. And whilst I was wondering, I saw exactly the man I was pretending to be. Alone in another corner, bottle, inscrutability and all.

I probably glared at him at first and in the course of the next hour my glare turned to a stare and, in the end, a gape of astonishment.

Let me try to describe Richard Rangward, though I am not much of a hand at description, particularly of a man.

Richard was one of those people who might be any age, not less than forty, possibly, and not more than fifty, I have never known. He was the sort of chap at whom you would certainly turn round and have another look—interesting. He was of medium height with dark hair, greying at the temples—of course. It was quite considerably grey at the temples, almost white, in two wing-like locks that were brushed back over each ear and contrasted strangely with the rest of his black hair. His face was interesting in that it looked as though he had lived the life, with great libidinous lines engraved deeply on either cheek. Oddly enough, knowing him as well as I do, I think I can say Richard was not lustful, though he may have been at one time. Indeed Richard was a complete paradox for where, from the look of him, you would expect lust, you got—of all odd things—hypochondria! His eyes were deeply set and an unhealthy pigment surrounded them so that, at first sight, you felt he had some secret vice, like drug-taking, or worse. He hadn't though. At least . . . I don't know now; in the light of what has happened, he might have had, but all the time I have known him his only vice *has seemed* to be that of taking patent medicines and talking about his health. You can hardly call wife-neglect a vice—or can you?

Well, Annabel came back to the piano, she was again wearing that golden dress which showed all the lovely curves of her body, and what-have-you. She sat down and started to play and blow me, but she was smiling across the room—at him!

So that's it, I thought bitterly. Floosie was wrong about the pack of kids and the husband in the suburbs; she's that dago chap's mistress.

But I was wrong, once again, as I learned later.

She did not know Richard any better than she knew me, but it seemed that the proprietress of the club—a hell of a woman, the procuress-with-the-heart-of-gold type—had been giving her a lecture on her inviolability which, she said, was not an asset at Two Lovely Black Eyes. She must be more charming with the guests.

So Annabel, always ready to oblige, so long as she doesn't have to put herself out too much, gave one of her

warm, heaven-sent, God-given, altogether adorable smiles
to that blighter, I mean, to Richard Rangward, simply,
I choose to believe, because he happened to be in the
direct line of her vision.

But he didn't rush his fences. Taking his time, he
smoked another cigarette. There were two or three
couples dancing and, in due course, he threaded his way
between the tables and across the dance floor and leaned
on the white piano, looking at her. Richard was always
well dressed and that night he was wearing a dinner-
jacket; leaning there on the piano, he looked impeccable,
like an advertisement for the best obtainable brand
of cigarettes. She, too, fitted perfectly into the picture.
The shining floor, the white piano, the golden gown, all
enhanced and glamorised by the soft candle-light. Even
the proprietress, though she didn't exactly approve, left
them to it, it was so clearly a high-life picture.

The question of turning over the music did not arise,
she played everything from ear, so Richard idly leaned
there, looking quite struck, until the proprietress, unable
to bear it any longer, came across to adjust the lid of the
piano, as an excuse for shifting him. He bent down and
said something to Annabel and then went back to his seat
in the corner and presently, when the interval in the
dancing arrived, she went over to his table and sat with
him, drinking pink champagne.

Leaning on the piano, he had looked so at home that
he might have owned the place but, clearly, the boss-
female, for all she had instructed Annabel that she was
to be charming to the customers, would have preferred
it if Rangward's interest had centred upon her rather than
the pianist. She buzzed around their table like a blue-
bottle after the smell of bad meat. I suddenly felt rather

70

sick, and tired of the whole thing. I drank up and departed hurriedly.

If only that could have been the end of an abortive affair! But falling for (as the saying goes) an Annabel isn't an ordinary, plain-sailing experience. It's like having an inoculation, you get her into your blood-stream and are never quite the same again.

" It was lovely while it lasted " is one of the dreamy songs Annabel bewitches you with, but there is nothing like that about what happened between Annabel and me. It had an unsatisfactory beginning, our affair (if it can possibly be called such), it limped along over the years with a few quiet, happy moments, and it has had a very unhappy end (if, indeed, this is the end). There has been no glorious culmination to contemplate retrospectively; I have, in fact, practically nothing to look back on but a curve, like a temperature chart, up, not very high and down, down, down, then up a little, then down, down. A great many more downs than ups. The chart is recorded on the papyrus of hope, without which we cannot live.

Do I sound a little sorry for myself? Well, dammit, I am.

After that miserable evening when I shook the dust of Two Lovely Black Eyes off my shoes and departed, I determined to put the whole thing out of my mind. But during the three weeks which followed, the picture, the thought, of that pianist-girl kept creeping up and nudging my elbow. Irritably I shrugged her off, but she was back. She came between me and what I happened to be doing in the most subtle and baneful way, but when I found this singularly hypostatic shadow in my arms at a time when

71

I was, in fact, clasping the current girl, I realised that I must really rid myself of it; I threw up my engagements and went west again to Pendlehead, where I spent a chilly time tramping round the estate with the agent and generally throwing myself into the affairs of the manor with all the interest and enthusiasm for which the aged parent could wish.

Ha, ha! I thought as I drove back to town in the old Bentley, which was going like a bird, I'm cured. I felt free, light-hearted; even broke into a song and it was only a little damping to discover that, practically all the way back to London, I had been crooning to myself " I've got that dame right under my skin."

I really believe that it was in this mood of relief that I went back to Two Lovely Black Eyes just to show myself (sic) that I had completely recovered.

The piano was playing as I entered and for the first few minutes I kept my eyes away from it, to show myself (sic again) how easy I found it not to look. Whilst waiting for my bottle of pink champagne, I allowed my eyes to rove round the vile mustard-coloured varnish of the roof, the candle sconces on the walls, anywhere. Alas, poor me! I was like child eating the pastry round and round a jam tart, keeping the really jammy bit till last.

And the fun of it was that, when I finally looked, a young man was playing the piano. He was spotty and his black tie trembled ludicrously as it balanced on his protruding larynx. I felt like breaking the bottle of pink champagne on his curiously-shaped head, but I refrained from this to ask the waiter where " the young lady " was. He was only too pleased to tell me; with some pleasure, even delight, he informed me that there had been " a ro-mance." Their client, Mr. Rangward. had fallen in love with Miss Annabel, he had come every night for a fortnight and, at the end of it, he had swept Miss Annabel away—to be married. I could have hit his silly, simpering face.

I looked across to the table where the boss-female sat; she was looking like a thunder cloud and I could understand why. Not only had Miss Annabel captured the rich client, but her defection caused one great big gap in Two Lovely Black Eyes' schedule of attractions.

I sat there, at my table, burning with a kind of white-hot rage and misery, like smokeless fuel. I tried to sort out my thoughts and feelings, but it was impossible; they seemed to have been replaced by *intention—purpose*—and *ultimate aim*. Cunning as a fox, I called the waiter over to me. When was the marriage to be? I asked. He could not say, but round about now. Almost a runaway marriage. Did I not think it romantic? I did not, but, civil, I asked him if he knew who the man was. Mr. Rangward, Mr. Richard Rangward, a company director, the owner of a new Bentley, and a member of Heron's Club.

" You mean *the* Heron's Club? In St. James's Street? "

" Definitely! "

" Do you know where he lives? "

" I couldn't say. Mr. Richard Rangward, it says on his card, Heron's Club, St. James's. She had it stuck up in a corner of the piano for days, to remind her of him," he giggled. " We used to call him the Honourable, between ourselves."

" Known him long? "

" Definitely not, sir. But I've not been here long myself. After that first night he was here, about a month ago, less, maybe, he came very often, every night, until he got her to go out with him and after that—well, they were off. Easy come, easy go in a place like this, sir; as I always say . . ."

The time I spent tracking down Richard Rangward is of no more interest to me now than the period at my prep. school when I decided to collect snail shells and spent one solid week doing just that, wholly devoted to the collection, in old churchyards mainly, of different species of snail.

I started off by looking up an old friend who was a member of Heron's Club. If I could have told him straight out that I wanted to meet a chap called Rangward, a fellow-member of his club, I would have saved myself infinite time and a great deal of money. As it was, I did it the hard way, seeking the company of this friendly bloke.

Let's face it. I was a man acting under an impulse stronger than himself; something over which he had little or no control. When an impulse like that takes charge, reason and common sense creep away, vitiated. I suppose it's a matter of juices. And the worst aspect of it is that I'm still under that influence—there doesn't seem to be anything I can do to throw it off.

I wonder whether this Heron's Club friend of mine guessed at what was going on under my extraordinary partiality for his company; if he ever questioned my dead-pan expression, my false manner, my gregariousness.

Weeks and months can pass without a fellow going to his club and, if I had not been so single of purpose, I might still have been sponging on my friend for meals and drinks at his club in the frail hope of my visit synchronising with a visit from Rangward. But single of purpose as I was, and having a little ordinary luck, after a while I managed to be walking out of the club with my friend as Rangward

74

was collecting his mail from the hall-porter. I went straight up to him and said: " Hallo, old boy." It was not at all what I had planned but it worked. He thought I was high, and mistaking him for someone else.

I was drunkenly apologetic on discovering my error. He accepted my invitation to forgive the insult by having a drink with me. My poor friend must have felt a little bewildered as he accompanied us along to the Ritz bar, but in due course he left us to it.

Rangward was not nearly so stand-offish as one might have expected him to be. He was distinctly friendly, and even partial to me, from the first. Though he told me nothing about himself, he learned quite a lot about me. I drivelled on, I felt I must, at all costs, avoid asking him questions or he might guess that our meeting was contrived. So on I went, about the aged parent in Albany and about the mouldering family mansion in the West country and all that. At one stage he said vaguely that he was sure he had seen me before somewhere and I hurriedly gabbled on before he could remember that it was at the Two Lovely Black Eyes.

I parted from him on the doorstep in Arlington Street with a definite date to meet him a week later in the long bar at Kempton Park, where I would have some obscure and probably false information for him about a horse.

So one thing led to another; I managed to keep it convincingly gradual, and before many weeks had passed I was invited to a house-warming party at No. 51, Park Row.

At none of the half-dozen or so meetings between the first and the invitation to the party did I meet his wife. I was not, in fact, told that he was married until I arrived at the party and discovered that it was by way of being a delayed wedding-celebration as well. I might have known that Rangward and his wife had little or nothing in common. When a chap is newly married, he usually takes his wife round in tow, doesn't he? Whenever I saw Rangward, he was alone. A cold fish, an icy-cold fish.

I was like a gangling boy of seventeen on my way to that party, hands sticky and trembling, mouth dry, voice husky with emotion. Pathetic. And when, at last I saw her (oh, horror; oh, shame), my face flooded, but flooded, with colour and heat so that it felt as though it had been immersed in hot water.

Fortunately, she thought it was drink. " You drink too much, Charles," she has said more than once. " I thought so the first time I met you and I still think so." My God, as if I hadn't enough to make me drink! A gangling youth, that's me, an *elderly* gangling youth.

It would have been like life if I had found her tinny and thoroughly commonplace, after all this high endeavour, and I have no doubt it would have served me right.

She was, however, neither tinny or commonplace. She was . . . What is Annabel? " *Who is Annabel . . . what is she . . . that all her swains commend her?* " I thought that mystery was no longer part of the female make-up, that a woman's mystery went out of fashion with the death of King Edward the Seventh, or round about then. Annabel is an anachronism and it is, perhaps, therein that her attraction lies. I had better make it clear, here and now, that I have never possessed Annabel. With any ordinary woman, a man would have got sick and tired of hoping but with Annabel you hope on, hope ever and in the fascination of the chase you practically lose sight of the goal. With Annabel you never *know*, you don't know

76

what she is going to do, you cannot guess with any hope of accuracy what she is thinking and she is so quiet that you wait, almost breathlessly, for any comment or remark she may be about to make in regard to any situation. It is not that the remark, when it does come, is particularly pungent, it is simply that it is so *rare*. My god! A silent woman is a wonderful thing, and if, too, she has the sort of looks Annabel has—well, there might as well be a notice over the dwelling: "Abandon hope all ye who enter here." No other woman is any good to you so long as you are under Annabel's thrall. You might as well become a monk and have done with it.

The last five years is an uninspiring record of me, tagging along hopefully in the wake of a married woman. The old man would like me to marry and beget a son so that the estate might be secure. And though he and I get on fine in most other ways, this subject lies festering between us, which is a pity. It is possible, if one knew that Annabel was happily married, in love with her husband and completely satisfied with her lot, that would be that. One could draw a sigh of relief and look round for some nice healthy girl, keeping an Annabel-fixation in one's innermost self to gladden the heart in one's old age.

But the trouble is that Annabel is, was, not happily married, was not satisfied and contented with her lot. Richard treated her with an air of possessive pride; he showed exactly the same sort of pleasure in her that he had in his favourite pictures or items of furniture. I do not think she impinged upon his personal life in any way whatever; she was an appendage to which he was reasonably kind and that is all.

How I could make Annabel happy, I could light her up like a torch and make her shine! If I had the chance, I could make her smile that lovely slow smile a hundred times a day, for me alone.

Oddly enough, the only person with whom Annabel troubles herself in the least is an old chap they call Mr. Toby, who occupies the maisonette above them in Park Row; he is practically blind, and has a couple of tin legs and a Pekinese which looks as though it owned the place; yet Annabel seems to prefer his company to that of any of us.

As far as I know, she has no relatives; most young married women spend some time with their mothers or married sisters, shopping and gossiping, but there is nothing like that in Annabel's life. She's lonely with the kind of loneliness that is not cured in the company of people like me, or any other doting male, for that matter. I dare say she finds it restful to be with Mr. Toby.

It is hardly credible that I have been hanging around the fringe of the Rangwards' ménage for five years now and, when it all comes out, things are going to look fairly unpleasant. I suppose, as a relic of that almost lost race of landed gentry, a man without a job, I have been able to call at Park Row at times when other men are " at the office," times when " the husband was at business." Yes, I'm a piece of cake to the popular press. Of course, I'm going to be the wife's devoted lover in the minds of everybody, if not actually on paper. I'm in it up to the neck, whatever I may say to the contrary. I've told the old man, roughly, what is happening, so that he won't get too much of a shock. His attitude is: " What a fool you are, Charles." But as he has always known this, there is no change.

And that is why it is not going to matter much if I fling

78

myself into this thing wholeheartedly; I'm in it body and soul anyway. Not that there is now any danger of their hanging Annabel, but she'll have to go to a woman's prison and work like a donkey, wear prison clothes and associate with—no, I can't let it happen.

Neither the state, nor anyone else, likes poisoners; but a person can be goaded to the point when things become unendurable and then have recourse to poison; the idea may not, necessarily, lie rotting in their minds. I cannot think that Annabel was planning this rather nasty type of death for Richard all these past weeks, months and years. I think she was desperately unhappy and suddenly, goodness knows quite how, she had access to this exceptionally quick poison capsule. I think that she then decided to kill Richard, quickly, just like that.

These particular capsules were in almost general issue on the Continent in the early days of the last war, and it is perfectly possible that Annabel may have met someone in Portugal who told her about them, showed her one and even, perhaps, gave her one. Whatever it was, I am certain that it was a matter of opportunity. Annabel is no Borgia but simply, as I have said, a woman goaded beyond the limits of her endurance.

Pray for her all you good, kind people; there, but for the grace of God . . .

The last evening, then, at Park Row, No. 51.

I was back in circulation after a long spell at Pendlehead with the old man. The first thing I intended to do when back in town was to call at Park Row to see if they were home but I found a postcard from Richard awaiting me. It was a photograph of Pena Palace, and on the back: " Getting nicely cooked, but the food is much too oily;

79

shall be glad to be back in Eddy's care once more. Come and dine to celebrate return, Wednesday as ever is. Yours, Richard."

On Wednesday morning I rang up Eddy; he was expecting me, he said, and Baron Halvorsen for dinner; he was killing the fatted duck. Richard, by the way, keeps an extremely good table. I don't think Annabel gives a damn what she eats or drinks but Richard fancies himself as a bit of an epicure and, in Eddy, he has the perfect servant.

Whatever may be the outcome of this ghastly affair I hope at least, to salvage Eddy from the wreckage. That particular piece of loot may serve to console the aged parent when I am sewing mail bags or—worse.

I had quite an amusing day at Hurst Park and I fetched up at the Rangwards' in good fettle.

Now, thinking carefully in reverse, can I, by any stretch of the old imagination, say that there was anything different that evening from any similar evening I have spent dining at No. 51 Park Row? Can I possibly say there was a particular tension in the atmosphere?

I . . . think . . . maybe . . . I . . . can.

There was something not quite the same about Annabel. It was not that she was tense, because Annabel couldn't, I think, feel mental strain or excitement, simply a kind of nerveless misery. But that was always with her to a greater or lesser degree. It was that she seemed, somehow, all bunged-up with unshed tears; it is a pity I can't put it more poetically, but there it is. But, mind you, it is only on looking back most carefully that I come to this conclusion. At the time I noticed nothing unusual; one of the worst things about drinking is that it dulls your faculty of intuition. Without being actually drunk, you can be thoroughly dim and lacking in perception, thinking you're having a good time and only afterwards realising that you weren't because you were only half-alive.

Richard looked absolutely tip-top, the perfect type of British Raj, bronzed and fit, but he talked like an elderly gentleman doddering about Aix-and-Pains, complaining bitterly about his innards and his insomnia.

Annabel was changing when I arrived; Richard was alone in the living-room. He was standing in front of the fire, fiddling about with a scrap of paper that looked like a motto from a cracker. He said something in German and asked me if I knew what it meant and, when I said no, he said it was a quotation: " He giveth His beloved sleep." Did I know where it came from? he asked, and I said, Yes, the Psalms, wasn't it? and he said, Yes, how on earth did I know? and I said, Well, how did he know? and he said it was written underneath beside the translation, ha, ha! And as he laughed he crumpled up the scrap of paper and threw it into the fire. I said what was this, was he going to join a quiz team on TV? He had stopped laughing and was making that long face he makes when he starts thinking about himself. He repeated that bit out of the Psalms and said too right: *He giveth His beloved sleep,* when you could not sleep it was a lot worse than being blackballed from the most exclusive club.

" Ah, ha! " I said, over the White Lady. " You probably have been, that's why you don't sleep, Richard, my lad, guilty conscience! "

" That's all very well, Charles. You've never *not* been able to sleep when you wanted to—you don't know what it is like. I went to see a doctor in Lisbon who has a big reputation and he said it was probably due to indigestion and that I must keep off alcohol! Where have I heard

81

those words before? Why can't they think up something new to say! Mr. Toby, upstairs, is the only doctor-chappy I have ever met who looks at things from a new angle. I've a great respect for the old boy. It was a big loss to medicine the day he got in the light of that bomb."

" I always thought he was a surgeon."

" Both, old boy. F.R.C.S., F.R.C.P. Highest degrees you can get."

" What does he have to say about your troubles? "

Irritably Richard kicked the logs in the grate, causing a shower of sparks to go up the chimney. He did not answer my half-hearted question; he seemed annoyed about something and neither of us spoke again until Annabel came into the room.

Yes, she was a bit different, in some way I cannot quite place. But she was still the same in that she *looked* the same and that old organ called my heart turned right over in my chest. I reckon there aren't many people of my age and type who can still feel that. They probably got that all over in their early youth; I didn't, evidently.

She was wearing a brown satin frock. I think she must have put on a bit of weight, I had seen her in the frock before but it had not seemed quite so skin-tight. It is a short dinner-dress with a low, round neck and no sleeves, as simple as an Edwardian vest, quite wicked in its simplicity. She wore no adornment whatever in the way of jewels. Richard once gave her some pearls, but I have hardly ever seen her wear them; any pearl would put up a pretty poor show against her skin, anyway.

I looked at her eagerly, refreshing my memory after all those barren weeks without her. " Dear Charles," she said lightly, and ran her fingers over the top of my head as she passed. " Richard, have you been up to see Mr. Toby? "

" Of course. Why? "

" I just wondered. He appreciates it when we go up to say ' Hallo ' or ' Good-bye.' "

Richard made a sound that was like " Hrumph."

Now was she, or was she not, carrying a handbag, pochette, reticule or what-have-you? I simply cannot remember. Did she have a pocket handkerchief, because, if she did, where did she put it? Was it tucked into the narrow gold belt round her waist? And if it was, would, could it contain a glass capsule of poison?

No, far more likely that the capsule was concealed somewhere about the room. However much I may try to explain it away, a poisoning must be premeditated, even if by only half an hour or so. Was she, as she helped herself to a White Lady, making a mental note where she had hidden the poison? Was she, as she sat down with her drink and looked across at me, smiling a little, thinking . . . wondering at what exact moment she would administer it? Or had she known then that she would wait until the meal was practically over? Oh, Annabel, it isn't true, you could not have done it! It is impossible, it didn't happen. And yet, as the old man sometimes says: " What's difficult we do immediately, what is impossible takes a little longer." And it *has* happened.

We must have been talking about something but, Annabel being in the room, my thoughts were occupied entirely by her. No doubt Richard was droning on about his dyspepsia and no doubt I answered absently. Annabel was sitting in a wing-chair covered in pale-blue silk, her elbows rested on the arms and from time to time she sipped from her glass, which she was holding with both hands.

Sometimes she looked at me and sometimes Richard, but she did not smile again after that first one.

Then Anders Halvorsen arrived—that blasted Swede!

Anders Halvorsen's head, being so far away from the rest of his organs, suffers from isolation and he undergoes a lack of mental nourishment. In short, I think he is stupid. He would, however, never have reached the high position he holds in the Swedish Foreign Office had this been so. In fact, I have been given to understand that he is extremely able. Be that as it may, in the carrying out of his ordinary everyday life, the man is an ass.

Even I must admit that he is quite staggeringly good-looking. He is a kind of Sir Lancelot, with a great deal of fair hair that will curl in spite of all his efforts to prevent it, and a singularly young, unhappy face.

Now if it had been Anders Halvorsen who, at the end of a pleasant meal, suddenly decided to do away with himself in front of his wife and two friends in a particularly horrible and spectacular way, I should not have been too surprised. That is the kind of thing he might do. There is a nervous tension about him, as though he had reached the end of his tether and could endure no longer.

Neither am I surprised to hear he is divorced from his wife, who has the custody of the three children; any woman married to Halvorsen might feel she had been caught up in the works of a roundabout; most uncomfortable.

No, I'm wrong about Sir Lancelot. Halvorsen is a cold Norse god, capable of dreadful violence, the kind that would strike off a man's head with an axe as soon as dammit.

I ought to feel loathing for him because he is quite

ludicrously in love with Annabel. I don't, because I know he isn't getting anywhere, any more than I am. I can, at a pinch, understand any woman liking to have him around the place.

I think Richard not only tolerates but welcomes his presence because it is all part of the décor, a tall, handsome and wealthy baron adds something to the social scene rather than detracts therefrom.

Well, in came Halvorsen, late because of a cocktail party at the Embassy, looking young and eager and full of hope. He did not want a White Lady and, as Eddy clearly had the meal ready, we all took our places at Richard's round dining-table and started on the potted shrimps and brown bread and butter.

What did we talk about? Halvorsen was back from a month's vacation in Sweden where he and a friend had been sailing, the weather had not been good, but he had enjoyed it, nevertheless. Richard said he should take his sailing boat down to Portugal and Halvorsen said he preferred the hazards of the Swedish waters. That sort of thing. I cannot remember the conversation taking a turn for the better, nor can I think of anything that was said which had any bearing whatever on what happened at the end of the meal. Annabel smiled a little, nodded in agreement and put in an occasional word. Richard, as usual, drew attention to himself by asking Eddy to bring him some water, leaving the Forster Jesuitengarten for Annabel, Halvorsen and me with a martyred air which he did nothing to hide. This led, of course, to a discussion of Richard's health. Halvorsen asked him if he felt a lot better after his holiday and Richard answered that he did but that he still couldn't sleep and I waffled on about guilty conscience, just to keep the ball rolling. Richard said he would have to get Dr. Trench round for a serious talk since Mr. Toby hadn't proved very helpful. Annabel said why should Mr. Toby help; it was years since he had practised medicine, it was hardly fair of Richard to pick his brain as much as he did. " Besides, Richard," she said gently, " Mr. Toby has told you repeatedly *not to worry.* He says it doesn't matter whether you sleep or not."

And then—oh, dear God, I remember now! I said, with a guffaw, " After all, you're a long time dead." But it was only party-talk and I bet nobody else remembers it if they heard.

It was an excellent meal, at the end of which I confess I felt thoroughly relaxed, almost happy, certainly philosophical. It had the reverse effect on Halvorsen; with some amusement I watched him getting all tensed up. Swedes sit at meals with their hands and arms on the table. It is not considered polite to put your arms down below the level of the table top. I noticed Halvorsen's huge pale hands were tightly clenched, with the knuckles showing white; when he was not giving quick nervous looks at Annabel, he was staring down at his plate. If Richard noticed anything at all, he gave no sign of it. It may be that he thoroughly enjoyed watching us both in the various stages of discomfort which we underwent on these social occasions. Happy in the pride of his possession, he liked, perhaps, to see us taunted and teased by a desire which there was no hope of having fulfilled. He was like a child with a splendid toy of which he can make other children wildly envious.

Eddy cleared away and dusted the polished surface of the table, put down fruit plates, glasses and decanter and left the room, turning out the lights. Three of us helped ourselves to port and passed it on, but Richard conspicuously took the decanter from his right side and put it firmly down on his left without helping himself. Annabel drank her wine a little hurriedly and then got up from the table. She threw a couple of logs on to the fire in the living-room and then went over to the gramophone. She put on a record which she had brought back from Portugal. It was a folk song, *fado* as it is called, sung by a famous *fado* singer; queer, shouting, tuneless kind of singing.

" Horrid, isn't it? " Richard remarked.

But the song was clearly something about which Annabel felt quite strongly. She came back to the table and looked at Richard across the candles. " It is a woman who has a coloured husband," she said slowly; " she is going to have a child and is asking God that it should be white." Quite a long sentence for Annabel.

" What rubbish," snapped Richard; " she should have thought of that sooner."

" You wouldn't understand," Annabel said sadly, slipping back into her chair and helping herself to wine.

" The sad voice of the Orient," Halvorsen said pacifically.

I'm afraid I said: " Hellish sexy," or something of the sort. Then we sat in silence and listened to the music. Presently Richard said: " Well, Annabel, I hope you don't start singing like that."

" She could not," Halvorsen protested, " that is harsh and coarse; Annabel's voice is exactly opposite."

Annabel turned and looked at him, she was not smiling, she said heavily: " The heart of the woman is breaking, Anders, it is a cry of pain." The whole thing had suddenly got too deep and serious. When the record was finished I got up and chose a dance tune. The first was a samba but when Annabel shook her head and would not get up to dance I changed it to a slow, dreamy waltz tune and almost lifted her out of her chair into my arms.

She is a trifle heavy on hand, but it is a blessed heaviness, a burden which you carry with a kind of stupefied delight, so long as it is Annabel. She likes dancing, I think, in a dreamy, lazy kind of way. There was a desultory conversation going on between Richard and Halvorsen but, beneath his brows, the Swede was watching us, almost dribbling for his turn, like a dog watching the cutting-up of his meat. When I was passing the gramophone, I put the needle back to the start without interruption, to annoy him. But he was not going to have that a second time because, when the record neared the end again, he got up and stood guard over it.

At this moment Richard was sitting alone at the table and, as the record finished, Annabel detached herself from my arms and went across to him, leaning over his chair evidently persuading him to have some port, and, I think, it was now that she broke the little glass cylinder and let the fluid slip between her fingers into his glass, just the few drops it contained. I went over to the chimney-piece to get a cigarette so I cannot be sure exactly what happened; but looking back, I find only this moment that was possible. Halvorsen was finding another record, his back to the room. Annabel was being rather pleasant to Richard, possibly, I thought, to make up for the sharp little interlude over the Portuguese record. I think she coaxed him into having a little port; I do remember seeing her lean over him, the loving wife to the life.

Yes, the more I think about it, the more sure I am that it was then. And, drawing away, she dropped the empty capsule, carefully put her foot over it and ground it into the carpet.

Then she went into Halvorsen's arms and they slid into a slow foxtrot. I stood for a moment beside the chimney-piece, watching them, then went back to my host.

There was some port in his glass. He was twisting the glass stem thoughtfully between his fingers. We may have said something to each other but, if we did, it was so trivial as to be of no importance whatever. I was, as usual, thinking about Annabel and I was uncomfortable when she was dancing with Halvorsen. I was waiting for the record to finish and not giving a thought to Richard.

I leaped up helpfully to change it and received a black look from Halvorsen. The record was not quite finished; I idly turned over the pages of the record-book, looking for another slow waltz. After a minute, I took off the needle. I simply do not know what Halvorsen and Annabel were doing, behind my back. But I guess they were just standing there, Annabel preoccupied and Halvorsen looking down on her adoringly. There was a loud and rather horrible cry. I turned round, thoroughly startled, to see Richard apparently acting the part of some tragic actor. He was standing up, clutching his throat, then he turned away from the table and took three or four staggering steps forward and crashed to the ground, where he lay twitching and grimacing.

It was thoroughly nasty.

We all three stood stock-still throughout the performance, absolutely rooted to the spot with astonishment. He had been on the ground for several seconds before any of us thought to go to his aid. When we did, we all three rushed forward together.

It must be clear that I have not begun to understand Annabel, that I have no clue whatever to what she might be thinking, nor, indeed, what she is really like. If, in the foregoing, I have quite failed to give an impression of what sort of mood Annabel was in that evening, it is because I do not know. I have no idea in what mood a woman must be when she pours poison into her husband's wine. I only know that it was done. One of the many things I did not know about Annabel was that she is a superbly good actress.

Kneeling there on the floor beside the dreadful travesty of her husband, Annabel broke into loud, hysterical sobs. Her wrists pressed to her eyeballs, tears were pouring profusely beneath her lashes. Now that I have time to think about it, she brings to mind a little girl who discovers her best doll has been smashed to smithereens. There was nothing phoney or unconvincing about that sobbing.

" What is that terrible smell? " Halvorsen asked me across the body.

" God knows," I replied.

" We had better get a doctor, quick."

" Yes . . . yes. . . ." I looked down at Rangward; he was clearly beyond any medical aid. I have an idea I knelt down and closed his eyes and then I must have staggered over to the telephone. Dr. Trench's number was in a small folder for current numbers which lay beside the instrument. I dialled. The doctor was at his dinner, but I asked him to come at once. He lives in Harley House, a block of flats which is not more than a couple of minutes run away from No. 51. During that minute or so I stood beside the telephone, trying to sort out my thoughts, and Annabel remained in Halvorsen's arms, not in any way other than that of a child being comforted. I have an idea that in the last few minutes Eddy had come into the room and that he was afflicted with the same shock and distress as the rest of us. I can remember nothing significant about him then, simply that he was there.

As soon as I heard the doctor's step on the pavement outside, I rushed to the door. He brushed past me and straight into the living-room. Half-way across the room he stopped, sniffed the air, and then looked quickly round at each of us in turn. Then he looked down at Rangward's body. " What's this? " he said. " Murder? " He got down on his knees and turned the body over on its back, looking at the eyes, feeling the heart, smelling the face, then he sat back on his heels and said: " My God, this is murder! "

He is a friend of the Rangwards and I guess the shock he got was as great as ours. I took a tumbler from Richard's grog tray and poured out a stiff whisky for him. He stood up and took the glass from my hand. " What is it all about? " he asked, looking again from one to the other of us. None of us seemed to be able to tell him anything. Eddy was frantically excited, verging on the hysterical, Annabel calmer now but still giving great shuddering sobs, Anders Halvorsen's face was set and white. The only coherent word seemed to be suicide, it emanated from Eddy.

" Nonsense," Trench said, " this is not suicide. It is cyanide poisoning. I saw it twice in Germany, it is un-mistakable. If I know anything about Rangward, and I have known him well these last five years, ending his life like this was the last thing he would do."

He swirled his whisky round and round in his glass thoughtfully, drank it in one gulp, then went to the telephone.

For the next hour or so we moved about like actors in a mime play, whilst the police took charge of the situation as impassively and impartially as undertakers. They had not been in the room more than a couple of minutes before they found the remains of the capsule, broken into small fragments, crushed into the carpet. It might, of course, have been anybody's foot which crushed it out of recognition and beyond the possibility of examination for finger-prints. It was lying beside Rangward's chair, where all of us had trodden. But when they discovered it, I looked at Anders Halvorsen and quite suddenly I knew that he was thinking what I was thinking, that Annabel's heel had broken it—deliberately. I don't know quite how I knew, because I am not an adept at reading people's thoughts; it was, perhaps, the surprise which took over on his unguarded face as he looked at me to see whether I had the same thought, that told me what he was thinking.

A sheet was brought to cover the corpse and my copy of the *Evening Standard* was opened out and laid over the broken capsule. Each of us, in turn and separately, was interviewed in Richard's dressing-room by the inspector. All we were asked for was an account of the evening. When that was over we were free to go home.

Halvorsen was waiting for me in the hall; we went out together and on the pavement in front of the house, out of earshot of the policeman who was on duty in the hall, he said in a nervy, almost threatening manner: " What are you going to do about this, Shefford? "

" Do? " I repeated, puzzled, playing for time.

In the light from the lamp-post I could see him, glaring down at me, looking, I can only call it fierce. Clearly some remark was expected of me. I said: " We can only wait to see how things pan out."

" Cannot you see already what they think? "

" No," I said firmly.

· " Can you not? " he made a Scandinavian sound denoting disgust.

"I don't know what you are getting at, Halvorsen. But if there arises any question of the poison having been administered by one of us. . . ."

" What do you mean, ' one of us '? " he interrupted.

" One of the three of us. Then," I said slowly, " I shall have to confess to it. There is nothing more to it."

I bowed slightly, forestalling him, he is a great one for bowing. And I walked off towards the main road. I found, when I had walked the mile and a half to Albany, that I had left the Bentley outside No. 51. Forgotten all about it in the stress of the moment. But it did not matter. My decision made, there being no turning back, I fell into bed and slept the sleep of the just.

AS ANDERS HALVORSEN SAW IT

THERE MUST BE, in the life of every man of the world, an episode, or episodes which he would prefer to forget and, with ordinary good luck, he is able to do so. There are others who are not lucky, like myself. My one excursion into low-class life will, I am sure, follow me now to the end of my time. I shall never be rid of it.

When Napoleon was shown a list of generals from which he could choose his staff for a specific campaign, he would ignore their qualifications and ask: " Is he lucky? "

It is important to be lucky and this I know because I am not.

An Englishwoman next to whom I sat at dinner one evening and who became a little drunk during the meal told me that she did not like Swedish men. " I am sorry," I said. " Why not? "

" Please don't think I mean anything personal in this, Baron," she answered; " but I find Swedes are so stiff and formal to begin with and they remain so until they have absorbed a certain amount of alcohol. You can see it coming, like a thermometer rising—at a given moment the top blows off—they become quite squalidly amorous."

I had to think for a minute what she meant by " squalidly amorous " and I confess that I was deeply hurt for my countrymen. It was far too strongly put and too widely inferred. I looked up " squalid " and " amorous " later in the Oxford Dictionary and I did not like what I found the words to mean. But after the passage of some time, I do understand her feeling. Furthermore I, too, am not exempt from such criticism. It is a pity but it is so.

We high-born Swedes are proud of our lineage, we consider ourselves above the ordinary people; we keep ourselves aloof in a way that British aristocracy do not understand and it is perhaps for this reason that one does not take easily to low life. The strictness of my parents and the rigid discipline of our household may account for the way my life has gone astray.

Firstly, my marriage. I wonder if there are any aristocratic families in England in which the marriages are arranged by the parents? That was so in my family. On leaving Upsala University, I went into the Foreign Office in Stockholm and my marriage with Ulla was arranged; that is, my father told me that he would like me to marry Ulla, my father's first cousin's child, and therefore my second cousin. Ulla, it seemed, was willing to marry me and there was no choice for us. She was a beautiful girl, amiable and capable. Above all, she had plenty of money. I, too, was considered to be not undesirable and I, too, had enough money. I could find no valid objection and she, it would seem, did not look for one. We were married in our little family church at Hanghö and spent our honeymoon ski-ing in the high mountains.

For the first three years we lived in a flat on the Strandvagen, in Stockholm, and we had our first son. Then I was sent to Rome as Second Secretary and we began to grow up. After a period in Rome, we went to Moscow for some time, then back to Stockholm. There followed service in London and in Washington. During these years Ulla and I had two more children but we

95

grew steadily away from each other. Each year Ulla took the children back to Sweden for the summer months and on her return, each time, we looked at one another like strangers. It seemed quite wrong to go to bed together.

And so we ended it, with no hard words on either side.

It was as simple as that. My children do not in the least require me. Bjorn, the elder boy, and his brother Sven go to school in Upsala and the little girl stays with her mother, who has remarried. Sometimes I take Bjorn and Sven sailing but we are not particularly good friends; I feel they are always on their best behaviour when I am with them and there is mutual relief when the visit is over. I am not complaining, that is the way things have been with me.

When next I came to England I was promoted and now hold a higher position than when I was last here. I do not trouble to have a flat, with the consequent household worries, but I have a suite of rooms in a small hotel in St. James's, which suits me very well.

And now I must tell you of the episode of which I am ashamed, which I might have hoped would pass out of my life and be forgotten.

I had been to dine with a Swedish couple who had a flat in Seamore Place, which turns out of Curzon Street. We had a very fine evening, with good food and, needless to say, plenty of wine. I started to walk back to my hotel in the company of a colleague.

When I was last in London, Curzon Street was considered exclusive, but in the interval I have been in other countries that street has become more ordinary; there are now cars parked along either side, outside the great houses, like that in which Disraeli lived and died. Teddy boys, as they are called, stroll up and down from coffee bar to coffee bar. The street has no longer the dignity and aristocracy it once possessed. On the steps of some of the great houses street women were standing—English, French, negresses, with their strange eyes and their wonderful clothes.

My friend and I, as we walked along the street, were both a little ribald from the drink we had taken; we were clearly what Charles Shefford would call " a piece of cake " for the ladies of the town. We shook them all off, however, and arrived, still on our own, at the little passage which leads into Berkeley Square.

It was here that trouble happened; a girl stood in the shadows crying quietly. My companion nudged me as much as to say: " There is your chance." But I had no idea other than to go to the help of a lady in distress. She was pitiably young, so poorly dressed compared with the splendid ladies we had seen. It would make the heart of any man sore to see her. My drunken friend became very silly; he went off by himself after tapping me on the shoulder and, with a wink, saying: " Bye-bye! "

I shall not go into details, because it is an ordinary story; and I am not a little ashamed of the part I played in it. I can but say, by way of excusing myself, that I must have been a good deal more drunk than I thought.

First I took her to a coffee bar, just round the corner. On the way there I believe I dried her eyes; anyhow, when we arrived she seemed to have recovered from her tears. She told me that she was unhappy because she no longer desired to continue the life she had unwittingly taken up. She told me by what mischance she had got into the power of a man who lived from her immoral earnings. I was shocked and moved, for such a thing we have not in Sweden. She had tried to escape from him

97

but he kept a watch on her, and she could not get away. She wanted to return to her home in Ireland and marry a boy there who was in love with her, but now she feared that she would never be able to do so. My sense of chivalry was much roused by this story and presently I took her home in a taxi-cab. She lived in Earl's Court, which was rather a long way off my usual haunts, and when we arrived at the tall, gloomy house in which she said she lived, I paid and dismissed the taxi-driver. She asked me up to her bed-sitting-room, which was at the top of the house, a long way up. It was a room which, she said, she rented furnished, it was clean and neat and in no way the sort of room I would have expected.

Since I am being honest, I may as well say that I became amorous and, no doubt, my Englishwoman friend would have called it " squalid." I must also confess that I enjoyed the episode; what I complain of is that other men, no doubt, may have these little *affaires* and they are over and done with. I, for instance, embark upon such an affair with some reluctance and it develops into a major episode from the repercussions of which I am still suffering. I stayed with her some hours; before I left I bent over her and whispered, " My dear little Irish girl, good-bye," and I did not forget to leave a folded five-pound note under the handle of her hand-mirror.

No sooner was I outside on the landing, carrying my shoes in order that I should not disturb the other people in the house, than the door of the next room burst open and out came a short dark man. He seemed to be very angry. He demanded what I thought I was up to. I think he was getting round to blackmailing me. This is a very ordinary, almost painfully ordinary, story and I can only think it must be because I look, as Charles Shefford has told me, a "mug," that all this happened to me. I suppose I look the sort of man who does not do this sort of thing (as, indeed, I am); a sitting bird for a blackmailer. I had twenty pounds or so in my wallet and I might have been quite willing to hand this over rather than that he should follow me back to my hotel, find out who I was, and proceed to pester me with the information he held against me.

As it turned out, I was in a reckless mood. I did not wait to hear what he had to say, I dropped my shoes and hit out, hard. My opponent was two feet, at least, shorter than I, but he knew how to fight. Within a few seconds we were fighting like hell, the noise must have been awful. The top landing of that house was only small, a few yards square, and surrounded by doors out of which people appeared. But we were locked in a really frantic struggle and I paid no attention to what was happening about me. There was a plain balustrade round the landing and down the stairs, the sort of simple hand-rail and light banister old English houses have as the stairs mount to the attics. I managed to unlock myself from the little demon I was fighting and stepped back to give him one knock-out blow, but he was too clever for me; he was somewhere down below my waist and in the quickest way possible he got his foot behind mine and I tripped up backwards and crashed right through the balustrade, which splintered like matchwood, and down on the stair below amid shrieks and screams from the various people who had appeared to watch.

I do not understand how it was that my back was not broken but it may be that all the time, as I have said, I was a great deal more drunk than I thought and I fell as a drunken man, loosely, so that no real damage was done. I sat up to feel where I was hurt and then passed out.

About an hour later, or so I was told, I came round. I was lying on a Knole settee and a perfectly awful woman was leaning over me. If I did not know she was the madam of a brothel I would certainly have guessed her to be such a one. The thought of her now gives me shivers down my back. She was holding some strong smelling-salts beneath my nose which caused my eyes to water. " Better? " I drew my head back sharply, and it hurt.

" You aren't half a one," she said admiringly, " you've smashed the place up. A foreigner, are you, dear? " I did not answer. I looked at the loudly-ticking clock and tried to figure out how long I had been unconscious.

" I must go," I said.

" Yes, you must. But you ought to remember, never fight an Irishman."

" How could I know? "

" You couldn't know, but if you take my advice, in future you'll stop to find out before you strike the first blow."

I stood up. My shoes were beside the sofa. I put them on.

" Can you walk? " she asked anxiously.

" Please telephone for a taxi-cab," I said curtly. I had no desire to be friendly with the woman.

" Don't worry. I've got a hired car from an all-night garage waiting outside, that's why I was in a hurry to get you round. It's past five o'clock now. You must get away before it gets any lighter. I don't want any talk from the neighbours. Won't do to give the house a bad name."

" Does the house belong to you? " I asked, but she was

in no mood to answer my questions, any more than I was to answer hers. Moreover, I felt extremely sick and wanted to get away.

I was staggering a bit and she guided me to the front door, taking a firm grip of my arm. She thrust ten shillings into my hand. " That's the fare for the car," she said. " There you are, dear, go home to mum."

She gave me a sharp push and shut the door behind me. At the bottom of the steps I turned round and had a good look at the house, which I could see quite well from the lighted lamp-posts. Oliver Lodge was written in shabby gilt lettering on the fanlight, and underneath, in newer letters was the number—15.

" Oliver Lodge, 15 Texas Crescent, S.W.5.," I said to myself. I had remembered the name of the street from the years and years before when I had arrived there in the taxi-cab with the girl and I was quite pleased with my feat of memory.

" Kermorn! " the car driver shouted and, as I wavered towards the edge of the pavement, he leaned over confidentially and said:

" Wot address? "

I really congratulated myself on the sharpness of my mind, it is a pity it could not have been sharper earlier on. But it made up for it now. Beware of blackmailers! I thought. Very cunning I said:

" Piccadilly Circus," and got into the car.

" Piccadilly Circus! That's no address."

" Piccadilly Circus," I repeated firmly.

I paid him off with the ten shillings I still had in my hand and sat down on the edge of the fountain in the wilderness that was Piccadilly Circus. My sickness was beginning to wear off but it was replaced by a dreadful

101

depression. I sat there, drained of all hope, and watched the dawn creeping up the sky. When the day was at last established I got up and walked back to my hotel.

It was only when I was undressing that I discovered my wallet was missing. It had contained the money, but what was a great deal worse, it had also contained a small supply of my visiting-cards, my international driving-licence and my diplomatic passport.

I got through the day somehow, but I felt too wretched even to collect my thoughts. After a good night's sleep, however, I woke up on the next day feeling quite recovered and ready to take any action that might be required. My wallet, I felt, was really something which I must make an attempt to recover. Besides, I was angry and sore about the whole thing. I decided to tackle the question before going to my office, so after breakfast I walked down to Piccadilly and hailed a cab which I took to Oliver Lodge, Texas Crescent, and I told him to wait.

The door was opened by the madam, who did not seem willing to let me in. I placed my foot in the space to prevent her slamming the door in my face and asked if I might speak to the young lady who lived on the top floor.

" If you mean the Irish girl and her boy-friend—they're gone! "

Unhappily conscious of the watching taxi-driver I had some difficulty in persuading her to let me in to discuss the matter with her. She said she had nothing to discuss.

When, after some little argument, I was at last inside in the room where I had regained consciousness, I turned to her at once and said, as coldly as I was able, that I was Baron Anders Halvorsen of Sweden and I intended to

102

take immediate steps to have her charged with the theft of my wallet which contained, etc., etc. I was going, I said, at once to the local police station. I was, in fact, on my way there now, but I had stopped off in the hope that she would return my property to me without any further argument, in which case, I said, I would consider the matter finished with.

It could not have been the first time that this sort of thing had happened to her, and I would have thought she could deal with it quite satisfactorily. But I could see that she was shaken.

She said that she was shocked to hear what I had to tell her but that it was nothing to do with her. She had, she said, had the Irish couple in one of her top-floor rooms for less than a week. She realised at once that she had made a mistake in taking them, they were shanty-Irish of the type she did not like. They had now gone.

Had they gone of their own free will, I wondered, or had she told them to go?

I told her to be honest with me. I had realised, I said, that this was not an ordinary boarding-house but a bordel. I said that I had no idea what the law relating to bordels was, but I did not think they included common thieving amongst their attractions.

It seemed, then, that she had decided what attitude she must take up. It was to tell me the truth. The house did not belong to her, she was simply the housekeeper. The tenants paid an ordinary rental and, when required, a proportion of their earnings were given up each week to pay for their food. The trouble, in this case, lay with the fact that she did not know the girl and had had no recommendations with her, how the Irish boy-friend had come to be in the next room was something which she

103

hoped to find out. It was possible that the girl in the next room had allowed him to stay there until I emerged; she intended, she said, to get to the bottom of the affair. There was no doubt whatever, she said, that the Irish girl had taken my wallet whilst I was asleep. It was an old trick, surely I must have known that such a thing might happen?

I did not for one moment believe this, I thought that the madam herself had taken it whilst I was unconscious. There had been no opportunity for the girl to remove my wallet, and it had been with me when I left her room. I looked at her for a long time, wondering what was the best thing to do.

Then, more friendly, she repeated that the house did not belong to her, but was owned by a company who employed her as a housekeeper. She said that there was nothing in ordinary brothel-keeping these days. The thing had to be run on proper business lines with proper insurance rates. " It's like everything else," she said, becoming explanatory, " the little man is getting pushed out of business. The overheads are too much, the risks too great. There was a time when you could run a house with quite a decent profit and a good time had by all, but it's changing now," she sighed.

" Do you mean to tell me," I said, " that there are companies who make a profit out of the immoral earnings of women? "

" Oh, dear, yes," she said, picking her teeth thoughtfully. " Where have you been all your life, dear? You're not the chicken you looked the night before last, by any means."

I wondered, really, where I had been all my life, as she put it.

104

She was really a horrible woman, but she was good-tempered and it did occur to me that perhaps I was wrong about who had taken the wallet. She could not have carried me downstairs and on to that settee alone; it was more than likely that the Irishman had helped, possibly others had given a hand. The wallet could easily have been removed during the process.

" Are you really going to the police, dear? " she asked, a familiar hand on my arm. Of course I was not. I could not, in my position, afford to go to the police in connection with such a disreputable affair.

She was not to know this, however. " I shall see," I said sternly.

" You must remember," she reminded me, " that it is nothing to do with me. I can't be responsible entirely for what goes on. I was cheated just as much as you."

I nodded thoughtfully, whilst she got herself indignantly worked up.

" The company will have to protect me against this sort of thing," she went on, " there might have been a murder the night before last, and then where would we have been? It's not all beer and skittles running a place like this. I shall have to tell the boss. There's a lot of risk attached, they'll have to give me a rise or I'll hop it. I really will."

" The boss? "

" Yes, Mr. Southern Star Estates, Limited. He's got a lot of property around here. A busy man; he's not easy to get hold of. But I'll tell him, I'll let him know just what sort of thing I have to cope with."

" I should," I said soothingly.

When she turned her attention to me and started to ask me tenderly how I was after my " accident," I felt I could not stay another minute. I remembered to thank her for the ten-shilling note, returning one to her, and then I fled.

" Southern Star Estates, Limited," I repeated to myself. Then I leaned forward and told the taxi-driver to go to Bush House.

At the Registry of Companies I paid my shilling and asked for the file of Southern Star Estates, Ltd. I waited, fully expecting to be told that such a company did not exist but, to my surprise, I was presently handed their file.

The address of the company, somewhere in the City, was given. There were not more than half a dozen names but the principal name was that of the chairman and chief shareholder, one Richard Rangward, of 51 Park Row, Regent's Park. No other occupation was ascribed to him but the potential business of the company was stated to be the buying and selling of residential and business premises.

I wasted no time but took another taxi-cab into the City, where, after a little difficulty, I found the office of Southern Star Estates, Limited, situated in a small alley off the maze of streets at the back of Liverpool Street Station. There were other firms in the building, as I read from a shabby board in the small entrance-hall. There was no lift so I walked up, and up, once more to the top of a building, where a door bore the white-painted words: Southern Star Estates, Limited.

I knocked and went in without waiting to be invited. It would seem that the office did not receive many visitors. The elderly woman in charge looked surprised. When I entered she had exactly one tooth and a few seconds later she had a shining set top and bottom. I said I would like to see Mr. Rangward and she asked me what was my business. I said it was private and she said that Mr. Rangward never gave personal interviews. If I could give her some idea of my business she might be able to attend to it. I said it was impossible. And she said: " In that case . . ." and intended me to go. But I remained. She fussed about with her papers and at last started to type, but I still stood there. She began to get annoyed. " You'd better go, you know," she said. " Anything you want to say you can write. It will be attended to."

" I cannot put what I have to say on paper," I said with some meaning.

" Then I am afraid your business will have to go unattended to, Mr.—er——"

" Look here," I said, trying to sound as English as I could, " you cannot treat me like that. I *wish* to see Mr. Rangward."

She stopped typing and looked at me over the top of her eye-glasses. " Are you trying to make a nuisance of yourself? Because I have only to knock the floor with this stick and friends from the office downstairs will come up and throw you out."

It might have been true, it might not. I was still sore, I had no mind for another knockabout, for the time being. I withdrew as gracefully as I was able. I stood outside the door for a moment and in that moment I heard the telephone ring in the office I had left. I put my ear close to the thin door.

" Yes, Mr. Rangward," I heard a woman say; " yes . . . oh, yes, sir. . . ."

A head had appeared, a young man was standing on the stairs below, craning his neck up to see what I was doing. He saw at once that I was eavesdropping. "Anything you want? " he asked.

107

I ran past him down the stairs to the street, into the taxi-cab and back to my office.

But I cannot say that my morning's movements had achieved nothing. The name Rangward, for instance. When time allowed I got out the telephone book L to R and looked up the name. There was only one Rangward, R., 51 Park Row, Regent's Park, Zoo 0929. Making sure that I would not be disturbed in my office I dialled the number. " Is that Mr. Rangward?" I asked. " This is Mr. Rangward's house," a male voice answered. " Mr. Rangward is not at home, can I take a message? "

" When will he be at home? "

" I am sorry, I cannot answer unless I know who I am speaking to."

" It is a customer," I said boldly.

There was a pause. " Beg pardon, sir. I don't understand."

Another pause. " I think you have the wrong number, this is Zoo 0929." When I said that was the number I wanted he went on: " If you are a business acquaintance of Mr. Rangward I cannot help you, this is his private address; he sees no business people here."

" Can you give me his business number? "

Pause. " I am afraid not, sir. I do not know it."

" Isn't that rather peculiar? " I asked. I could hear heavy breathing as of one thinking hard. The voice said: " Sorry, I cannot help you," and rang off.

I was quite determined that I was going to get to see this mysterious Mr. Rangward somehow, but for the next few days I was really busy with a Board of Trade conference. During this day or so something happened which certainly took the urgency out of my determination. I received a bulky grubby envelope with the postmark

" Dun Laoghaire " on the Irish stamp. I think I guessed
what it was before I opened it. My wallet, complete with
all its contents except the banknotes. I searched through
it for a note of some kind but there was no word. So
the little Irish girl had not forgotten me, I had meant
something to her after all. I felt quite sure that this was
her doing and not that of her male companion. Possibly
she had stolen the wallet from him to return it to me,
possibly he beat her for it. I felt that the envelope
contained some heart-felt message for me as well as the
welcome wallet, and I was pleased and comforted.

" Tell me," I said to an English friend of mine, " is it a
criminal offence in this country to live off a woman's
immoral earnings? "

" Oh, no," he threw off, then paused to think. " Well
. . . I don't know . . . of course, it must be."

" Is it? Yes or no? "

" To tell you the truth, old boy, I'm not sure. But I
think it must be. The police have clean-ups from time to
time and I suppose there are prosecutions. One doesn't
often hear about them, I must say."

" In Sweden we have no bordels," I said.

My friend laughed. " There is nothing much I can say
to that but oh! No bordels—well, well! "

" But you have here."

" My dear chap. What are you glaring at me for? If
you want me to make some sort of justification for it I will
say they are a safety valve. There have been bordels, as
you call them, since the days of Moses. One doesn't talk
about them, that's all." He laughed again but I did not
find it a laughing matter. " There is a name for a chap
who lives on a woman's immoral earnings, know it? "

I did.

" Frankly," he said, " I do not claim acquaintance-
ship with anybody of that kind. So I don't give it a
thought."

But I did; I gave it a lot of thought.

Park Row lies some half-mile to the north of my
Embassy. I have often passed along there on my way into
the park for a walk, or back from a stroll in the rose
gardens. I passed it now more frequently, fascinated by
the mental picture I had of Mr. Rangward, who lived
there.

Many of those houses have been converted into govern-
ment offices but this house stands amongst them, still
proud to be privately owned. There are soft drapes in the
windows and through them one can see shaded lamps.
On the front door is a brass plate with the name, " Mr.
Tobias Totterdell." One day I saw a Pekinese dog sitting
on the doorstep, watching me. I could not resist stopping
for a moment. " Yes," the Pekinese seemed to be saying;
" my house is a nice house. Have a good look, please."
I could not help smiling as I passed on my way. Shortly
afterwards on my way back, I met, face to face as they
walked up towards the park, an elderly man in sunglasses, limping, with a white walking-stick, and a young
woman, who walked along at his side and held his arm.
They were talking as I passed them and I knew they came
from No. 51 because the Pekinese was following close to
their heels. He seemed to wink at me as I passed. Could
that old man, I wondered, be Mr. Rangward?

More than ever I was intrigued. A day or two later, it
was a Sunday morning, I saw a Bentley standing beside
the pavement. A young man in a sports jacket ran up

from the basement of the house and put a folded rug into the back of the car. He went down again. I walked to the end of the road and turned back. I saw a man, smartly dressed as though for golf, come out of the front door. He was followed by a man-servant in a white jacket who put a camel-hair overcoat on to the back seat. I hurried so that I might have a better look at the man in the car, but he drove off before I got there, the man-servant withdrew into the house and the door was slammed just as I re-passed. That, I felt quite sure, had been Mr. Rangward.

This fleeting glimpse, far from satisfying my curiosity, doubled my determination to get to know him. I was fascinated. I decided that it was no good my being too fussy about the regularity of my behaviour; Mr. Rangward, I considered, could hardly be too particular about the nice points of introduction. I could think of no pretext of calling at the house other than the Pekinese. Shortly after this I drove up to the front door in my Cadillac with the CD number plate. Taking the risk of the servant recognising my voice from the previous telephone conversation, I rang at the bell and asked to see Mr. Rangward. The manservant asked me who I was, I told him, proffering my card. He asked me if Mr. Rangward knew I was calling and, when I said no, he prepared to shut the door, saying that he would tell Mr. Rangward when he came home that I had called, and give him my card. But I was not to be put off. Could I see Mrs. Rangward? In desperation I said I had come about the black Pekinese. I was a Pekinese-lover, I said, I very much wanted to possess one similar. At that he said that the dog belonged to a Mr. Totterdell, who lived in the upper maisonette. I don't know how we should have gone

111

on if it had not been that the young woman I had already seen came out into the hall, ready to go out. The man-servant turned round. " Oh, madam, this gentleman is making inquiries about Tiddly Push."

She smiled at me and, as she came forward, I knew that, in more ways than one, I had reached the end of my journey—or the beginning.

The shock I had recently received made me feel a good deal older and wiser, a man of the world. Though what I had been before I do not quite know. Here was Mrs. Rangward, the beautiful and young wife of a man who lived on the immoral earnings of women. I had to keep telling myself that, and even so I do not think I really believed it, though I knew it to be a fact.

I think, perhaps, I was in love with her from that first moment, though I should have strongly denied it if charged with it. To feel an overwhelming curiosity about a woman is, surely, a better beginning to a relationship than to feel instant desire for her. Possibly I felt the second, but the first was so much greater that I cannot even remember the desire. That came later.

Perhaps it is important always to feel curiosity about a woman; I know that I never had the least curiosity about Ulla and that my curiosity for Annabel has grown rather than decreased in the single year I have known her. Right up to this minute I do not know whether she knows what her husband's " business " is. But now, as I write, after what has happened, I am inclined to the opinion that she must know.

Otherwise I cannot see that she had any motive for murdering him. If I have a great many doubts about the first, I have no doubt at all about the second. I saw her do it. Or rather, I must say, it happened before my eyes.

Starting off on the Pekinese basis I had, naturally, to strengthen my foundation and this I found none too easy, as I know nothing whatever about the breed. I have made the pleasant discovery, however, that there are English people who will go out of their way to be pleasant to foreigners. It makes me happy because I always feel that we, in Sweden, go out of our way to be pleasant to English people, or I hope so.

Mrs. Rangward was one of these kind people. She said she was sure that Mr. Totterdell, to whom the dog belonged, would be only too pleased to tell me from what breeders I could buy a Pekinese of that sort; if I had time she would take me up to see him now. She rang through first, on the house telephone, to ask if she might bring up " someone to see Mr. Totterdell " and up we went.

" This is Baron Halvorsen from the Swedish Embassy. He has fallen for Tiddly Push, Mr. Toby. He wants to talk to you about him."

Though he was indoors, he was still wearing his sunglasses and, as I was unable to see his eyes, I felt a little strange with him at first. But he soon put me at my ease, and presently we were all three sitting round talking about dogs, and a servant brought in coffee.

I was told that Tiddly Push was a direct descendant of the lion dogs of the Emperor Kubla Khan. The dogs lived in the fabulous palace of Xanadu and hunted with the emperor's lions. He told me the legend about their progenitor; a lion, the favourite of Buddha, had so loved his master that he had changed himself into a tiny dog

113

so that he might lie in his sleeve. The descendants of this favourite became the Imperial dogs of Peking, guardians of the sacred person of the emperor, Master of the World, the Heaven-born.

I laughed very much, since the old man was eccentric. I said that was very nice, but must I go to Peking to get a dog like Tiddly Push, and he said, No, there was no need to go any farther than the so-and-so kennels, somewhere in Dorset. In the meantime, Tiddly Push, as though to show me what a fine little dog he was, brought out from somewhere a ping-pong ball which he played with like a kitten.

" He is showing his paces," Mr. Toby said. " He rather fancies himself as a retriever, he's too undershot to carry things around comfortably in his mouth, but he's always at it."

There was a red cotton cushion on the hearth and the dog sat on it, very upright and imperial as though he knew how well it suited him.

" Your Royal Highness is the only form of address Tiddly Push answers to," Mr. Toby said. We laughed very much and I marvelled to myself at the ease with which one can get into an English household if one really tries.

When I left Annabel shook hands with me on the doorstep, and said: " Do come again, Baron."

" Thank you, I will," I said, and I did. I went again very soon, at cocktail time, when I thought the husband might be at home, because, in spite of the friendly atmosphere of that first visit, I did not lose sight of my initial reason for wanting to get to know the Rangwards.

That second time I called, Charles Shefford was there. He was sitting in the drawing-room with Mrs. Rangward and at first I thought it was Rangward himself. But no, he was introduced to me as Mr. Charles Shefford and as I sat back and sipped my cocktail I thought very much about him. Was he a lover of Mrs. Rangward?

I must say at once that I have been wondering about this ever since, and, as in so many other aspects of Annabel, I have not yet come to a conclusion. He may be, he may not. It is even possible that by now he entertains the same thought about me. I would like to be Annabel's lover, but I have never had the opportunity.

Charles Shefford is what the English call " very good value." He drinks too much, but I must say that drink makes him into a more amusing person; he does not become sullen, or "squalidly amorous," he becomes extremely lively and schoolboy-like, and when he comes away from the house to return home he may take a flying leap over his car. He has tremendous vitality, and, though he is older than I, probably as much as eight or nine years, it is I who feel older by a score of years. I do not think he is very deep, I do not think he is ever hurt to the heart, or that he worries much about the soul or the meaning of life. It is perhaps because of this that he seems so cheerful. Unlike me, he does not worry about anything.

Not saying a great deal but observing much, I sipped the cocktail and awaited the arrival of the *raison d'être* of my presence. For some weeks now I had lived with the image of Richard Rangward, the arch-pander, ace of evil-doers, and it came as no little shock, certainly a big anti-climax, to see him in his own charming home, a typical well-to-do English business-man.

But not quite typical; charming, generous and genial a little querulously self-centred, perhaps; he was withal not a nice man. The English are so fond of the word nice,

but I find the French word *sympathique* is better. I found
Richard Rangward quite lacking in *sympathie*. He had
deep lines scored down either side of his mouth and there
was much pigment round his eyes that made him look
older, possibly, than he was. His eyes were hard and
though it might seem that he laughed as much as any
other Englishman of the type, a loud, frequent guffaw,
he was not really diverted; his eyes were not amused and
his laugh shut off quickly, before other people had stopped
laughing.

Annabel explained my presence at once. I felt the
Pekinese pretext would begin to wear rather thin if
used much more often, but I enlarged upon it, telling
them what Mr. Toby had told me about Buddha's
lion.

" You speak excellent English, Baron."

" And I can talk American if I want, sure I can," I
lapsed into American which I sometimes do to amuse my
colleagues in Stockholm.

They laughed very much and soon we were like friends
of long standing. When I left, Richard Rangward came
with me to the door.

" If you get a dog like this you won't be able to call
your soul your own," he said. " Tiddly Push keeps a
sharp eye on us all in this house. There he is now. . . ."
The little black dog was watching my departure. " He
never hears the front door open or shut without going to
see who it is." He bent down and tickled him behind the
ears.

There seems to be no limit to the amount of time English
people will spend in discussing animals, dogs in particular.
I felt that my choice of subject for introduction to the
household had been a happy one. I have no doubt that

when Richard returned to the drawing-room they decided that I was " a nice man."

And so, for a whole year now, I have spent much time with the Rangwards. They have kept open house for me, as for Charles Shefford, whom they have known for longer. They have become my greatest friends, and yet how little have I known about either of them!

I have come to love Annabel as I did not know it was possible to love a woman; I would do anything for her, though she gives me nothing. She is always detached and impartial and always I hope for the day when she will not be, when she will come into my arms, realising, at last, how much I love her. And perhaps this day is not so far away.

You could not say that the Rangwards were an un-happily-married couple in the sense that Ulla and I were unhappily married. There was a bitter tension between us two. Between the Rangwards, however, there exists no more than between Rangward and the manservant; simply, she was part of his household and she, on her part, seemed sadly resigned, that is all.

On the Rangwards' return from their holiday in Portugal I was invited to dine with them. I had hoped that, during my summer holiday in Sweden, I should cease to think about Annabel, but the opposite was the case. I do not believe that five minutes passed when she was out of my mind, and all night I saw her in my dreams.

What was I going to do? Something, some change, I felt, must happen. The situation could not go on as it was. I knew that I would do something but what that was to be I had not decided. I had thought of challenging

117

Rangward in front of them all, asking him to tell us what his means of livelihood were and whether he was proud of living on the immoral earnings of women. But, as always, in the comfortable, unemotional atmosphere of 51 Park Row, I found that could not be done. What else could I do? I could take Annabel into my arms and tell her how much I loved her and ask her to come away with me. But I dare not risk that. If she were to say a definite no, and I had no reason to think she would do otherwise, how could I continue to come to the house, and how, without seeing her, could I continue to live?

I could tell Annabel how Richard lived, but how was I to know that she did not already know?

Curiously enough, there were times when it was not Richard I wanted to knock about but Annabel. I wanted to shake her, to hit her until she begged me to stop; I felt a desperate urge to do something, anything to get below her surface calm, to discover what was really going on in her head, anything to make her realise *me*.

Like the character in Ibsen's play, I found that my thoughts went round and round in the well-worn groove from which there seemed no deliverance.

The cocktail party to which I went before going to the Rangwards' did nothing to give me confidence or comfort; I arrived at Park Row with the unhappy certainty that I would do nothing whatever, there would be no release, this would be an evening like any other and I would return to my hotel in the company of my worn-out feelings.

I found Charles Shefford there, we were a party of four. I hope that I have made it quite clear that I have not had, nor have I now, any idea whatever of what was going on in Annabel's mind, but it is possible that she had not decided to kill Richard until a given moment came. It is possible that the moment came after a discussion of a gramophone record which she had brought back from Portugal. Richard was certainly sneering about it and it may be that she had some special feeling about that record. Richard said that he hoped Annabel would never sing like that and I said, in her defence, that she could not, her voice was quite different. Annabel seemed suddenly to notice my presence because she turned to me, and said: " The heart of the woman is breaking, Anders, it is a cry of pain."

I stared at her as, I am afraid, I so often do, because I find it difficult to take my eyes away.

I must try and be quite clear in my mind what exactly happened next, so that there is no confusion when I am questioned at the inquest. I had had, unfortunately, enough to drink to cause my mind to be less than acute; the far end of the room, where we were dining, was lighted only from two candles. I remember talking to Richard about nothing much; I was watching Charles Shefford and Annabel dancing, waiting for my chance to dance with her, but Shefford put the needle back to the start of the record and I was obliged to sit on at the table. It annoyed me very much and I did not want this to happen again, consequently, I left the table rather sooner than was polite, leaving my host alone.

I think it was when the dance ended that Annabel, leaning over his chair in the semi-darkness, poured the contents of the small phial into his port glass. There was no other opportunity. I had my back to the room, looking for a record I wanted, and I think Shefford was standing by the fireplace, because when, at the start of the music, I turned round and Annabel came across the floor to me and we began to dance, Shefford had not returned to the table to keep Richard company, but was looking at us through his cigarette smoke with that mocking, amused look which makes me want to strike him. He did return to the table, however, but was up again as the record neared its end. He stood by the gramophone until it was finished and it was then that Richard must, at last, have raised the port glass to his lips and drunk the contents. It is a curious thing that he should have delayed drinking from his glass until all of us had left that part of the room.

Annabel now says that she wanted to dance and that, in order that Richard might not be annoyed at being left, she whispered to him to have a little port. I have never witnessed any such charming solicitousness on her part before and that is possibly why I noticed it this time.

I wonder whether Annabel had the poison concealed in the palm of her hand. It is a tiny glass capsule, I am told, which when broken pours out enough potassium cyanide to poison a man instantly. I am told that the drug paralyses the central nervous system and artificial respiration is no antidote because the heart stops almost at once and the red blood corpuscles are destroyed.

Poor Richard, he was always so fussy about his red corpuscles, making sure that he had the right diet for keeping them in good condition. Within five minutes after the first cry of agony, his face was nearly violet in colour, his jaw fixed and there was slight froth about his lips. His eyes were prominent and glistening, his hands were clenched. When we unclasped his fingers we found his finger-nails purple and the veins on his hands standing out and swollen.

Poor Annabel, too. I am certain that if she had known of the vile death that the poison induced, she would never

120

have done it. Anyone could see that she was horrified by what she had done, her whole body was shaking violently and she sobbed loudly.

If she had not put her foot on the little glass phial after dropping it to the ground, things might have turned out very differently. The police would have found it and would have been able to detect at least part of a fingerprint on the glass and this would have left us all without any doubt in our minds, if, indeed, doubt existed.

It was clever of her. That was one of the many things I did not, until now, know about Annabel. She is clever.

I had mixed feelings as I looked down at the dreadful corpse, lying there beside his civilised dining-table. Those who live on the edge of the underworld, I thought, must expect to meet a violent end. Single words like *retribution*, *judgment*, and *justice* flashed across my mind like captions in an old-fashioned movie, and a verse from the Bible:

" Thou shalt not bring the hire of a whore, or the price of a dog, into the house of the Lord thy God . . . for even both these are an abomination. . . ."

I was trying to think this out when the doctor arrived. His behaviour was unprofessional in the extreme and I can only attribute this to his being as shocked as we all were.

Throughout the rest of that horrible evening I watched people coming in and out. It was not difficult to see what they thought. Sooner or later everybody looked at Annabel.

But what made me angry was Charles Shefford's attitude. I know a great many Englishmen who think they are born to command and, at certain moments in life, it

121

is a good thing. But, at a time like this, such an attitude only serves to annoy. His air of being an old friend of the family, calm and possessive, made me want to strike him. His manner, too, with Annabel, was unendurable. Could he not see that the more possessive he became with her the more the police would begin to wonder? The kindest thing we could both have done would have been to treat Annabel with the utmost coolness. For some hours I had to fight down an almost unendurable urge to hit Charles Shefford to pulp and when, finally, the opportunity came and we were leaving the house together in the small hours of the morning, I had to remind myself that one murder in an evening at 51 Park Row was more than enough.

I think he was either very drunk or else he had taken leave of his senses for, as we parted, he seemed to be trying to tell me that it was he who poisoned Richard. I followed him down Portland Place, past my Embassy, through Hanover Square and right down to Burlington Street where he turned into the Albany.

I could see there was going to be trouble.

AS EDWARD BOLTON SAW IT (I)

WELL, THERE WE all were in the news, right on the front page, and no mistake. We'd got ourselves worked up and primed for the inquest, going over in our minds what we were going to say and all in a dither about it. There we were, huddled together in the passage outside the court, at least the Ormers and I, and Miss Emms were huddled, whilst Mrs. Rangward and the Lovers, as everyone is calling them, sat on a bench a bit away from us. One thing that struck me was how lonely Mrs. Rangward seems, for all that she has the two men hanging around. Most young married women, suddenly becoming widows, like that, would have other women about them, their mums, or their sisters or even their aunties, but she seemed to have nobody and I was sorry for her.

I have never disliked her, like Edna Ormer does, she's always been decent to me, in all these five years we've never had a wrong word, so far as I can recall. And she's never interfered, either, she's left me to get on with it, never poking around, niggling about, sticking her nose into the store-cupboard and such, like a lot of mistresses. " What do you want, Eddy? " she would ask me, sleepy-like, and I would give her the list. " Well, ring up and order it for yourself, there's a dear," she would say. There are not many mistresses like that, I must say.

I didn't like the insinuations that were going on. You could see people were thinking she did old Rangward in, it was written all over their faces. I'd willingly stake my

last farthing that it wasn't she who did it. I had my own
theories about who done it, which I will leave for the
moment.

I was asked a lot of questions about the other people
in the house, and things right off the point like how often
was I paid and whether it was in notes or cheque, and
how long everybody in the house had been there, and
how much time I had off and how much entertaining they
did. They even asked me whether a lot of alcohol was
consumed on the premises and I had to show them the
wine store, under the stairs.

When they got round to asking me if Mr. and Mrs.
Rangward got on all right together, whether I ever overheard any quarrelling and how often Mr. Shefford and
Baron Halvorsen came, and whether they came when
Mr. Rangward was out, I thought they had gone a bit
far, and told them so. One chap, trying to be clever, said
he thought that murder *was* going a bit far, wasn't it?
You had to use drastic methods, he said, in investigating
drastic crimes. So I had to try to answer the questions
to the best of my ability and no sooner had I done that
than up comes another chap and starts asking me a lot
more questions. And the things they think up!

All the same, I told them as little as I could because I
don't think it's right, tramping all over decent people's
houses and asking a lot of personal questions; you can't
call your soul your own.

They never left Mrs. Rangward alone neither. Not that
she was eating a lot, but you have to keep body and soul
together and I got her nice little snack meals, Welsh
rarebit, which she likes and a nice bit of sole done with
green grapes and such-like. And I took in the tray
regardless. " Here's Madam's lunch," I'd say, with a

look, and they'd have to stop their questions for a bit, anyway.

Miss Emms was another got on my nerves too. I could have strangled the old cow. Treated the whole thing like a personal insult, she did. Kept telling us all she'd never been used to this kind of thing, as if any of us had! Kept saying how sorry she was she'd not gone to Lady Horwich like she'd been asked. Upon my word it was all I could do not to tell her how sorry we all were that she hadn't. I really pity Mr. Toby having to put up with the old hag. I reckon he daren't sack her, the way things are at present. But she's an old misery, thinking of herself all the time when there's others, poor Mrs. Rangward for one, is a lot worse off than she is. Not that she's badly off at all, she's got things pretty much the way she likes and Mr. Toby has to lump it. I could tell Mr. Toby a thing or two about Miss Emms, too, if I was one to make mischief. She doesn't like Tiddly Push, that I do know, there's many a time and oft I've seen her shove him off with her foot, almost a kick, and when she takes him down the street for a bit of exercise she drags him along till he's flying the air at the end of the lead, more like a kite than a dog. It's a shame!

She's given Mrs. Rangward some dirty looks, too. All over her before there was any trouble (such *nice* people, she was always saying), and now . . . looks at her like she was dirt, the same way she looks at Edna Ormer.

Did I say we were all huddled together outside the court? Well, Miss Emms, though she looked as miserable as the lot of us, kept herself just that much off of us, a few feet away down the bench, and she kept her mouth screwed up like she had a nasty smell underneath her nose.

We'd got ourselves all tensed up for this here inquest

when one of the court officials came tiptoeing out, his thick shoes creaking like anything, and whispered behind his hand, " Adjourned siney dee." None of us knew what that meant until a lawyer came out, with a file of papers under his arm, and told Mrs. Rangward that the inquest had been put off, pending police investigations, which sounded pretty sinister to me. I think we all looked like we'd had a bit of a kick in the stomach. And Edna says: " Well, we'd best get off home and get ourselves a cuppa."

The Baron drove Mrs. Rangward home in his big American car. Mr. Shefford followed in his old Bentley and the rest of us crowded into the Jag, driven by Ormer.

Miss Emms went off up to the top of the house and I was glad to see her go; the Ormers asked me to join them for a cup of tea in the basement and I said yes, when I'd seen Madam was comfortable. But when I went up from the garage and into my kitchen to put on the kettle, I heard the two men talking in the living-room.

" I think I can deal with the situation, Halvorsen," I heard Mr. Shefford say.

" No doubt you think you can," I heard the Baron reply. " But I feel sure Annabel would like me to stay and keep her company."

There was a silence you could have cut with a knife, I stopped messing about with the teacups so I should miss nothing.

Then Mr. Shefford said: " I'm getting a bit tired of you, Halvorsen. You're not an old friend of the family, by any means. A year ago, if I remember rightly, they did not know of your existence. At a time like this it is *old* friends that count."

" You know nothing of my friendship with the Rang-wards," I heard the Baron say, all tense and angry.

126

" I know that they thought you a damn' bore," Mr.
Shefford answered; he was angry too.

"I don't want to lay hands on you, Shefford," I heard
the Baron reply, " because you're an older man and you'd
get the worst of it. One murder in the house is quite
enough for the moment."

" Don't be a fool, I'm in far better condition than
you. . . ."

Before I knew where I was they were at it, like two
schoolboys; I dashed into the drawing-room just as Mr.
Shefford's foot went through the glass of the marquetry
china cabinet, caught it with his heel, he did.

" Gentlemen," I shouted, " stop it for the love of mike!
You ought to be ashamed," I went on when they did
stop and pulled down their silk cuffs and straightened
their ties, glaring at each other: " Ashamed," I said,
" behaving like two school kids! "

I started to pick up the bits of glass off the carpet.
Bless me if the Baron didn't sit down, like he was there
for keeps. And so did Mr. Shefford!

I heard Miss Emms's voice calling me over the banisters.
It always annoys me the way she will call me " Eddy."
" It's Mr. Bolton to you," I've said many a time and oft.
But she reckons she's a lady and she goes on calling me
" Eddy."

" Mrs. Rangward is staying upstairs with Mr. Toby for
tea," she says.

I went back to the drawing-room. " Well, gentlemen,"
I said, " Mrs. Rangward is staying upstairs, so I'd go
home if I was you." I would never have thought of talking
to them like that before Mr. Rangward died; but now
everything's different.

There's not a thing goes on in the house without Master

127

Tiddly Push knows all about it. In he came as much as to say: " Now, what was all that noise about? " He went up to the broken pane of glass and sniffed it.

I could have given them both tea, but I reckoned it was high time they went. So I opened the front door and stood waiting, taking a firm line, kind of thing. The Baron got up and smoothed his hair back nervous-like with his hand. He's got a bit of a nerve, though. He stood in the drawing-room doorway, bowing slightly so's Mr. Shefford could pass out first. I saw Mr. Shefford eyeing his backside like he'd willingly give it a good kick, but he kept his temper and came out into the hall.

" We're clear of the police for the moment," I said to cover the awkwardness; " let's enjoy it whilst we can."

The Baron, hatless, kept well behind Mr. Shefford like he was making sure he, the Baron, would be the last out of the house. Mr. Shefford stuck on his bowler hat, comic-like, right on the front of his head. He looked real arrogant and, as he went down the steps in front of the Baron, I fully expected to see the Baron give his backside the kick that Mr. Shefford had himself been thinking about. I would have had a good laugh if it hadn't all been so serious.

But our Edna was enjoying herself. I could see that when I went down for the cuppa she had suggested. She'd got her face all arranged like you take your hat off in the presence of death, but there was a look in her eye would have made me laugh if I felt like laughing. What she didn't seem to notice was that there was anything wrong with Rudie Ormer.

I said: " There'll be another corpse around before long, I reckon," I says, " they're out for each other's blood, those two," I said, with a jerk of my head meaning the

Baron and Mr. Shefford. "It's a pity really," I said; "duelling's over and done with. If those two went and had a duel they'd feel a lot better. As it is . . ." And I told them about the scene upstairs.

I said: "They're regular old-fashioned. It's not often you get men feel the way those two do about a lady."

Edna sniffed, a regular nasty sniff, I thought it best not to inquire what she had in mind.

Ormer was quiet. I kept looking at him. He'd been pale and not like himself these last few days but then, hadn't we all? We'd all had a nasty shock but Ormer, I fancied, had taken it worse than the rest of us.

I asked him what was wrong and Edna answered for him. Rudie was worried, she said. Didn't I realise we were all going to be out of a job, and it was a lot worse for them because they'd be out of house and home as well?

Then Edna and I got talking about what was behind it all, Edna had got the same feeling I had, there was something at the back of it all. I said, Was it something to do with racing? Was he bankrupt? I wondered. All the race meetings he went to, there was big money changed hands, that I knew. I'd heard Mr. Rangward on the telephone sometimes; it wasn't chicken food he was talking to bookies about. I said maybe he'd gone bankrupt and did himself in, though, even as I said it, I knew it wasn't right, the doing-himself-in part. You'd only got to know Mr. Rangward to know he'd never do that.

The one thing frightened him was death, he couldn't let himself have nothing much to do in case he got thinking, it scared the lights out of him. It was like he knew that death was something he could do nothing

129

about, but all the same, he was going to do what he could. How did you keep from getting cancer? he used to ask Mr. Toby. And what did Mr. Toby think was the real cause of thrombosis? And did Mr. Toby reckon continued sleeplessness caused heart trouble and an early death? A regular hypo-whatever they're called. That type don't take their own lives.

This morning when I was dusting the dressing-room, got to keep the place dusted even if the boss has gone, I looked into his little cupboard, stands on his boot-rack. Jammed, it is, packed with patent medicines. There's a lot of them free samples he's got from Mr. Toby, but there is a lot more he's bought, tried once or twice and given up. He was always getting Dr. Trench to make him out prescriptions and the doctor used to pull his leg, saying he ought to be under a National Health doctor and then he'd get all his dope on the cheap. He was the sort would send threepence in stamps for a free sample of some quack remedy or other. His health was his hobby.

Thinking it over, I said to Edna and Rudie, I says: " If a mixture of patent remedies could kill people I'd say it was that."

" Go on! " Rudie exclaimed. " There's no denying cyanide, can't get round that."

I says, very casual, doing a bit of detection of my own: " What's this here capsule of cyanide? What's it like? Is it really glass? "

" It's like a small ampoule, as you might say," Rudie explained. " Yes, glass, not more than three-quarters of an inch long, you break off the top in the mouth and whiff—you're a goner."

" Or else," Edna says, " you break off the top and pour out what's in the ampoule, as you call it, into a glass."

" No," Rudie says; " it's got to be properly broke. Air won't let it come out of the top. You've got to smash it proper."

" Well, then," I says, " that's a lot of hot air about the ampoule being smashed till it's powder by . . . someone's foot right into the carpet."

" Yep. All of us was tramping round, it's no wonder the empty container got trodden on, more than once, I'd say."

I says: " Rudie," I says, " how come you know such a lot about it? "

I could feel Edna let out with her foot underneath the table, for all she looked so casual. He's all there, though, he wasn't going to give anything away, not he.

" Oh," he says, nice as nice, " when I did ambulance driving I did a bit of hospital orderly work thrown in. You pick up things, you know."

" So it seems," I remarked; " so it seems." And then after a bit I says: " Rudie," I says, " how did you get this job in the first place? "

I could see I'd jumped right into the middle of something. Rudie's neck went red as a turkey cock. He says, right out: " Eddy, are you trying to pick a quarrel? " he says.

" By no means. I only wondered."

" It's a funny time to start wondering. I could begin thinking how did you come to have the job."

" I can tell you that," I says, quite ratty. " I got sick of hotel work, wanted a job on my own, and better-class work at that. Went to the Crown and Anchor Domestic Agency and picked this job right off the assembly line."

To tide over the nasty pause Edna asked:

131

" What's up with us all? We must hang together whatever else."

Rudie gave a sharp laugh. " Might of been better put," he said.

Whatever else, I repeated to myself, it is my duty to look after Mrs. Rangward's interests. I'm still in her employment, I'm still being paid (I hope) and therefore, I kept reminding myself, I owe loyalty to Mrs. Rangward. So I set myself to keep off the reporters, and giving a nasty look to those people who came and stood outside the house, having a good stare. And I did my best over the police, treating them polite but that much coldly and not falling over myself to offer them cups of tea, like others I could mention.

It was the Baron and Mr. Shefford I couldn't stomach. In and out, in and out, and it wasn't as though she seemed pleased to see either of them. She spent a lot of time upstairs with Mr. Toby and she went out and stayed out quite a long time, goodness knows where she went, to a movie to be by herself, most likely. But I could see Mr. Shefford and the Baron bothering around weren't doing her no good.

The Baron came when she was out and seemed quite annoyed. " Where's she gone? "

I gave him such a look. I said: " It is not my business to ask Madam where she is going to when she goes out," as much as to tell him that it wasn't his business either.

He was like a cat on hot bricks. " You mustn't let her go out, on her own, like that," he says, very much annoyed.

" And pray, why not? " I couldn't be polite, I couldn't. It was such cheek, I reckoned.

132

" You never know," he said. " You never know what she might do. She might never come back."

" And for why? "

" Well, look at the way the police are persecuting her."

" That's natural. They've got to find out who done it."

" Well, they won't find out that way. It's third degree."

I got him suddenly. I knew he was one of those think she did it. I couldn't understand for why, I could not. They reckon they love her, but they don't have a clue what she is like if they think she done it. If you'd got that much knowledge of human nature you'd know she couldn't have done it. It's not in her, no more than a baby in arms could have done it. She wouldn't have got that sort of thing in her mind in the first place, let alone carry it out. It seems as clear as daylight to me, and I can't understand how other people can't see it the way I see it. Maybe it is because I am not in love with her, nor ever likely to be, that I see the thing so clearly. They say love is blind. I don't reckon love is blind, seems much more, love makes you see things what aren't there at all.

I looked the Baron straight in the eye, or rather I tried to, but he is a goodish bit taller than me. I thought, shall I tell him straight? And then I thought, but I'm only Eddy; the pansy, they call me, with a laugh. The queer. I don't know anything. I don't exist. They never think people like me might observe a lot more than people like them. When people are in love, as they call it, they get their sight all cluttered up with it, can't see straight, for the time being. Oh, I know I get myself worked up, but when that's over and things settle down, I can see what's left pretty clear.

I thought all this before I answered the Baron. I knew full well what he meant by third degree, he meant the

133

police was wearing her down, talking away at her, until they got her tired out and ready to confess to anything.

I had to say something. I couldn't leave it at that for all I'm the servant and it's supposed to be none of my business. I reckon it was the business of all of us, this lot.

" It doesn't matter how much they question her. She no more did it than you did," I said.

He jumped at that. " I'm glad you think that," he said, talking to me, for once, as though I really was there. " But how do you know I didn't do it? "

That was a surprise. " I reckon you didn't, that's all." A lame reply, I grant.

" You could be wrong, Eddy. Think it over. You could be wrong."

Yes, I could be wrong, but I firmly believe Rudie Ormer did it, and why I think Ormer done it is this: It's always been like Mr. Rangward had a hold over Ormer, to my way of thinking. It's like Ormer's got something at the back of his mind he's afraid of. I reckon he's an ex-gaol-bird or something of the sort. Being the business gentle-man he was, I dare say Mr. Rangward came in touch with all sorts in the day's work and I shouldn't be at all surprised to hear Ormer had done his stretch and that Mr. Rangward had given him a chance to go straight. He was like that, Mr. Rangward, not fussy. This last five years, I reckon, Ormer's grown sick and tired of the hold Mr. Rangward had over him till at last he couldn't bear it and when the opportunity came along he took it.

The opportunity . . . that's what I can't make up my mind about for sure. When did Rudie give him the cyanide capsule?

Fanciful? Yes, but you've got to be a bit fanciful planning out a murder. I don't read all those detective stories for nothing; murder is fanciful and that's that.

It is like this: this sudden death is one of three things.

(1) Suicide. We're all of one mind that it's not that.

(2) Accident. How could it be that?

(3) Murder. Well, they do happen, it's two a week they say they know of, isn't it? And I reckon there's more murders take place than we ever hear of, it's only the flops get into the news. Well, here is a murder right in our midst and if Rudie Ormer done it it's only fair he should be brought to justice. Though, at the moment, the police are about as far off the mark as they could be.

The opportunity again . . . now Rudie seems about as familiar with cyanide as with Beecham's Powders. Mr. Rangward and Rudie were quite friendly, master and chauffeur, sort of thing. Mr. Rangward would talk away to him about his little troubles by the hour, sitting beside him in the Jag. I can see Rudie saying, slyly: " Ever tried these? " and bringing out one of those capsules he's so familiar with. I can hear Mr. Rangward laughing. " Try anything once," and slipping it into his pocket. It wouldn't matter to Rudie when he took it, any old time would do just so long as he took it.

Come to think of it, it wouldn't have been a bad idea at all if Rudie had given him the capsule on the way to the airport the day they flew to Lisbon. If Mr. Rangward had taken it whilst he was staying with his sister and dropped dead there nobody would have been any the wiser how he came by the poison. They're a bit soft in foreign parts, so I've heard, about crime. It takes them years to catch a murderer and I reckon if Mr. Rangward had died sudden in Portugal, they'd still have been scratching their heads this time next year.

So maybe Rudie intended him to take it in Portugal and maybe he saved it till he got home. . . .

Roughly, that's my idea of what happened. Brains, eh?

Part Two

THE TALL, haggard-looking man, erstwhile creature of the fog, looked a good deal more mortal standing in the livid light of Piccadilly Circus Underground with his violin case under his arm. There was nothing startlingly distinctive about him, his face and his duffle coat looked almost the same colour but he had a certain Byron-like romantic appeal.

There was a number of other men standing around waiting, their faces all wearing the same sort of look, which would alter only when the particular person for whom they were waiting arrived. There was, however, a small moment of hesitation before the face of the man with the violin case lighted up, for Annabel looked oddly different in a way that he could not for the moment fathom.

" Good gracious! " he exclaimed. " Black stockings! "

She smiled wanly at the attempt to cheer her up, looking back over her shoulder. There was a man following her who was quite wilfully like any other man, hatless, hands deep in the pockets of his elephant-coloured raincoat and a look of boredom on his face. He had been with her from Regent's Park station, and now he was standing with his back to her, looking at the magazines arranged on the bookstall. But Annabel was not deceived.

She took the arm of the violinist. " Let's go to Lyons," she said, " it's nice and cheerful there."

A cold draught blew down the steps from the street and,

as she drew her mink coat round her, Annabel once more glanced back. He was there all right, walking up the steps after them, but looking over their heads to the roof tops where the lights of an advertisement seemed to chase each other round and round a rectangle, like playful coloured mice.

The name of Annabel's lover ought, of course, to have been Sebastian. But it was simply Clement Williams, Clem. He was a Welshman and complied with conformity except in that he had a minor genius for playing the violin and that Annabel Rangward loved him as much as a woman can love a man. She loved him dearly, and tenderly and passionately and possessively and exclusively and too late.

He was her man, he done her wrong; but that did not matter to Annabel because she was utterly monogamous and what the rest of the world might consider to be wrong, Annabel found completely right.

There was a queue, of course, but Annabel and her lover stood patiently amongst the typists, and the long-haired young men in curious garments, and the stout women " up West " for a matinée, until a table was available. She clung on to the arm of her Clem and took pleasure from his proximity.

When, at last, they got a table and Clem had given their order, Annabel drew off her gloves. " I'm not really hungry," she said.

Clem put his hand over hers. " Come now, you must eat, love."

" Oh, Clem." There was an interlude for a few gentle tears. Annabel had come from Richard Rangward's funeral and she held no malice in her heart.

" Was it bad, love? "

138

" No, not bad. The parson said ever such nice things. The horrid bit was when the doors at the end opened and the coffin slid away. I nearly fainted, Clem, honestly."

" Thank goodness he's been put decently to rest."

Annabel nodded. " If only we'd got all the police business over."

" Now, Anny. That's what I want to talk to you about. There's nothing for us to wait for now. What's to stop us getting married right away? "

Annabel sighed. "How's Mum? " she asked evasively.

" She's worried about you, naturally, but I've had a word with her. She's all for us marrying straight away. She says people'll talk whatever happens. You're in it up to the neck is her idea and she says, if you marry me now, at least you'll have that comfort, whatever else you may have to face."

Annabel nodded. But she was not looking at Clem, her eyes were searching the room. . . .

" What is it, love? "

" It—it's not as easy as that, Clem. You think you've no more worries. Richard is dead, that's all you think matters."

" That's all I care about. You've been Richard's all this past five years. Haven't you any idea of the misery it's been for me, Anny? "

" I haven't been his. I never was his. I've been yours all the time."

He moved the cutlery about impatiently. " I know all about that, but in actual fact you were his," he said, ignoring the shake of her head. " His death is a blooming miracle to me. I'm feeling fine, it's like I've been ill and now I'm better. And it's just happened at the right moment, that's what makes it so marvellous. Another

139

few weeks and anybody could see what was wrong with you, Anny."

Annabel shuddered. " Don't let's think about it." She slipped her coat over the back of her chair and sat staring at him. " You don't think, do you? "

" Think? What do you know? "

" I mean—*think*, Clem. You know they're all saying it's murder. Well, a murder has to be done by somebody."

" I reckon there's many a chap would have liked to murder Richard Rangward."

" Maybe. But who did? "

There he was, the elephant-coloured sleuth, sitting at a table where sat a large, red-faced woman. He was sipping coffee, or perhaps it was tea, and munching a biscuit. He was looking, ostensibly, at the *Evening News* lunchtime edition and taking no notice at all of Annabel. But he could see her all right.

" That's nothing to do with us." Comfortably Clem plunged his knife into the heart of his poached egg and watched the yolk flood over the white and down on to the soggy toast. He had gone through his agony, his hours of watching outside the house, imagining; his hours of practising his violin in his bed-sitting-room in Brixton, putting all the misery of his heart into a squeaking torture of gut against string, it was all behind him. With the death of Rangward, Clem had come out into the sunshine and he felt as though nothing would ever hurt any more.

" Clemmy, darling," Annabel looked at him as tenderly and sweetly as a mother looks at her newly-born babe. " Richard has gone just at the right time, as you say. But things like that don't happen by chance, not in real life, they don't, *not accidentally*. You must see what I'm getting at? "

Clem, eggy, shook his head.

Annabel's eyes filled with tears. She could bring Clement back to real life, she knew, if she were to tell him about the man who was even now watching them as he read his *Evening News*, but she wanted to protect him from further misery and distress whilst, at the same time, reminding him of the seriousness of their situation.

" It's so plain to me," Annabel wailed softly. " He's unselfish, for all he's alone in the world. He loves me the way he might have loved a daughter if he'd ever had one. He doesn't care what happens to him just so long as I'm happy, so long as everything comes all right for me."

Clement stared at her in astonishment, then, recollecting, said: " Oh, your friend Mr. Totterdell! "

Annabel nodded, tearfully. " He's been right all along. He said years ago that I ought never to have married Richard. Well, we all know that. I do know that he's made life much happier for me whilst I had to stay married to Richard." Annabel did not touch her food, but now she took a sip of her coffee. " Can't you see what I'm getting at? "

But it would be many weeks before Clem took life seriously again; he knew that the tremendous weight was lifted from his heart, that it was replaced by a song and it would be very difficult to worry about anything for a long time.

" It was my fault," Annabel went on. " No sooner had we got back from the airport than I went upstairs to him. I was longing to see Mr. Toby. Oh, Clem, I'd been feeling so sick in Portugal, so sick and yet so thrilled about the baby! After I went to that doctor in Lisbon and he said it was a baby all right, I thought it must have shown

141

on my face. I caught myself laughing at my reflection in the mirror. I thought somebody *must* know, and yet nobody seemed to. Richard's sister might if she hadn't been thinking so hard about herself that she never sees anybody else. So when I got back, I had to dash upstairs and tell it all to Mr. Toby."

The man in the elephant-coloured raincoat had ordered another cup of coffee. The large woman, having finished her meal, had left the table and he sat on alone.

" And when I'd told him everything I felt a lot better. ' Richard will have to divorce you now,' he said. ' If he were a normal man he wouldn't want to keep you, *and* the child of another man. As it is he may still want to keep you, *but*——' ' Yes,' I said, ' but what? ' ' But I won't let him. I shall blackmail him. I shall tell him he will have to divorce you—or else! ' You know the teasing, half-serious way he has of talking. Then he asked me exactly when the baby should come and when I told him, he said there was no time to be lost. We had a long talk about everything and then I went down and had tea with Richard. I was practically certain Richard would be going up to see Mr. Toby afterwards, as we had a dinner-party that night. He often goes up at that time of day. He said he was going up to tell Mr. Toby about the holiday." Annabel twisted her small handkerchief about. " Do you think it happened then, Clem? "

" What? "

Annabel leaned forward across the table. " Do you think Mr. Toby gave him the poison when he went up before dinner? " she whispered.

Clement stared at her in astonishment. " Even so . . . why would he take it? "

" Mr. Toby was always giving him patent remedies.

142

He might easily have given him the poison capsule and told him it was for his lumbago."

"And was Richard such a fool as to take it?"

Annabel shook her head impatiently. "You don't understand, Richard wasn't a fool. It was just that over his health—well, I've often told you what a child he was about himself."

"Then serve him right," Clement returned stoutly as he cleaned up his plate with a piece of roll. He leaned back and took out a cigarette. "Don't worry, Anny. You're worrying yourself a lot and it won't do our baby any good. Let things take their course."

"Take their course," Annabel repeated wonderingly. "Let Mr. Toby get arrested for murder, a murder which he did for us?"

Clement shifted uneasily in his chair.

"He wouldn't get hanged, anyway."

"You don't believe it, Clem, do you? You don't believe that Richard's death wasn't an act of God, the act of a God whose only desire was to see Clem and his Annabel happily married and their baby born in wedlock. Things don't happen like that."

Annabel glanced through the smoke-laden atmosphere. The man in the elephant-coloured raincoat was looking across at her and for the first time she met his eyes. A policeman, or not even a policeman, a poorly-paid sleuth . . . and yet he was looking at Annabel in the way she was used to men looking at her.

Williams was a man of strong ambition, though a visionary and capable of standing outside Annabel's home, ⁺orturing himself, he combined a practical strain with his Celtic ideology and he owed his success as much to sheer hard work as to genius. There was a time for dreaming, a time for making love and a time for practising. At present, in his mind, he was going over a difficult phrase of music. He looked fondly at Annabel, but already he had flown in spirit.

Whereas Richard Rangward had treated Annabel with a callous indifference which, at first, had hurt considerably, Clement Williams evinced a tangy air of domination which Annabel adored; it was a refreshing change.

" Back to work, love," he said, tucking his violin under one arm and Annabel's hand under the other. Annabel looked up at him, her own face glowing with the love she felt for him. " There are times," she teased, " when I think you like your violin more than me."

He squeezed her hand to his side.

" Clemmy, what if Richard has left me his money? "

" What's made you think about his money all of a sudden? "

" I've got to go and see the solicitor. He was at the funeral, he told me to go and see him to-morrow morning. Oh, I do hope . . ." she burst out suddenly. For Annabel to be emphatic was a surprise. Williams looked down at her with interest. " What do you hope? "

" I do hope it won't be much, the money he's left. What are they going to say. . . . Clemmy, when we're married, so soon, I mean? "

" It will be my wife they're saying things about," he answered darkly; " they won't have to forget that." They turned into a small side-street and into the doorway of a shop. " I won't press you for an answer now but next time I shall want to know what day you're going to marry me, and it had better be soon, isn't it? " The Welsh upward lift at the end of his sentence brought a smile to

Annabel's face. They kissed good-bye in the shop doorway and the man standing on the opposite side of the road shuffled his feet uncomfortably and averted his gaze.

Waiting on the platform, the sleuth gave his attention to the advertisements stuck on the walls. He was completely nonplussed when the woman whose movements he was observing came up to him and said good evening.

" Er—good evening," he stammered politely.

" Why are you following me? " Annabel asked point blank.

" Instructions, miss."

" From whom? "

" My—er—my employers."

" The police, I suppose? "

" Well—er——"

" Well, you silly little man, what do you hope to find out? "

Stung, he answered a trifle testily: " I haven't done too badly, not for one afternoon, I haven't." He jerked his head, indicating the departed Williams. " Gent with the violin case. You'll have to get used to it, lady. My instructions are to keep you watched till further notice, taking notes."

At the moment the train came in and they both entered and sat down side by side.

" That was my fiancé," Annabel told him.

" Oh, yes? "

" We're getting married very soon."

" Oh, yes? "

Annabel bit her lip. " If there is anything else you want to know, please ask me." There was not a trace of sarcasm in her voice and the little sleuth's sharp look melted to one just something short of admiration. His

145

meagre professional attributes were dropped, he rapidly became another man under the spell of a fascinating woman.

"Don't think I'm enjoying it," he said, "it proper hurts me, following you around. But if you've nothing to hide, well, there's no harm done, eh?"

Annabel turned her big eyes slowly in his direction. "I've nothing to hide, now." Nor had she; only she knew what pleasure it had given her to say, a minute ago: that was my fiancé.

"Do you know," he said as though coming to a great decision, "I don't think you have anything to hide. It's a shame, what everyone is thinking."

"How do you mean?" Annabel asked candidly.

"Well" he shrugged his shoulders, "I mean. And look at the papers with all their incinerations."

"I don't. But what do you mean?" she persisted.

He moved a little closer, not too close because the leather arm between them prevented it, but quite close enough.

"They're saying you poisoned Mr. Rangward and what I say is, if you've nothing to hide—well, you didn't. Not "—he laid an officious hand on her fur-covered arm —" not that I for one moment agree with them. But if I follow you around and show them how innocent all your movements are—well, it's going to be all the better for you." He wondered just how innocent her afternoon's movements had been.

"Why should I, Mr.—er——?"

"Bell's the name."

"Mr. Bell . . ."—Annabel lowered her voice as the train had now stopped at Oxford Circus, "why should I poison my husband?"

146

The expression on Mr. Bell's face was like that of someone very much enjoying a film, he was enraptured. " To leave you free to carry on your nefarious love affairs," he said with juicy erudition, in a hoarse and confidential whisper.

" Oh." Annabel looked down at her neat-gloved hands.

" And yet," Mr. Bell continued, raising his voice as the train started, " it isn't neither of them, what a lark! "

So great was the shock she had sustained that she scarcely heard; she felt dizzy and sick and deafened by it. When the train stopped at Regent's Park, as she stood up she staggered slightly and Mr. Bell solicitously steadied her with a firm grip on her elbow. He guided her towards the lift, feeling twice the size and half as much again.

Up the steps, through the driving wind that always blows out of Regent's Park tube and out into Marylebone Road, over the crossing and along the railings under the plane trees. " Bless me," Mr. Bell said as they turned into Park Row, " I dare say both the gentlemen are there, they don't give you much peace, do they? "

Roused out of her dreamy half-life, Annabel suddenly saw everything with dreadful clarity. She gasped. " Those two! "

Mr. Bell nodded with ill-concealed delight. " Yes! Mr. Shefford and the Baron! "

She might have given way to wild hysterical laughter, she might have turned and hit Mr. Bell hard, she might have rushed screaming into the house, but it was not in her to do any of these things. Outside No. 51 she stopped and turned to Mr. Bell. " You won't be coming any farther? "

" No, I'm taking quarter of an hour off for a pint at

the Dover Castle. I take it you won't be leaving home again before I'm back? "

" No "—Annabel shook her head slowly—" no, I won't be going out again this evening. Well, thank you Mr.—er—Bell."

Wrung with pity, Mr. Bell protested that she had nothing to thank him for.

" Oh, but I have," Annabel said seriously. " I have." Without a smile she held out her hand. " Good-bye, and thank you again."

Uncomfortable, Mr. Bell put out his hand, the newspaper dropped from under his arm, nervously he stooped to pick it up and when he stood up Annabel's hand was still outstretched. Mr. Bell clasped it with his own, sticky with nerves.

" Bye-bye, till next time, Mrs. Rangward. It's been a pleasure, I'm sure."

Annabel stepped into the living-room, shutting the door behind her, stood with her back to it and looked, as it were for the first time, at her two so-called lovers. Dressed in dark clothes and black ties they had worn for the funeral, both presented the perfect prototype of the young-man-about-town. Both looked like the magazine illustration of the male escort, the young-man-that-never-was-on-land-or-sea. Charles had kissed her, many a time, she remembered, and she had hardly noticed it. Anders had not gone so far as to kiss her but his manner towards her had always been charged with nervous emotion.

" Have a drink, Annabel? Let me mix you a White Lady? " Annabel shook her head, slowly she drew off her gloves, finger by finger. " But I'm glad," she said, " that you have helped yourselves to drink." She was incapable of sarcasm, but a twinge of unhappiness twisted Halvorsen's face. He made a formal remark, however, about their drinking to Richard's memory and the memory of the many happy hours, etc. Nor could Annabel give him a withering look.

" Let's cut out the formalities," Charles suggested. He was standing in front of the fire, in a position of authority as befitted one who had known the Rangwards for some time. " I would like to know what your plans are, Annabel. What is going to happen to you? "

" How can she know that? " Anders Halvorsen asked angrily. " It is much too soon for Annabel to have made any plans. The police . . . the solicitors . . . all Richard's affairs have to be looked into."

" I was talking to Annabel," Charles reminded him coldly.

" I am answering for Annabel."

" I think Annabel is capable of answering for herself," Charles stated, not in the least believing it.

Halvorsen said: " You must make your own decisions, Annabel, you must not be influenced by anyone. We all . . . that is . . . we both have your interests at heart and we are both ready to do everything in our power. . . ."

" Cut it out," Charles snapped. " I, too, am capable of speaking for myself. This isn't the time for one of your formal addresses. Skol! " he added insolently, emptying his glass.

Halvorsen went a degree paler but he controlled himself admirably; nothing, he realised, would be gained by losing his temper. He was, however, certain that if Annabel were left alone with Shefford she might be persuaded into allowing him to take charge of her affairs, if not of Annabel herself. It was a crucial time and, if he were to go carefully, he might himself step into the rôle of protector; it was clear that Shefford had already had enough to drink. With this last thought in mind, Halvorsen held his hand out for Charles's empty glass, refilled it, topped-up his own glass, said: "Skol!" And drank from it.

"We do not know," he said, "how Annabel will be left. She may be well-to-do, she may be penniless. It may be that we shall have to help her very much."

Charles made a sound signifying disagreement. "Richard was a good business-man," he said, "apart from the question of a will, I don't believe that his affairs will be anything but cut-and-dried."

"Ah!" Halvorsen looked from one to the other. "A good business-man. He did not talk about his affairs."

"Property," Charles said shortly.

"Property?" Halvorsen repeated wonderingly.

"Real estate," Charles qualified.

"*Real* estate," Halvorsen echoed. "What is that?"

"Immovable property, lands—houses."

"Ah . . . so!"

"He has big interests in outlying districts, Earl's Court, Baron's Court, Hammersmith."

Halvorsen repeated, "Ah . . . so!" in such a way that Charles gave him a sharp look.

Charles said: "Richard didn't like the idea of dying at all. It would not surprise me to hear that he has made no will. Richard, God rest his soul, *de mortuis*, and so forth, was captain of his soul, up to the point of departure. He had everything the way he wanted it and I admired him for it. He knew what he wanted and he got it. It was only death he couldn't do anything about, poor chap. That's why he got so fussed about himself. I used to think he was old-maidish, I couldn't fit his hypochondria on to him, somehow. It's only now he's gone that I can see it clearly."

" I thought you said it was no time for formal addresses. You may be right about Richard, *as far as you go*. But that is not far. I see that I know a *great* deal more about our late friend than you."

After delivering this shot, Halvorsen sat down, as though there for life; it only remained for Charles to take his departure.

" Is that so? " Charles said slowly.

" It is so."

" What do you propose to do with your knowledge, Halvorsen? "

" I shall wait and see, as you say."

" Wait and see, eh? Don't you think that anything you may know that—er—that is not common knowledge, might be of interest to the police? "

" Possibly."

" Then you will see, Halvorsen, that anything you may tell the police will also be of help to Annabel."

" No, I cannot see that follows."

" Are you trying to tell us that Richard led a double life? He had a mistress, perhaps? Another establishment? It would not surprise me over much."

" You English! " Halvorsen exclaimed. " You will never cease to astonish me! "

" That is because you Swedes try to generalise and you can't generalise with people like us. It can't be done."

Annabel, still wearing her coat, was sitting on the arm of a chair, stroking her gloves which hung from one hand, her eyes were lowered. Both of them turned to her suddenly.

151

Everything was changed now, for Annabel. It was as though she had stepped right out of her old self. For the first time she spoke to them about something which was important.

"Perhaps you would like to know," she said, "how things really were between Richard and me. We did not live together as man and wife, Richard did not want me that way. He only wanted to marry me because to be married and to live in a nice house was the right thing to do, like having a Bentley and going to the races, belonging to Heron's Club and going to Portugal for a holiday. Richard did not marry out of his class. We belong to the same class; my mother keeps a lodging-house in Brixton, my father was a third-rate actor who lodged with her. It is from him that I have inherited the ability to act, to act the part of a . . . lady. My mother wanted me to go on the stage and I wanted to, too, but I could not act well enough. They told me I was very bad. So I gave it up and took to my music. I got poorly-paid jobs in night-clubs. And then I met Richard. I thought that by marrying him I was going up in the world. I thought he was a gentleman, the Honourable, they called him at the night-club where I worked. It seemed a wonderful chance for me, and I took it."

Annabel stroked her gloves, eyes still lowered. "In a way I have gone up in the world, I have done well for myself. Only this"—she waved vaguely round the room —"isn't what I want. None of it, nothing, is any good if you don't . . . have love with it," she ended in a whisper.

"Did you hate Richard, Annabel?" Charles asked. Both men had put down their glasses and were now standing near her.

"No. I don't hate anybody."

152

Then why? The unspoken question hung in the air.

Halvorsen, conquering the acute irritation that Shefford's presence was giving him, went down on one knee, so that his face was level with Annabel's face. " I have an idea for you," he said, very intense. " Please, please consider it for it is a good one. I have a house in Sweden, not far from Stockholm, inland, on the edge of a large lake. It is an old wooden house, Annabel, warm and comfortable, and there are servants there all the time. I would like you to go there until all the trouble is over. There is a big piano, a Bechstein. I have two horses, for riding, and a groom who looks after them. And when the snows come there is a sleigh and a pony to draw it."

" Look here, Halvorsen. Pendlehead is a lot nearer. . . ."

Halvorsen shook Shefford's remark off angrily. He laid a hand on Annabel's fur-covered arm. " Don't you see? It would be the best for you? Peaceful . . . away from it all. Please . . ."

Shefford looked sulky, he thrust his hands into his pockets and stood with legs apart, in front of the fireplace.

" And while you are away, Annabel, I will deal with everything, the police and the lawyers. There will be nothing for you to worry about."

" She can't possibly go before the inquest."

" I cannot go," Annabel said slowly, " because they will not let me. I am being watched. I could never get out of the country."

Halvorsen made no attempt to conceal his horror and dismay. " This is getting serious." He jumped to his feet.

" Getting serious "—Charles Shefford's laugh was slightly sneering—" my poor fellow. My poor drivelling chap! "

There was but one thing left he could do and that was

to wipe the sneer off Shefford's face. Halvorsen did so, acting instinctively, as he had so unwisely done before.

It was quite a splendid fight; unfortunately it was to do nothing to further Annabel's cause.

The grog tray went over with a prolonged noise which brought Edna and Rudie Ormer up from the basement. Eddy shouted at them to stop, Edna cried to Ormer to part them, and Miss Emms, who happened to be passing, started shrieking and squeaking in many different sharps and flats.

Ormer felt it his duty to do something but was afraid of getting hurt.

Eddy's main concern was the furniture, the Queen Anne tallboy with the three *famille rose* bowls, the china cabinet with the Rockingham tea-service, the Georgian whatnot with the yellow Liverpool Transfer. He stood protectively in front of first one and then another valuable piece as they fought towards it. He could not save the whatnot, however, it went with a splendid crash, and a piercing scream from Edna.

Annabel was not there, she had fled upstairs to fetch Mr. Toby, but her small gloves were being trampled to and fro, underfoot.

Mr. Toby arrived quietly, he carried Tiddly Push under one arm and had his stick in his hand.

" Are they drunk? " he asked.

It was clear that Halvorsen was getting the better of the fight. He was the younger man and though he was not fighting skilfully he was, possibly, the angrier. His long arms were swinging, out of control but none the less dangerously. It seems that the aggressor always has the advantage and Charles Shefford was receiving some unpleasant blows in spite of his skill in parrying them.

When he realised that he was at the front door and on the point of being driven from the house he was off his guard for a moment. The mighty right hand at the end of Halvorsen's wildly flailing arm caught him under the chin and out he went on to the pavement.

The Baron waited a minute to see that Shefford did not get up, then pushed his way back through the gaping onlookers into the living-room. He was badly short of breath, but with an assumed nonchalance he picked up his neglected glass from the chimney-piece and grandly took a drink from it.

Annabel came slowly down the last few stairs and into the wreck of her living-room. Everyone else was outside on the pavement. Halvorsen held up his glass. His face was bloody and battered but he was in a state of exultation and could not resist a fine theatrical gesture; " Skol! " he said, raising his glass.

Had the murder at 51 Park Row been something less than a week old, there would have been observers on the pavement, people who had nothing to do but stand and stare, watching whatever might occur. And upon this occasion they would not have been disappointed.

The affair, however, had now been relegated to a small column in the Press, and public interest was reduced to a trickle of abusive anonymous letters which arrived daily and were annexed on arrival by Eddy and taken to Mr. Toby on his express instructions.

There was no police car outside and a merciful darkness shrouded the scene; Mr. Toby realised there was much to be thankful for.

" I hope to God he's not killed him," he said, " it would

155

be a bit too much in the way of a complication. Can you find out, Rudie? "

Ormer knelt down on the pavement and felt above Shefford's heart.

" Knocked him out stone-cold, sir."

" Is Mr. Shefford's car here? " It was not.

" Edna, you go down to the corner and get a cab," Mr. Toby directed, " you can tell the cabby there's a drunk to be taken home. And Eddy "—Mr. Toby fumbled in his hip pocket and brought out a pound note—" you take Mr. Shefford home. It's a flat in Albany. If the old man Shefford is at home, you'll have to explain. Get their family doctor anyway, and make sure he's comfortable before you come back. Now, Eddy, I charge you. Don't come back till you're sure he'll live. He could be very badly concussed, he came a fearful smack on the pavement; but maybe, if he's got enough alcohol in him, he'll have got off lightly."

Feeling first with his stick, Mr. Toby knelt clumsily down beside the recumbent Shefford and felt his pulse. " Is that cab coming? " he asked irritably. " There might be a cerebral hæmorrhage, this pulse is damned weak. . . ."

A taxi, with Edna clinging dramatically to it, came round the corner on two wheels. The cabby, clearly an ex-commando, leaped from it and he and Rudie scooped the body up and into the cab in a matter of seconds.

" Well done! " As the cab drew away, Mr. Toby rose and dusted the knees of his trousers.

Apart from the ubiquitous Mr. Bell it cannot be said that nobody observed the scene. One or two passers-by slowed down and looked back, and half a dozen or so people on the other side of the street stopped and stared.

But on the whole, as Mr. Toby remarked, they had " got off very lightly."

" You'd better go and see what you can do for the Baron," he told Ormer, " and you, Edna, you'd better take yourself into Eddy's kitchen and get us all a cup of tea." Mr. Toby groped round for his stick, retrieving it from the pavement beside him. " Are you there, Miss Emms? " Miss Emms was there, she was having a small scuffle with Tiddly Push, who was endeavouring to evade her. Mr. Toby stood quite still, like a gun-dog pointing. " Who else is here? There is someone else! "

There was, in fact, someone else. A smartly-dressed woman was standing under the lamp-post inscribed William IV. Elsewhere in this story she has been loosely referred to as " a perfectly horrible woman." This was an exaggeration but she had a distinctly raffish air which, under certain circumstances, became roguish with an underlying hardness and could well give rise to the epithet " perfectly horrible." But now she was no more than a worried-looking earnest woman. She stood hesitating in the circle of light by the lamp-post.

" The excitement is all over," Mr. Toby said, " I should go off home." He turned towards the house, clicking his fingers to Tiddly Push. " Where are you, Miss Emms? "

" Here, and never, in all my born days, have I known such goings on. In a respectable house—disgraceful. Mr. Rangward not dead a week and his house turned into something like a low-class public house! "

" My house, Miss Emms, my house." Gently Mr. Toby began to shut the front door. The woman had followed him in and was now standing on the threshold. " Excuse me, is this number 51? "

" It is, Madam."

157

" The late Mr. Rangward's house? "

" He lived here, but I'm afraid we cannot do anything for you."

" I would like to see Mrs. Rangward, as they call her."

" I'm sorry," Mr. Toby replied; " but you really can't, you know. If there is anything you feel you must say to her, perhaps you would write it. Many other people are doing so." Mr. Toby cleared his throat, leaving a great deal unsaid.

" It is very urgent indeed! I'm sure she would want to see me. I know she would."

" Who are you? "

The woman hesitated. " Why should I tell you? Who are you? "

" I am Tobias Totterdell, the owner of this house, and for the moment I am acting as Mrs. Rangward's guardian."

" In that case, perhaps you had better tell her—it's Mrs. Rangward."

" I don't understand."

" Mrs. Dicky Rangward. I have my marriage lines here with me, in my bag. They're shabby, but you can still read them."

Tiddly Push was sniffing round her feet. Miss Emms was like one of the memorable figures at Pompeii, arrested for ever in the stilly heart of time.

Mr Toby ran a hand across his forehead. " This," he said, " is getting beyond me. I'm out of my depth." Recovering himself a little, he said: " But, still; you've won. You'd better come inside."

She stepped into the hall.

" Can you find out where Mrs. Rangward is, Miss Emms? I can't have her bothered now with this."

Annabel had gone up to her room to find first-aid

appliances for Halvorsen. Edna was getting tea in Eddy's kitchen, Rudie Ormer, with a basin of warm water and cotton-wool, was doing what he could for the Baron's face.

" You'd better come up to my room," Mr. Toby said distractedly.

" It is her I want to see," the woman reiterated.

" You know, you've come at a very awkward moment," Mr. Toby told her, " there's been a fight and the living-room down here has been a bit knocked about. If you'll come upstairs quietly with me, you can tell me your business and I'll see what I can do."

Annabel was showing an unusual briskness and efficiency. She came downstairs, her hands full of bandages, plaster and lint. She glanced, as she passed, at Mr. Toby, Miss Emms, Tiddly Push and the new arrival and hurried into the living-room, leaving the door wide open as she had no hand free with which to shut it.

" Is that her? " the woman asked. " Dick always had taste. I can see she's busy. I'd best come again in the morning. I want to catch her before that solicitor gets hold of her. Give her less of a shock, that's what I felt. Well, I *never*! "

From where she stood, irresolute, the woman could see right into the living-room. Halvorsen lay on the settee; Ormer had cleaned the blood off his face and it was swelling rapidly. He was holding his eyes open with both hands raised to see how much he could see when he saw her.

" Oh, my God! " he groaned, as though this were one too many.

" Oh, yes, sir," Ormer agreed. " I'm afraid it'll be a lot more painful before you're through."

159

The woman had moved into the open doorway. " If it isn't the Baron," she exclaimed, " I thought it was you from the photograph in the *Sunday Cordial*, but I couldn't be sure! Been getting into trouble again, Baron? My word, you are a one for a fight, and no mistake! " she said admiringly.

" What's that woman doing here? " Halvorsen shouted.

" Now, dear . . . now, dear! "

" It's that damned woman from Oliver Lodge. I have no luck! " With his voice thickened from the rapid puffing-up of his lips, and his eyes swelling almost visibly, Halvorsen was, indeed, an object for pity; he was speedily losing such control as he had been able to gather round him. " It is a nightmare," he shouted, " or else I am going mad! "

" Sh—sh "—Annabel laid a gentle hand on his shoulder —" don't get yourself worked up again, Anders. We've all had enough for the present."

" But what is this bordel-keeper doing here? " There was a Strindberg-like, hysterical edge to his cry.

" I don't know," Annabel replied calmly, " and I don't much care. Here is the wych-hazel, Ormer, if you soak the lint in this and lay it on his eyelids, it will reduce the swelling."

Mr. Toby remonstrated gently with the woman, asking her again to go up with him to his room. But it was a great deal more interesting down here in the living-room, this was where things were happening, and this was where she intended to stay. Edna gave substance to this resolve by coming in with a tray of cups and saucers.

" Tea won't be a tick," she said, coming over to inspect the Baron. " How is he? "

" Bordel-keeper " had stung; Halvorsen's face was not

the only thing to swell, the woman was quietly expanding with indignation until she reached boiling point.

" I don't know who you all are," she said, looking round at the five other people present. " But you had better know who I am. I am Dicky Rangward's lawful wife." She gave an unpleasant laugh. " If it was only a bigamist he was, it'd be simple. But there's a lot more to it than that. I'm sorry," she said harshly, " if this has been a shock to you," turning to Annabel, " but I've got to make myself felt. I wanted to go to Dicky's funeral, and there was nothing to stop me going, but I thought it might create an awkward situation so I spared you all that, and I'd hoped to spare you the shock you'll get to-morrow when you see the lawyer, but I can see I've no need to bother myself. It's myself I've got to look after."

Annabel sat down quickly and said wearily: " You get to the stage when you don't get any more shocks. I've had my big shock for to-day and nothing will surprise me any more. As a matter of fact, it is not a shock to hear that Richard was a bigamist, it's quite a relief. If it is of any interest to you, Richard and I were nothing to each other." It would seem that shock had released Annabel's tongue; she had never been given to utterance and now the words seemed to flow from her.

" But it's the scandal," the woman returned angrily. " Aren't you going to mind that? "

" Just a minute," Mr. Toby cried; " let us behave in a civilised manner even if we are caught up in fantastic events. Edna, bring tea for us all. Then you will come upstairs with me, Madam."

There was a small hiss from his side which Mr. Toby realised was Miss Emms tautly repeating the word " civilised."

161

In a weird silence Edna poured out tea, politely asked people if they took milk and sugar. " This is like after an air raid," she remarked, blowing the hot tea in her cup; " does you good! " Presently she said: " Would you like me and Rudie to retire? You don't want to wash your dirty linen in public."

Talking became increasingly difficult for Halvorsen but talk he must, and, though he sounded as though his mouth were packed with dry biscuit, he was determined to have it out with Annabel whilst he had the chance.

" How is it possible," he asked when they were alone, " that I feel as I have felt for you, Annabel, and that you have known nothing about it? Are you a woman without a heart? What is your secret? What are you thinking? Who are you that you can escape me so? "

" I have told you already once this evening who I am. Do you want me to repeat it? "

" I do not mean literally who are you, but what *kind* of woman are you? "

" You seem to know what kind of woman I am. You believe I poisoned the man I thought was my husband. That is a foolish question."

" I believe that only because I cannot, otherwise, see how it happened."

" What about Charles Shefford? He was alone at the table with Richard while we were dancing. Don't you think he might have done it? "

There was a long pause. " But why? "

Annabel shrugged her shoulders. " If Charles loves me, too, you might find that a reason."

Annabel watched such expression as was apparent on Halvorsen's stiff features.

162

" It is extraordinary," she went on, " you do not even stop to think. I *did* it. You have no shadow of doubt."

It was quite true. And even now he had no shadow of doubt that Annabel did it. He saw it happen.

" And why should I do it? " Annabel asked. " What have I to gain? "

He knew the answer to that, she had a great deal to gain by Richard's death—her freedom, his money. It was, possibly, the motive aspect of the case that had brought him to his conclusion rather than any other.

" It is extraordinary, and sad," Annabel protested, " how wrong people can be about other people! Everyone thinks I have no brains at all, that I am utterly selfish, and even that I am a lady! And now everyone thinks I am a cunning murderess too! People take me at my face value. Nobody ever learns not to believe what they see."

Halvorsen stared at her in amazement, this was a new Annabel indeed.

" If I tell you the truth," Annabel went on, " you won't believe me, so why should I? "

" You should, because I am in this with you. You must, because I want to know where I am. This might ruin me, Annabel. After this affair I shall be finished professionally. We have a high standard to keep up in our Foreign Office and I am far from living up to it. You owe it to me to tell me the truth."

" Very well, then. I was frightened to death of Richard. He wasn't the good fellow you thought him. He was bad. Really wicked people are those who would go to any length to harm others for some personal gain. Richard was one of those. Whoever killed him, killed him to save acute misery to other people."

Halvorsen looked unconvinced.

163

" That woman who is now upstairs with Mr. Toby says she is his wife, and if that is so I am glad, for it means I was never married to Richard Rangward, and I am not Annabel Rangward but still Anne Brown. But think of the unhappiness *she* must have suffered, Anders."

Halvorsen made a sound like a snort of disbelief. " The less we say about that woman the better," he said. " I cannot help it, Annabel. I do not understand you at all. I only love you. I do not mind that you killed Richard. I am silly about you. You have ruined me and I am no longer a sane man, but a raving fool. I cannot reason. I cannot do anything but love you." He held his head in his arms. " And for all these reasons which are not reasons, *I* shall take the blame for the murder. *I* shall ' confess.' "

" You would not do anything so foolish," Annabel exclaimed aghast.

" I am ruined anyway."

" Pull yourself together, Anders."

" And it is not so foolish as you think. I have had it in mind these last few days and I have read up the position in a law book. I have diplomatic immunity, I am exempt from the criminal jurisdiction of the state in which I reside."

Annabel, wide-eyed, hands to her mouth, stared at him.

" Furthermore," he went on, " I had a motive for murdering Richard which might shock the world, which might discredit you English people, indeed, one aspect of your British way of life. If *I* confess to the murder, Annabel, there will be no trial, no more publicity. The matter will be dealt with by my own country and I believe it will be dropped because, to use an English slang which I much dislike, it stinks! "

164

She took his hand, and touched gently the bruised and grazed knuckles. " That could be an answer. It could be an answer to everything. Do you really think it would work out that way? "

He nodded, breathlessly watching how she took his proposition.

" Dear Anders. . . ." She stroked his hand. As Halvorsen watched her, he was aware of feeling some new emotion, but blinded as he was by the violent feelings of love he had experienced for so long, he was quite unable to recognise this new emotion for what it was—dislike.

Mr. Bell, refreshed by his visit to the Dover Castle, took over the evening watch. When Charles Shefford was lightly tossed out of the house on to the pavement and lay there as one dead, it was all Mr. Bell could do not to run forward. But he stayed where he was, chewing frantically at his scrap of gum.

When Charles Shefford and Eddy were loaded into the cab and it moved off, a second vehicle containing Mr. Bell followed it. This was not in his terms of reference, but he felt it was more important to investigate the present happenings than to stand around awaiting some hypothetical movements on the part of the murdered man's wife.

Thus, when Eddy's cab arrived at Albany, Mr. Bell sprang out and ran forward officiously with offers of help.

Charles Shefford was delivered home like a large unwieldy parcel. His father, who had just finished his dinner and was enjoying a quiet cigar by his fireside, was shocked and alarmed. But when his doctor had been called and had administered first-aid, when Charles came round and when he heard Eddy's explanations, he

165

became extremely angry and greatly overdid the use of the old-fashioned word " zany."

He glared at Eddy. " Who are you? " he barked. Eddy told him. " And you? " Eddy looked confused and puzzled how Mr. Bell had got there at all, but that was not amongst his more pressing anxieties.

Old Mr. Shefford was what Eddy afterwards described as " proper worked-up." He stormed up and down Charles's bedroom raving: " He's not been the same since he first met that damned woman! The fool deserves everything he gets, but I'm damned if I know what I've done to deserve a zany for a son. The only one I've got, God help me," he added bitterly. " That woman's put a hoodoo on him. A couple of hundred years ago she'd have been hanged for a witch, and a good job too! I'm all for hanging witches! Let them live and what happens? They poison their husbands. No man's safe when there's women like that around."

Eddy was busy sponging Charles's face, but the patient brushed him aside and leaned up on one elbow. " You don't know anything about it, Dad," he shouted. " Take that back! "

Mr. Shefford senior looked at the ceiling, at the doctor, at Eddy and Mr. Bell. " Listen to the zany! Let's hope, policeman, that your people are going to make a good quick job of it and get the wife convicted as soon as possible or there will be another murder before we've finished. I've never yet heard of two men having a good fight over a decent woman. It's the tarts that like to get men fighting over them."

" An outrageous statement! " Charles groaned and lay back against his pillows. " Who are you? " he asked, suddenly noticing Mr. Bell.

" Attached to the police force, sir," he returned promptly.

" You'd better get your inspector, or someone who is in charge of the Rangward case to come round pronto. I've got an important statement to make. Now."

" He's concussed," the doctor said quickly. " I don't think Charles is responsible for his actions, Mr. Shefford."

"That will make no change," old Mr. Shefford declared, but he looked nervously at Charles all the same. " Could you give him an injection or something to put him out for the time being? "

" I can't do that," the doctor said, shocked. " And he's not bad enough for morphia. But I certainly think it will be some time before Charles is himself. I would advocate sending him down to Pendlehead with a nurse in an ambulance to-morrow morning. He'd be out of the way there until this trouble is over. Concussion needs rest, part of the treatment. I'm off now to make the arrangements."

Old Mr. Shefford, delighted with his medical practitioner, followed him to the front door.

Charles lay with his eyes shut whilst Eddy continued to minister to his face with soft white hands. " Did you hear that, Eddy? "

" Yes, sir. Quite right too, I'd say."

" I might die."

" Possibly, sir. These here hæmorrhages——"

" Baron Halvorsen will have killed me."

" That's right, sir."

" And so he's won."

" Too true, sir." Eddy squeezed out the sponge and took up the bottle of Pond's extract and a dab of cotton-wool. " You've a couple of black eyes now! "

167

" It all started with Two Lovely Black Eyes," Charles murmured. Eddy thought he was raving.

" I don't suppose the Baron is unscathed, is he, Eddy? "

" No. He won't be exactly an oil painting to-morrow, he won't."

" But what a fighter, Eddy! I had no idea these tall, cold-blooded Scandinavians had it in them."

" Who says they're cold-blooded? "

Charles frowned. " But he's not going to have it all his own way. Do you really not know who poisoned Mr. Rangward, Eddy? "

" I have no idea."

Charles nodded. " I bet you're surprised to hear that I did it."

" You did, sir? "

" Um."

" Well, that is a surprise! " Eddy took away the bowl of blood-stained water. There was a click from the telephone; in the next room, Mr. Bell had replaced the receiver. He came back into the bedroom. " They'll be along in three or four minutes, sir."

Eddy came back. " Where did you get the cyanide, sir? " he asked conversationally.

" Eh? " Charles, startled, opened his eyes. " The cyanide? I had that by me. Captured it off a German officer we took prisoner. Had it years. It doesn't deteriorate with keeping."

" Well," Eddy remarked, " this is a spot of news and no mistake. Just lift up your head a minute, sir; *that's* right."

" Look "—Charles leaned against his elbow—" will you keep the old man out of the room whilst I talk to the police? "

168

" Me, sir? But I'm busy with your face."

" You can't be doing that when I'm talking to the police, Eddy." He paused. " Look, you're virtually out of a job now, aren't you? "

" Except for looking after Mrs. Rangward."

" I think we can take it the Rangward ménage will have finished with you, Eddy, very soon now. How about looking after my old pop? "

" Do you mean that, sir? "

" Mean it? Isn't this my death bed? Of course I mean it."

The front-door bell rang and Mr. Bell sprang towards it.

" There is going to be trouble with my father, now. Go on, Eddy, go to it. Keep the old man quiet whilst I see the inspector."

AS RUDOLPH ORMER SAW IT (II)

WELL, WE'VE LIVED with this murder for over a week now and it is become as familiar as the back of my hand. We wake up with it in the morning, spend the day walking around with it and go to bed with it at night. It's like there's another person come to live in the house, a skeleton-like character, this, and none of us like it, but we're getting used to it. It seems like years since life was normal, me and Mr. Rangward off to business in the Jaguar, back home in the evening and me and Edna off to the Dover Castle for a quickie. We don't go to the Dover Castle now, seeing that we're one of the chief topics of conversation.

But the thing that gets me is *me* and Mr. Totterdell! We're never anything but icy polite now.

I want to say to him: It was you gave him the cyanide, wasn't it? Well, it's O.K. by me, I want to say. Reckon we've all of us that was in the war done our bit of killing, some mother's son who done us no harm. You killed Mr. Rangward and you've had your reasons, I want to say. But what's getting me down is that they're closing in on Mrs. Rangward. Before we know where we are there'll be a sudden arrest. She'll be taken off to Holloway like that Mrs. What's-it shot her lover not so long ago and got herself hanged. It's making me nervy, I want to say.

They tell me that's why the inquest was put off indefinite instead of to a date a week or so ahead. The police have

170

got a lot to look into and they can't say how long it will take them to have everything lined up.

Every day that passes the police can find out a bit more. I reckon they'll know all about Southern Estates by now, and it's only a matter of time before they're on to me with the everlasting questions. And there's nothing been said yet about Edna's Bert and the stretch he's doing for robbery with violence but—any day now. And when that's out, what are the chances of me finding another decent job?

And look at the dreadful goings-on the evening after the funeral!

Well, that's the kind of thing I mean. The Rangward set-up was all right while it lasted—oh, very much all right; respectable, nice, everything that could be desired. And then something happens (the murder in this case), and there's a hole bashed in the scenery and then you see, suddenly, that it is all scenery, all phoney; it's a cardboard, painted set and behind it there is all the rubble and the muck and you don't know where it's all going to end.

I decided I must do what I could to stop investigations. If Mr. Toby confesses he done it, I thought, what's he got to lose?

He might even get himself into one of them prisons without bars.

Of course, if it's all going to come out Mr. Rangward is a first-class pimp and a pander and lives on the fat of the land off of the immoral earnings of women, there'll be a proper palaver. But it won't. There's things even the papers won't publish . . . ex-army officer and member of Heron's Club . . . oh, dear me, no!

Well, thinking over these things, I decided I'd best give Mr. Toby a lead. So the morning after, upstairs I went.

On the landing outside Mr. Toby's sitting-room, Tiddly Push was messing about, playing like a puppy with something he'd got in his mouth, his ping-pong ball most likely. I usually stop and give him a tickle behind his ears, but this time I didn't; I'd too much on my mind.

" Is that you, Ormer? " he says as I went in. " Where's that dog of mine? "

" He's all right," I said, " out there, playing about."

He was sitting by the fire in his red brocade dressing-gown with the white silk scarf round his neck, he looked a proper old gentleman, but I didn't stop to think. I went for it like a bull at a gate. I said: " Mr. Totterdell, sir," I said, " it's like this." I looked round to make sure the door was shut and that Miss Emms wasn't snooping around.

" You remember the murder was on the day you wanted Tiddly Push wormed? "

" You wormed him, if I remember rightly."

" I did. But not before there was a bit of a scuffle about the pill."

" Scuffle? I don't recall any scuffle."

I was regular uncomfortable and I didn't seem to be able to choose my words right. " Well, you remember you said you wanted Tiddly Push wormed that day, that you'd been waiting till I came home to do it and the dog had been starved in readiness."

" I certainly remember all that."

" Seeing as it should be done in the morning you said you thought you had a worm pill by you, and to go and look in the bathroom cupboard."

" Yes, and then? "

" There was a small tin looked like it might have contained one large pill, there was some writing on the lid. I brought it in to you. I handed it to you. ' Is it this? *Toxicum, non sumendum?* ' and you said, ' Do you want to poison poor Tiddly Push? ' and you went on feeling it with your fingers. You said you hadn't known the thing was there, that it had been there for some time and that it had better not go back. Then you told me about Field-Marshal Goering and how he'd been holding on to one of these tiny capsules until right up to the last and when he knew there was no escape from hanging he took it and was dead in a couple of minutes. And then I asked you where you'd got the thing and you said you'd taken it off of a patient who was suicidal."

" Yes, I remember all that."

" Well, then . . ." I began to feel uncomfortable. His face was raised towards mine and I couldn't make out if he saw me or not. Made it very awkward. " Well, that was that. Then later on. . . . Mr. Rangward got home and all that. . . ." Yes, I didn't like saying this at all. " Mrs. Rangward was the first to come. She was upstairs with you quite a time, so they say. Talking about her holiday and so on, I reckon. Then later on he came up, like he often did." I paused again, but Mr. Toby stayed quite still, waiting for me to go on. " It was then you could of given him the thing."

" How? "

" Well, you know what he was like. Always asking you for free samples of this and that. You could of handed him the capsule and said: ' Take it later on, as a night-cap.' "

" You have a very fine imagination, Rudie. I've often thought so. I'm staggered with your imaginative gifts."

All blah. I waited.

" Then where is the container? Where is the small tin

with *Toxicum, non sumendum* on the lid? Where is the scrap of paper which was inside the tin with the capsule, on which there was something written in my handwriting, a whimsey of the moment? Where is the cotton-wool and the tiny silk container? "

" I don't know nothing at all about the scrap of paper. I know I put the tin down quick. I went on looking for that worm pill and it turned up in that little drawer in your bureau."

" Think, Rudie, think, man. *Where* did you put the tin down? "

" I tell you, I don't know."

" It beats me how you come to think *I* gave him the poison."

" It's motive," I said.

" I agree with you that motive is very important when trying to discover who committed a murder. Why pin a motive on me? "

" You didn't like him, did you? You've been in the know all along, haven't you, about the way he earns a living? And you like Mrs. Annabel," I said. " You thought it was all a crying scandal——"

" But you've got it all wrong, Rudie. That's not a motive. And unless you're a poisoner for the love of the thing you've got to have a good big motive before you can bring yourself to doing the dirty deed. An ordinary person can become a poisoner only if tried beyond his endurance. No, you haven't made out a case."

Something like relief was coming over me, from head to foot. I felt like crying.

" I find," Mr. Toby said; " I find that you have a bigger motive than I."

" Me! " No, I couldn't swallow that, I could not.

174

" Yes, you. You've got on with him all right on the surface. But he'd got a hold over you. Hadn't he now? Come clean."

I swallowed. The tables were turned all right.

" He had a hold over me," I said; " but it was not all that strong."

" Right. I could say where did you put that tin, Rudie? In your pocket? I could say that, but I won't. I'll accept your statement, if you can call it a statement, that you ' put the tin down in a hurry.' Right. From then on three people had access to that tin—Miss Emms, Mrs. Rangward and Mr. Rangward. All three were in my sitting-room that evening." Mr. Toby paused for a long time. " Now that I come to think about it," he said, " not one of those three could read Latin. None of them would know what *Toxicum, non sumendum* meant. Food for thought."

" Yes," I said. " See! You were the only one really knew what it was."

" So you have grounds for your suspicions."

" No, they aren't suspicions any more." I felt apologetic now. " About this hold he had over me. I'd best tell you and see what you think . . . but if ever Edna got wind of it I'd cut my throat. It happened before Edna and I was walking out. I never go near them places now."

" You visited brothels under the jurisdiction of Southern Estates? Is that it? "

" Just about it," I said. " It was Mum and Aunty Bess put the fear of death into me about getting young girls into trouble. Right from the very first Mum's told me I was ' over-sexed ' like Pa. I reckon she's right, poor Mum! She'd never believe it but it was she and Aunty

175

drove me into those places. Well, I got into the habit of going to a house in Earl's Court; I wanted to be as far off home as I could get. They're awful places. It's the atmosphere. Commercial. . . . I'll never set foot inside one of those houses again as long as I live, not as a customer, I won't. Well, one night I got plastered and the girl I'd been going with regular, she turned out a shocking tart. We had a bit of a row and there was one or two others joined in and it turned into a regular brawl and one of the ladies of the house had to lock me up by myself in a small room. I was there all night, lying on the floor, but I'd enough drink inside me to float a ship and I slept like the dead. When I woke up, half the day had gone and I was feeling like—well, you know the sort of thing. And ashamed of myself into the bargain. All I wanted was to get away. But she wasn't having any of that. She said I was to ' see the boss ' who was coming round that morning and she kept me there until he arrived. They've got a hold over you, those people. It was against the law, keeping me there, I could have sued her for it, but she knew full well I wouldn't. . . . I was far too frightened anyone would find out I was there to do anything but what she told me. So I sat there feeling every kind of a fool and after a bit ' the boss ' arrived. Yes, you know—it was Mr. Rangward. By that time I was in a pretty poor condition. He asked me what a youth like me wanted to come to a place like this for, lectured me like a Dutch uncle. I swallowed it. He talked to me like a blooming schoolmaster and when all was said and done I wasn't all that young! I reckon I'd been going downhill for some weeks and I could see now it was time to pull myself together so when he offered me the job of chauffeur I jumped at it."

" I understand you completely, Rudie. Mr. Rangward had a fascinating personality. Nobody could be more charming when he liked."

" But cor! What a blooming hypocrite! "

He smiled a little. " A whited sepulchre."

" You're right about the charm, if you like to call it that. You couldn't have found anyone nicer as an employer than Mr. Rangward. At first I thought I was in clover. I started on a period of good luck, I met Edna and she threw in her lot with me and we had this basement flat offered us. Well, I suppose the luck has held, so far. When I got to know him better, I began to despise him. When all's said and done, I thought, look what the man lives off of! "

" You shouldn't have done that, Rudie. So long as human beings have their weaknesses, their vices, if you like, there will always be people to supply the necessary. I need hardly say that the business of living off immoral earnings is older than history. You must not be smug and self-righteous."

I was astonished. " But don't it shock you? "

" I'm not easily shocked."

" I don't understand your class," I said, and nor do I, they do and say things we'd never do and say.

" Don't let's plunge into the ramifications of class distinction, Rudie. Anyway, it's nothing to do with class, it's the way you look at things. What it all boils down to is that Mr. Rangward *had* a hold over you." He paused. " But I can see it wasn't a very strong one, not strong enough to cause you to give him a lethal dose. Shall we take it, then, that neither you nor I is the murderer? "

By this time I couldn't hardly believe I ever thought he was. It's always best, when you've anything on your mind,

177

to talk it over with the person. Things soon sort themselves out.

And then Mr. Toby said something nice. He said that seeing Edna and me would be out of a job, how about staying on in the basement and me working for him? I says how about Miss Emms and he smiled and said Miss Emms didn't fancy staying in a house where there'd been such goings-on. I reminded him that cooking wasn't in my line and he said maybe Edna would give a hand; he said I might even get a driving job in addition, part-time perhaps, with one of the doctors in the district.

That would suit me all to pieces, but I didn't say so. I said I'd think about it and talk it over with Edna, and he said well, was that all I had on my mind? And I said, yes, and it wasn't half a relief to have got it off my mind. I said something about Mrs. Rangward and the police getting at her and he said it wasn't anything to worry about because she was innocent of the deed. I said that was what I thought, but you never knew but what the police might pin it on to her. And he said that was why it was important to hurry up and discover just who did it.

Then I remembered I'd better tell him about Edna and me not being married, and about Edna's Bert doing a stretch for robbery with violence. I had to, I couldn't have accepted his offer of a job without he knew.

Blow me if he didn't laugh, and then he apologised when he saw I didn't see the joke. He said he was only laughing because it was another nail in Miss Emms's coffin. I said it wasn't a laughing matter because Bert in prison might see all about this murder in the papers, see Edna's and my photograph and all. The first place he might come to when he was out was No. 51 Park Row. Then Mr. Toby said something about let's cross our bridges when we come to them. And I said—well, just so's he'd been warned. He said thanks for telling him and if Bert did turn up unexpected he, Mr. Toby, would deal with him.

That seemed to be the lot, only just as I was going I said there was one thing, I didn't want Edna to know about the kind of property business Mr. Rangward had, I didn't want her to get to know I was ever mixed up in that kind of thing and that when I went out in the mornings with Mr. Rangward we went the round collecting the rents for the week from those places. Edna would never get over it, I told him. He said I could rest assured that as far as he was concerned Edna's innocence would not suffer and I left him smiling away to himself, the queer old bird.

I left him and went off downstairs. Tiddly Push had stopped playing and was sitting at the top of the stairs, bang in the middle. He's a funny little dog, that. He didn't even look round when I came out, or move, so I had to step right over him. But he watched me going down the stairs all right; beats me how he can look so haughty when he's no nose to speak of!

AS MISS EMMS SAW IT (II)

I'VE WRITTEN to Lady Horwich and offered my services. It is the only way. I shall have to accept a much smaller salary, I am sadly aware of that, but I cannot afford to have my good name dragged through the mud. It is a great pity that after twenty years of absolute devotion, through no fault of my own, my connection with Mr. Totterdell should come to an end in a storm of publicity, crime and immorality.

Murder isn't a bit like you read about in novels; I shall never read another murder story, not after this because I know how different it is when it happens in real life.

But Lady Horwich will understand; it was nothing to do with me. She'll be only too pleased to get someone willing to do her chores to bother her head about the murder.

I've had it all out with Mr. Totterdell and we're still quite friends though I do feel he is laughing up his sleeve at me; he always has. I've told him how it was I couldn't stay on in such a house and he quite understood. I said I might be leaving him in the lurch, but there was plenty of gentlewomen placed like myself, in reduced circumstances, who would be willing to replace me. I promised I would whitewash the job when they came for an interview.

He said he didn't think I needed to do that.

"Your mind, Miss Emms!" he said, clicking his tongue.

That was the end.

I know he didn't mean it, but there are things you can't say to people and expect them to forget. My mind! No, I couldn't possibly stay on after that if he begged me on his bended knees.

AS EDNA ORMER SAW IT (II)

I DON'T KNOW what happened between Rudie and Mr. Totterdell, but all of a sudden Rudie dropped the idea he'd had about Mr. Toby.

The morning after the fight, I was that excited the way things were going, it was all I could do to get myself off to work. The girls in the shop are all over me about the murder, I've suddenly become somebody, overnight. But I've been careful what I said. You never know. I looked at the others as we were having our elevenses, and I thought; what dull lives you lead, girls, you don't know anything!

I thought about the fight last night and all of a sudden I laughed because what they are going to say when the Baron turns up at his posh Embassy I cannot think. He can't put it all down to slipping on a banana skin, even in Swedish!

Later on Eddy, who'd been out all night after he'd taken Mr. Shefford home, burst in on us having our dinner, and said: " Well, who do you think done it? "

Rudie and I stared.

" It was Mr. Charles Shefford," he said. He was tickled to death, spreading the bad news, or was it good news? Anyway, it was certainly news. It gave me quite a turn. " I can't believe it," I says at last.

" He's told the inspector. Made a statement in full and it was all taken down by the sergeant. They took hours over it. Meantime the old man, Mr. Charles's father, he couldn't be kept out of the room. So Mr. Charles shouted

182

at him he'd done it. Cor! " Eddy exclaimed. " I've never seen anyone so upset, thought the old man would have a fit, I was real sorry for him. Mr. Charles won't be brought to justice though, mark my words. I don't see it, somehow."

" I don't see it either," Rudie put in. " I don't see he done it." He looked at me to see what I had to say.

" But he *said* he done it."

" I could say I done it," Rudie said, sarcastic.

" But why say you done it if it's not true? "

" That's no answer. If Mr. Charles said he done it I reckon he done it and that's that! "

" Motive," Rudie says importantly. He's that wise when he's been upstairs with Mr. Toby, I could tell they'd been having a pow-wow that morning whilst I was out. Says Rudie, quoting Mr. Toby, I'm sure: " Motive. Unless you're a poisoner for the love of the thing you've got to have a good big motive before you can bring yourself to do the dirty deed."

" Hark at him! " I says.

I don't think Eddy is quite sure what a motive is; Rudie pointed out that if Mr. Rangward was a bigamist, then Mrs. Rangward was not his wife, which would leave it easy for the Baron or Mr. Shefford to marry her, so why bother to poison Mr. Rangward? There's no motive there, Rudie says, giving Eddy a dirty look.

" But," I says, " nobody *knew* Mr. Rangward was a bigamist, Mrs. Rangward least of all. And look what she said last night, it was quite a relief to know that he was a bigamist, she said, though I could tell she'd had a shock. But," I went on and I must say I quite enjoyed the sensation I was going to cause; " it don't make it any easier about the babe."

" Babe? " Rudie repeated.

" She's three months gone, anyway," I says, casual.

If you'd given them both a hard knock on the head they couldn't have looked softer, those two. Rudie was the first to get over it. " You don't say! "

" That makes things look a lot different," Eddy says. " Who's the father? "

" Mr. Rangward, of course, who else? " Rudie says.

" You don't believe that! " Eddy said.

" What do you know about it, Eddy? " I says, with a laugh.

" Enough to know he's not the father," Eddy says, blushing.

It was time I went back to work so I got up and went, leaving them to it. But I couldn't help smiling. It's the way men look at things makes me laugh. Always take the complicated line when it seems to me it's always the simple answer that's the right one. Seems to me as plain as plain that Mrs. Rangward got herself into trouble with somebody else; someone she went to see on those afternoons out when she went off alone. She was a woman going to meet her lover and it stuck out a mile. The way she walked down the road was enough to tell you, like a young girl, she almost skipped. I know why she was dreamy. She's not dopy, she was dreamy with love. And all the men could sense it, they could feel it but they couldn't understand. That's what kept the Baron and Mr. Shefford hanging on, hoping. Like children they were—they see one child happy, and they hang about thinking there's something for them.

I'm not much of a hand at description, but I do know what I'm getting at and I can't put it clearer. I know what it is makes other women dislike her and I reckon if I wasn't so happy with Rudie I'd feel the same way about her. Jealous, perhaps.

So now all the police have to do is to find out who she's been going to and that's who done it.

And as for Mr. Shefford " confessing " to the murder, I reckon that's all " my eye." It's to draw attention to himself, he must get himself noticed somehow and he's gone to desperate lengths to make her take some notice of him. He wants to show her how much he loves her and he doesn't give a damn about any other thing.

It's all quite clear to me, and it's simple.

But we shall see. . . .

WE HAVEN'T reached the end of our surprises yet, I reckon. Yesterday he was just a name I'd heard over the telephone, a voice, and to-day I can see Mr. Pethod is changing the whole course of events. This is how Mr. Pethod comes into it.

Going to see the solicitor was something hanging over Mrs. Rangward ever since Mr. Rangward died. Seeing she was so upset it was decided it should be left until the day after the funeral. I'd fixed the appointment over the phone with this Mr. Pethod's secretary. I've spoken to her once or twice before over the phone and I knew Mr. Rangward did business with this Mr. Pethod, though he's never been to the house that I know of.

Well, the day after the funeral, being the morning after the fight, I got back to Park Row a bit the worse for wear after my night out, all frowsty, I was, sleeping in my clothes on the Shefford sofa and I was reckoning on getting myself tidied up a bit before taking in Madam's coffee. I thought it would be best to say nothing at all at that particular time about what had taken place the night before in the Shefford apartment, I reckoned she'd gone through enough for the time being and with the appointment with the solicitor ahead I thought I'd keep the news to myself.

However, my lady was up and about, and as cheerful as a young lark. She asked me if Mr. Charles was all right and I said, yes, he'd gone into the country to recuperate and she said she was glad, that was the very best thing he could do. Then she started pulling open drawers and sorting things out and presently she asked me to fetch some suitcases up from the basement storeroom, and I says was she thinking of going away, and she says yes, she was planning to go back home. " Home! " I says, surprised. " Yes, Eddy," she says, " back to my home in Brixton."

She was ever so sweet. " Eddy," she says, " what about another job for you? " Then I told her I thought there was a job waiting for me, and I told her about old Mr. Shefford and how he needed a person like me to look after him and how I fancied living in Albany. She couldn't have been nicer, sweet as pie. Then I asked her if she'd like me to order the car for her to go to the solicitor's at two o'clock and she said no, it bothered her to have the car waiting about in the crowded streets, she'd go down to the corner and pick up a cab. So when she was getting herself ready to go out, I nipped down to the corner and got her a cab and saw her into it, and off up the street, and then I went down for a bit of a chat with the Ormers.

It was then I learned that Mrs. Rangward is in the family way and I went off upstairs to my own quarters to think it over. It made everything look a bit different, and I wanted some time to think it out. So I set myself to washing the alcohol off of the living-room carpet, as I can always think best when I'm busy. It was about teatime Madam was back from seeing this Mr. Pethod, the solicitor. I heard the taxi click up its meter outside and I heard her footsteps at the front door and in she comes, right into the living-room and flings herself down on a chair and bursts out crying. Great gasping sobs, shaking her from head to foot! I thought of a cup of tea for her, but it was something a lot worse than a cup of tea could put right. So I went upstairs at the double and brought Mr. Toby down, or rather I sent him down in the lift.

Miss Emms came out and wanted to know what was up but I'd no time for Miss Emms. I just gave her a look and Tiddly Push came off downstairs at my heels. Whoever else is left out of it, that dog isn't! He's in on everything —investigating and making his own conclusions. If you ask me Tiddly Push knows the lot. If he could only talk he'd tell us the whole story, there's nothing he misses! While we're all buzzing around in the dark getting a shock here, a surprise there, Tiddly Push has known it all along and there he sits and looks at you as much as to say: Didn't you know that, you B.F.? Except that he'd use more high-falutin' language, I reckon.

The living-room door was shut when we got down, and I could hear the murmur of voices but I couldn't hear a thing that was said. I went into my kitchen and Tiddly Push sat and watched me, looking ever so saucy.

I'd have given a lot to hear what was going on in the sitting-room. Presently, just what I was hoping for happened: Mr. Toby put his head out and called for tea and quick as a knife I made tea and took it in.

I was ashamed to look at Madam, I've never seen such a change in anybody in such a short time; she don't cry like those film stars, big tears which don't mess up her face. Her poor face looked like it had been wrung out, and her hair was all hanging—well, it usually hangs, but now it really *hung*, like damp clothes on a line on a wet Whit Monday. She hadn't even bothered to take off her coat, she sat there, all bedraggled. For all he couldn't see what she looked like, Mr. Toby was upset.

I fussed about the room, switching on the electric fire, drawing the curtains, turning on the lamps, pulling the rugs over the wet patches I'd been making scrubbing the carpet. I messed about as quiet as I could and I heard Mr. Toby say: " I shall telephone to Williams. . . . Whatever you say to the contrary, Annabel, I am convinced it is the right thing to do."

" I shall never forgive you if you do. I can't have Clement mixed up in this. You *must* see that I'm right. Besides . . . he's working to-night and I won't have him upset before a concert."

There was a long envelope lying on the carpet, face down, and a single sheet of writing-paper lying on the settee beside her. I gave it several looks, wondering if I should tidy it up, like. But I left it alone. Mr. Toby had been standing by the window, like he was looking out, when I came in, and even after I had drawn the curtains he was standing there, poor chap, staring into the curtains, just a foot or two off of his face.

" Perhaps it's going to be all right," she said in a small voice like a little girl. She'd stopped crying now but every now and then she was shaken with a kind of shudder you could see a mile off. " Once the shock is over maybe nothing has changed. It's going to be all right." She tried to smile at Tiddly Push, but it wasn't much of a thing.

" I'm uneasy," Mr. Toby said. " ' Hell knoweth no fury like a Pethod scorned.' If you could only have been nicer to him, Annabel, even for the time being! "

" After the shock of that letter! "

I knew that letter was the clue to it and that I shouldn't see light until I'd laid eyes on what was written in it.

When there wasn't another thing I could do in the living-room I went out and shut the doors after me.

Mr. Toby is a wizard, he is! He works wonders, that old man! He must have made a fine doctor in his day. Half an hour hadn't passed before I heard the piano going; he'd got Mrs. Rangward playing some of her old tunes which she hadn't done since the night of the tragedy. It did your heart good to hear her, husky and low, singing the negro songs she'd sung often enough: *Siddown, brother! I cain't siddown!* and *I wanna walk all over God's heaven . . . heaven . . . heaven. . . .*

I winked at Tiddly Push. " A storm in a teacup," I whispered and Tiddly Push winked back and I believe I whistled as I brushed away at the silver. Maybe things were coming all right after all.

Then the front-door bell rang and I tripped off to open it. One of our gentlemen friends, a policeman in plain clothes. Could he see Mrs. Rangward, please? I could see he'd heard the piano and the singing and he gave me ever such an old-fashioned look. If it comes to giving looks I can do my bit. I gave him a look could have burnt him up and he just pursed up his lips like he was going to start whistling, he threw up his eyes and—well, it was no time to stand in the open doorway playing dirty looks. He had another chap with him and they both came in, pushing past me. I hesitated a minute to show them where they got off and then, though it broke my heart, I opened the living room door and announced them. " The C.I.D., Madam," I said.

And I didn't shut the door and go back to the kitchen. Not on your life, I went on standing there and so did Tiddly Push.

Mrs. Rangward was wanted by the inspector at the

station, the police station, mark you. The inspector sent his compliments and asked her to be good enough to step down.

Mrs. Rangward stood up, looking like St. Joan of Arc; I was proud of her then. " So this is it," she says, and she goes across to the chair and picks up her fur coat and slips it on. No one went forward to help her, Mr. Toby couldn't see and the police officers were staring so hard they forgot their manners and me. . . . I was a blooming pillar of salt.

Mr. Toby was cross, he swore angrily, and said: " Pethod hasn't wasted much time."

Mrs. Rangward picked up her gloves and her handbag. She got a comb out of her handbag and went over to the chimney-piece and touched her hair with the comb in front of the looking-glass trying to tidy herself up. She said nothing else, but as she passed Mr. Toby she put her hand on his arm for a moment.

The police officers looked tactful, as though they had nothing to do with it. " Acting on instructions," one of them murmured apologetically.

It broke your heart to see the way she went. When I came back into the living-room Mr. Toby was holding aside the curtain and looking out of the window, though he wasn't *seeing*, of course.

" You know how it is going to end, Eddy? "

" You mean an arrest? It's not that I'm so worried about. I'm distressed to see the way Madam has been upset with that solicitor this afternoon. No, I'm not worried about an arrest."

" I wonder why? "

" Because," I said with some pleasure; " because Mr. Shefford has *confessed*! He done it."

191

He stood there with his back to me, ever so quiet, I wondered if he'd heard. But presently he says: " Don't you believe it. It's decent of him and all that. But he didn't do it."

" Then why say so, sir? "

" Ah! There are plenty of reasons why, the main one being to protect Mrs. Rangward. The police expect the odd confessions with every murder, you know. They have their own way of dealing with them."

" He'll have to have a story, he can't say he did it and leave it at that. Maybe he can prove he did it."

" That is what these would-be ' confessors ' are apt to forget. Sometimes it is as difficult to prove you did a thing as to prove you didn't.

" I'm afraid they'll treat that ' confession ' for what it is worth. Poor girl." Mr. Toby seemed without any of his usual cheerful spirits and optimism. " Poor girl, she's going to get herself lined up with the loose women of all time, with Cæsar's wife Julia, with Jane Shore, with Anne Boleyn and with Mrs. Edith Thompson. And she's not like that, Eddy, she's not like that."

" No, sir. She isn't," I agreed, eyeing that letter lying on the sofa.

" I'm glad you agree. If you hear people talking about her, Eddy, in that sort of way, you'll squash it at once, won't you? "

I said I would.

" I'd hate *her* to read one or two of the letters she's been sent. Anonymous letters from spiteful people."

" You don't say, sir! "

" And the trouble is, Eddy . . . Oh! " Mr. Toby thumped his forehead with his wrist. " I'm no good, I'm an old crock! There's nothing I can do but stand about trying to be wise. I'm not nearly wise enough. There's a simple answer to all this, if I could only put my finger on it."

He couldn't see, of course, so what was to stop me picking up the letter and reading it then and there?

" MY DEAR ANNABEL," I read, " I hope you will never receive this letter because, if you do, it will mean that I am no more and I do not particularly want to die. However, Pethod thinks it essential that I write it because, if I meet with an accident and *do* die, it will mean that things will be complicated.

" I want you to know that when we married at the Chelsea Registry Office I had a wife living. At the time of writing this, she is still alive and therefore you have no status as my wife. I gather from your behaviour that this will not distress you in the least, but I may be wrong. I do not know you, I have never been able to guess what you are thinking. I married you for reasons which I need not divulge; I thought it wise at the time and still think so.

" On the other hand, you do not know me. You have never loved me and you neither know nor care what I am thinking. You live in a world of your own and do not see me at all. Which, on the whole, is just as well.

" So long as I live, Annabel, you will never know that I married you bigamously; I have no doubt that is the one thing you would like to hear but I shall do everything in my power to see that it does not happen. Nobody knows but myself, my wife, and my partner and legal adviser, Pethod.

193

" I know you are unhappy, but do you not think you deserve to be?

" Sincerely and, though you don't like it, *ever your*
" RICHARD RANGWARD."

Mr. Toby snapped: " Are you reading that letter, Eddy? "

" Yes, sir." Why deny it? " I thought it might shed some light on the situation."

" What do you think now? "

" We know all this. Edna and Rudie are full of the bigamy story."

" But what is your impression of the letter? "

I read it through again, careful. Except for that spiteful remark at the end, I didn't think it was too bad, and I said as much.

" You might think him a badly-done-by husband? "

" Yes, sir," I returned, " that's exactly what I might think."

" Then," he said, " that is just exactly what the police are going to think."

" If they see this letter," I said, cunning.

" Mr. Pethod," Mr. Toby said as though he had tasted something nasty. " Mr. Pethod has evidently wasted no time in sending a copy of it to the inspector. By hand, judging by the speed with which Mrs. Rangward has been sent for."

" O-o-o-h." I was shocked, really I was.

" I suppose you liked Mr. Rangward, Eddy? "

" Liked him, sir? He was always very decent to me."

" Charming? "

" Oh, yes, sir."

" Good company? Plenty of friends? "

" Oh, yes, sir."

" Generous? "

" That too, sir."

Mr. Toby sighed heavily. " So was George Joseph Smith," he said, " so was Major Armstrong of Hay, so was Dr. Palmer of Rugeley." I didn't know what he was talking about, he often goes on a bit above your head, like. " Haigh, and even little Christie, too, had his appeal, a *nice* little man. All of them what Miss Emms would call nice gentlemen."

" But Mr. Rangward *was* a nice gentleman," I protested because I really didn't follow him.

" Oh, yes. Mr. Richard Rangward, too."

I was reading through the letter once more, trying to put myself in the inspector's place. There was nothing, really, could damn Mrs. Rangward at all, unless it was that last sentence: " *I know you are unhappy but do you not think you deserve to be?* " They might read a lot into that. I didn't have a clue what he meant, but it didn't sound nice. Sounded like something was very wrong somewhere. . . .

" It's a pity about this," I said.

Mr. Toby was feeling about for his stick. " An understatement, Eddy."

" Might do a lot of harm."

" We must do something quickly. Something practical. We must use our brains, Eddy! Oh, if only I could *see*! "

" How would that help, sir? "

" ' He that hath eyes to see . . .' "

" I reckon there isn't much you miss, sir."

" I've missed this all right."

He was standing near the piano and he ran a finger over the keys. *I'm gonna walk all over God's heaven . . . heaven . . .*

195

heaven . . . he hummed. Then he started to walk out of the room, he was leaning a bit on his stick and he looked quite an old man. " Here's the letter, sir. Don't want to leave that lying about."

He took the sheet of paper and folded it up. " No doubt it will be published in the *Sunday Cordial* before long." He clicked his fingers: " Come on, Tiddly Push."

Off they went, Tiddly Push carrying the envelope in his mouth.

As Mr. Toby went up in the lift Miss Emms was coming down the stairs. She was all buttoned up, her new winter coat buttoned up to the neck, her face buttoned up, her mouth buttoned up, her new plastic handbag hanging on her arm. She managed to unbutton her mouth enough to say: " Where's Mr. Toby? "

" Just gone up," I says.

She clicked her tongue importantly. " I can't go up again, I'm in a hurry. Will you give him a message from me, Eddy? "

" O.K." No I will not call her " Miss " just so long as she calls me " Eddy."

" Tell him I've had to go out on urgent business, but that I hope to be back in time to give him his dinner."

" O.K." She was waiting for me to ask her what her urgent business was, but I was not going to be drawn. She got as far as the front door, then, hesitating, she turned back. " You don't happen to know which particular police station the men who are investigating our case come from, do you? "

" Marylebone and Scotland Yard working together. You'll find our inspector down at the Yard, but—er—he'll be engaged. Won't have time to see you."

" Oh, yes, he'll have time to see me."

" Think so? " I said very casual.

" I have some information for him. A very vital clue."

" Oh! Been doing some detective work on your own? "

" I think I may say I have the key to the whole situation." Miss Emms patted her handbag, then she raised her hand, like a schoolteacher calming down a class of rowdy boys. " No, Eddy. I shall divulge nothing at this stage," she said, buttoned up her mouth again and got herself off.

" Mr. Bolton to you," I sent after her, but I doubt if she heard.

It was one damned thing after another. I've had a quiet enough life up to now, I told myself, and I dare say things will settle down again—but blow me! things kept happening with a vengeance. I felt like I was a character in a play.

The front-door bell rang just as I was going up to Mr. Toby with Miss Emms's message, so I went back to open it and this time it was the Baron; at least, it looked like the Baron, though I should never have recognised the mother's boy we've all got to know so well. His lips were blown out like a couple of aubergines and he was wearing dark glasses like Mr. Toby, to hide the bruises round his eyes. And there was a strip of plaster across his chin to complete the picture.

Talking like someone with his mouth full of dry biscuit, he asked for Madam. I told him she was out and he said could he come in and wait. I didn't like to keep him standing at the door, poor chap, so I asked him in while

197

I thought out the proper answer to that one. While I was
wondering what I'd best say, he asked could he possibly
have a drink. Pathetic. I said I'd see what I could find,
but the current drinks had had a nasty knock.

He stood in the door of the living-room and looked
round.

" Never be the same again," I remarked. " Women are
a lot of trouble."

" But we can't do without them, Eddy."

" I don't know about that," I says. I have my own ideas
on that score, but they are neither here nor there.

I said: " I didn't think there was a woman left alive
you'd have two chaps fighting over. Regular old-
fashioned."

" Is it not? " he said. " When will Mrs. Rangward be
back? "

I thought I'd best get the poor chap a drink, he needed
one. Then I told him Madam was down at the yard with
the C.I.D., they'd sent for her not above half an hour ago.
I reckoned she wouldn't be back till dinner-time, at the
earliest. " If then," I added, remembering what Mr.
Toby had said.

He sat down and started drinking his whisky, saying
nothing.

It wouldn't have been human nature if I'd not told him.
I was all burned up by what had happened last night, full
of it. So I told him, giving a rough outline of the goings-
on at the Shefford flat in the Albany after the fight.
". . . and the marvel is," I ended, " the police have let
him go to his house in the country. He's not been arrested
nor nothing. That's what happens when the well-to-do
confess to murder! But Mr. Toby says they're not taking
it serious."

The Baron was looking at me like I was a caterpillar he'd found in his greens.

" It's not me has confessed," I pointed out, " it's Mr. Shefford. He says he done it with a capsule he got from a German prisoner-of-war, but Mr. Toby thinks he'll have to prove he had it in his possession. But," I went on, " things aren't all that simple. There's a nasty piece of information makes things look black against Mrs. Rangward come to the fore in the shape of a letter from Mr. Rangward. It's that has made the police send for her for further ' talks.' And Miss Emms, from upstairs, she's just gone off to the police with what she calls ' a very vital clue.' So where are we? "

I don't know why he had to tell me unless he was proud of it. He drank up his whisky and put down his glass very careful. Then he says: " Soon all will be over. You will all return to your normal lives. And you will remember the poor Swede; you will say ' That one was not quite right in his head!' Is not that how you put it? I had a sudden impulse which came together with a favourable opportunity. *I* gave him the poison. I am sorry now. I regret it very much."

I'd gone a long way past being surprised. I took it quite calm. And I took it with a pinch of salt.

" You'll have to prove you had the poison."

" I can do so. I had a capsule of the poison in my possession, there was a time I was going to do away with myself when I was unhappy in my marriage." It sounded too glib, I must say. " So you can tell all your friends and the newspaper reporters and anyone else interested. The police have got a written account, I have delivered it to them."

He must have been a bit mad, talking wild like that.

" The reporters couldn't write up a thing like that before the inquest," I exclaimed, but he didn't seem to be listening.

I said, well, what about Mr. Shefford's confession? and he gave a grunt of a laugh, not a proper laugh by any means, and said Mr. Shefford could do what he liked with his " confession " or something of the sort.

I said, well, did you ever, but, as Mr. Toby says, I told the Baron, the police expect confessions with every murder. They have their own way of dealing with them, I told him, like Mr. Toby told me.

" My confession," the Baron said, very superior, " will not be a matter for your police. I have simply delivered the statement to them so that they may know how things stand. This affair will be dealt with by my own country. I have diplomatic immunity! "

It sounded all right and I exclaimed: " You don't say! Then you diplomats can go about behaving any old how! "

But he'd got tired of talking things over with a servant. He stood up and said as Mrs. Rangward wasn't back, could he see Mr. Toby, upstairs?

I remembered the message I'd got to give to Mr. Toby from Miss Emms, so I went up with the Baron, in the lift.

Mr. Toby was standing with his back to the room " looking " out of the window; he was holding Tiddly Push close up to his face.

" Excuse me, sir," I says. " Here's Baron Halvorsen to see you, sir. And there is a message from Miss Emms."

I'd have given something to hang about and try to overhear what the Baron and he were going to talk about, but it wasn't too easy the way that maisonette's arranged, with the kitchen at the top. I'd no good reason for staying around.

He'd put Tiddly Push down and the little dog followed me out of the room, very playful he was and started rummaging around, sniffing under the furniture.

"Here," I says, clicking my fingers, "looking for your ball? It's there!" The ping-pong ball was behind a Chinese vase Mr. Toby had on his landing. Tiddly Push picked it up in his mouth, then dropped it. He took no more notice of me; he didn't feel like a game, he turned his back and went on rooting about under the chest-of-drawers; all I could see was the black feathery tail.

I went on slowly down the stairs.

Part Three

AS TOBIAS TOTTERDELL SAW IT

As a doctor and a student of human nature I could hardly fail to be interested in Richard Rangward at any time in my career. But washed up, as I am, upon the lonely sands of blindness, Richard has offered me an opportunity for study.

I have mused often upon Duncan's statement in *Macbeth* that there is " no art to find the mind's construction in the face." When I had my sight, I fancied myself on reading character from appearance, I thought I had brought it to an art. And so I have wondered whether those words were Shakespeare's own sentiments or whether he simply put them into the mouth of his character.

Be that as it may, I have been obliged to abandon that art in favour of another; that of finding the mind's construction in the voice. It is a great deal more difficult, and open to even greater error.

It has, therefore, taken me quite some time to come to the conclusions which I have now reached with regard to Rangward. As a famous judge once said, kind-hearted people find it extremely difficult to believe that, in somebody of apparently good education and perfect sanity, there can exist real wickedness and by wickedness is meant the desire to harm another for gain. That a man of physical health and strength, brave, determined and energetic, can also be cruel, treacherous and avaricious, is hard to believe. I do not line myself up with kind-hearted people but at least I am not the man with the muck-rake; I do not look for evil in my friends.

I believe that everyone has their claim to immortality and that even those most heavily involved in moral darkness are not without the ability to experience moments of superhuman excellence. I once encountered the foulest homicidal sexual maniac, yet he played the piano divinely.

From Richard Rangward's voice, however, I could guess nothing. He has the kind of voice heard in R.A.F. messes all over the country. At first I put him down as a perfectly ordinary middle-aged man, a product of the mid-century with no distinctive doctrines or schisms. As I got to know him better, however, I found that he was a genuine sufferer from insomnia.

People who cannot sleep have always interested me. There are a great many secondary reasons why a man or woman cannot sleep. But primarily it is a refusal on the part of the subconscious to allow itself to float away into oblivion. They call sleep the brother of death. In other words, it may be that the man who cannot sleep harbours, subconsciously, a fear of death.

In the course of my career I have found that, on the whole, the happy people are not afraid of death and that the less happy people are. Like every categorical statement, this has many refutations. I repeat, *on the whole*.

Richard Rangward gave the impression of being a happy, successful man, and when he told me, repeatedly, that he could not sleep, I began to wonder if he were quite so successful and happy as he would seem. He had taken sleeping-tablets ever since I first knew him but, in the course of time, each brand became ineffective and he searched anxiously for a change. It was a subject which never failed to interest him.

Though I am a physical wreck and no longer practising, I am still a doctor and as such my name is still on the Medical Register. My secretary reads the more important items of interest in the British Medical Journal to me each week and thus, I like to think, I am keeping up with the times. From time to time I receive the free samples of medicines and drugs distributed to everyone on the Register.

It was certainly Rangward who made the first approaches towards friendship and it was he who began the habit of coming up for a chat in the early evening once or twice a week.

The progress of our friendship was slow and our conversations seldom touched upon the personal or, indeed, upon anything that mattered much. It was all rather superficial and, I must admit, quite pleasant; Rangward was good company. He always had a ready anecdote about the race meetings he attended, or the sales; he had lively opinions about politics and the world situation and he was deeply interested in stocks and shares. We always had plenty to talk about and he gave me the feeling that I was part of the busy, bustling into-the-city-every-day world.

His wife Annabel was a shadowy entity in the background—at first.

Then gradually a truer picture of the Rangward ménage began to form itself in my mind's eye. Rangward was egocentric, the happiness of people around him did not enter into his reckonings at all. I began to feel a certain sympathy with his wife and to wonder what she was like. She had a soft low voice with a very slight cockney intonation. I should have liked to ask her if I might run my hands over her face, her hair, her neck, but, this being impossible, I had to content myself with imagining what she looked like. Once I said: " How tall are you? " And she took my hand and put it on the top of her head. That is the only time I have ever touched her except for the occasions upon which she takes my arm, like a daughter.

Then I discovered that Annabel is musical and that formed the first link between us. After that, the discoveries I made about her read like a catalogue.

She is by no means the high-born lady that Miss Emms thinks her but a Brixton-born lass of unpretentious origins. Her mother, whom I imagine to be a hard-working, outspoken woman, the salt of the earth, but standing no nonsense, had ambitions for her which were dropped, one by one. Annabel worked in a night-club as a kind of hostess-cum-entertainer. She played the piano, for which she has some ability, and sang catchy and sentimental songs.

Annabel was not made to earn her own living. It is said that Eve was made of a limb of Adam and if that applies to any woman it certainly applies to Annabel. She is quite completely a man's woman; not, mark you, a fellow's friend, but a man's mate, the sort he could kick around as much as he likes, so long as he loved her truly. Annabel has to be loved and, in return, she flowers completely and gives utterly of herself. The reason she is so attractive to other men is that they sense this deep sexuality in her and they hang about her, warming themselves at the glow. What they do not understand is that her fire is for one man only. Once ignited, Annabel will burn brightly and truly and until death do part her from the object of her affections.

I hope that I do not sound a note of complaint when I say that the object of her affections was a young man studying music who came to lodge with them in Brixton. I would give a great deal to be able to see this paragon, but I am afraid I should find him nothing to write home about. I think he must have made a casual pass at Annabel, little dreaming of the bonfire he was igniting. He was, however, wholly absorbed in his study and determined to make good. Annabel became abjectly in love with him. Just about this time, she was employed in a night-club with the absurdly ambiguous name of Two Lovely Black Eyes. One night she was treated to a few drinks by a customer and when she arrived home (there was never any question of her going home with the customer, Annabel was strictly moral), she met young Williams in the narrow hall of the Brixton house. I have no doubt he essayed the odd kiss and was alarmed and startled by the response, out of all proportion to the feelings he had. I gather that there was some sort of show-down; Annabel, no doubt, passionately declared that she loved him and what was he going to do about it, and Williams backed clumsily out of a situation which frightened him. And no doubt wisely. Here was a boy from darkest Wales, sent up to London to study music at the Royal College because he had won a scholarship. He was here for one purpose and one purpose only—to study music. Time has shown him to be right; he is now established and doing well. I have no doubt his father is proud of him, as I should have been had he been my son.

Only when he was through his examinations and well

on the road to success did the young man's fancy lightly turn to love.

Alas, by that time it was too late.

Annabel, hurt to the heart by his flippant treatment of her abundant gift of love, dedicated herself to eternal chastity, like a nun. There must have been loud laughter amongst the Shades at this example of human folly.

Within a month she was married to Rangward.

I do not pretend to know what exactly the arrangement between the two was. I can only guess and my guess is no better than anybody else's. Whether Rangward demanded his marital rights or not, I do not know, nor would Annabel tell me. If he didn't, I cannot see what he hoped to get out of the marriage other than the appearance of being happily married to an extremely attractive woman.

On Annabel's side there was more to it; she had security, position, a lovely home and enough money to make life pleasant. As far as she was concerned, the Rangward arrangement might have continued indefinitely. But, unfortunately, there was always Mum to be visited. Mum never comes up west; Mum (Mrs. Brown is her name, I believe) has no ideas above her station. She is proud of her Anne's success in what she considers to be the smart world; she is entranced when her daughter's photograph appears in the *Tatler*, dining at an expensive night-club or attending Ascot. But nothing would induce her to come to Regent's Park and see her daughter's home. So every week or so Annabel, the dutiful daughter (she really loves her Mum) goes to Brixton. Sometimes she takes her out to tea at the Bon Marché and sometimes she takes her to the movies but, more often than not, they sit by the fire gossiping and have a cup of tea.

It was all too easy. Mr. Williams, scratching away at his violin upstairs, often came down to have a cup of tea with Mrs. Brown. He may have met Annabel again as many as a dozen times a year. But there was a psychological moment, and until that moment arrived, nothing happened. When that moment did arrive . . . they were off, there was nothing to hold them.

I have no doubt at all that Annabel went upstairs to see some piece of music, to help adjust some violin string. Any excuse would do. And Mrs. Brown would hook her shoes off with first one big toe and then the other, and smile to herself because she was pleased to see Annabel looking prosperous and happy. She was a good girl, was Annie.

There were no half-measures about Annabel, she flung herself wholly into her love. It was not an affair, it was her fulfilment, what she was born for.

Lucky, lucky Williams! He is a nice enough fellow but I sometimes wonder if he realises just how lucky he is. Yes, I think he does, it is unfair of me to have any doubts.

One of Rangward's charming attributes was that he was a splendid listener. He liked talking himself, but he also appeared to like listening and he had an altogether winning way of appearing to sit at the feet, learning all he could from a man of infinite wisdom, and experience, myself in this case. But I have no doubt at all it was to this quality that he owed most of his social success and his membership of the exclusive Heron's Club. I now know that his deferential manner was completely spurious, but it took me a long time to realise it.

Most people consider the anecdotes of an elderly man to be dull but Rangward seemed to want to hear all that one could tell him and I found myself telling him numerous narratives of my hospital days, some amusing and some gruesome. It was only quite recently that I found that this had passed beyond the anecdotal stage and that Rangward was doing something very like picking my brains. At various times in the past year he has asked me an isolated question such as: " How long is it before rigor mortis sets in? " or " What is the difference in rigor mortis time between someone who has been killed suddenly, shot for instance, and someone who has died a natural death? " or " What would be the appearance of the corpse of somebody who has died of carbon monoxide poisoning, would a doctor recognise it at once?" or " Would *you* be kidded, Mr. Toby, into thinking symptoms of arsenic poisoning were gastro-enteritis? " Only a day or so before they were off to Lisbon he asked: " How many tablets of luminal would be a fatal dose? " And when I told him, he said: " Less than that would make you sick, would it? You'd vomit up the lot? "

Not that the isolated question was of any significance at all; it was only when I looked back over the past months that I found these questions formed the core of an apparent desire to become well informed.

I began to wonder.

I began to wonder about the whole Rangward establishment. What did I really know about them? And the answer was that what I really knew was (I was going to say what I *saw*) . . . practically nothing.

So I set to work to discover what lay beneath the apparent normality. I should never, of course, have gone to the lengths to which I finally went, if it had not been that, sometime during last spring, I learned about Annabel's love-affair with the young musician. She took me to an orchestral concert where he was making a first appearance and I had my suspicions from then. Not so long after that, during a spell of glorious spring weather, when we were walking in the park, the young man was apparently waiting for Annabel, hanging about, hoping to meet her. Even to a blind man it was all too evident.

Sometime afterwards I challenged her: " You love that young Welshman, don't you? " Of course she did; with shining eyes (which I could only imagine) and warm husky voice, she told me how much she loved him. I was the only person to whom she could talk about her love and at first she took great delight in talking about it.

But that wasn't to last. Nobody as monogamous as Annabel could be happy for long, married to one man and in love with another. She soon wilted under the strain.

As spring turned into a warm summer, we had many strolls together in the park and it was evident that she was becoming increasingly unhappy. At last I advised her to tell Rangward. He was not unreasonable, I said, he would probably agree to divorce her.

And then I had my real surprise. Annabel was frightened of him. I tried to pin her down. " I can't understand you," I told her more than once, " Richard seems reasonably kind and understanding."

" But he isn't," she said, and left it at that.

Every good word I spoke for Richard she contradicted flatly and uncompromisingly. She was not disposed to discuss him, but simply disagreed with any good opinion of the man I might promulgate.

That made me wonder a lot more.

Why is she frightened of him? I asked myself over and over again. It was at the point when my wondering about

211

Rangward's curiosity with regard to criminal juris-
prudence and Annabel's fear of her husband met, that I
decided to take an equivocal step to find out something
more about Rangward.

I used a method which may seem curious, drastic and
even fantastic, but it was the special form of procedure
of a blind man. I employed a private eye. It cost
surprisingly little money because my requirements were
straightforward and easy to fulfil and I learned a great
deal in a very short time.

To say that I was astonished at what I heard is a
miserable understatement. I got a considerable shock,
but in a short time I had settled down quite easily with
my knowledge and I found that there was nothing I had
learned about Rangward which, now that I knew, did not
fit in with the man.

He was the owner of a good deal of real estate scattered
about London which was run in the name of " Southern
Estates, Limited." In addition, about half a dozen large
Victorian Houses due for demolition were included in this
property and I was astonished to learn that they were run
as brothels. The rooms were let to women who paid a
certain rental for their lodging, light, heat and hot water.
The rent was payable weekly but with each payment an
unspecified sum of money was handed over in addition
to the rent. In one of the houses there was a resident
housekeeper who was, in fact, responsible for the lot; it
was her job to keep the houses clean and warm and to
attend to all small domestic problems. Rangward kept a
firm hand on these properties; he was by no means the
absentee landlord and I imagine personal supervision to
be an essential if places of the kind are to be run success-
fully.

Now the law with regard to this kind of trade is somewhat obscure; it seems that men living on the immoral earnings of women can only be charged under the Vagrancy Act.

Only the other day, in the House of Commons (as my secretary read out to me) the Home Secretary said that as this problem was being considered by the Commission on Homosexuality and Prostitution, it would be wise to wait its report before considering legislation. An Honourable Member protested that the unequal operation of the law with regard to leaseholds did call for separate examination of the law on the use of property in this way. Another member asked if the Home Secretary really knew what was going on. Rents, he said, were soaring and criminals were transferring their affections to these quarters as the easiest way of making a living. The Home Secretary replied that he was trying to find out what was going on, but he still thought the best thing was to ask the Committee's opinion on the matter.

My private eye had, doubtless in the rôle of prospective customer, become on friendly terms with the housekeeper, whose headquarters were in one of the houses, called Oliver Lodge. He described her as being extremely discreet with regard to her employer, loyal, faithful but inclined to harbour unspecified feelings of resentment against him. There was nothing which my private eye could put his finger on, he simply felt that she considered herself " hard-done-by." He described her as being a plain woman, stout and past middle-age but reasonably kind and with a rich store of lubricious stories which, after a glass or two of port, she threw out with gales of salacious laughter.

Yes, I think my private eye quite enjoyed the Totterdell

213

commission. I paid his bill with a feeling of money well spent. What I was going to do with my information I had no idea, but I knew that knowledge is power, and, as such, might be useful.

I went on wondering; fortunately the process of wondering does not show on the face. My manner towards Rangward remained unchanged but his questions, it seemed to my heightened perceptions, increased three-fold. Is it possible . . . could it be——?

Was he, in fact, contemplating doing away with Annabel?

Fantastic, far-fetched, fabulous. Why not divorce Annabel and have done with her? Why go to the trouble of killing her?

And yet I could not wholly dismiss it from my mind because there was this fear of hers.

Then I began to wonder about Rudie Ormer. He is a boy of whom I have become very fond. A product of the age, on the whole Ormer is kind and a good boy, though he has considerable doubts about himself. As Rangward's chauffeur for the past five years, he must have had at least a smattering of knowledge about his employer's more profitable sources of income. I have recently wondered why Rangward employed a chauffeur at all, but I under-stand that the difficulties of a Londoner travelling about the metropolis now are manifold and that the services of a chauffeur are invaluable in the saving of time and trouble. I wondered whether the knowledge that Ormer must have had was troubling him. He is a conscientious youth with a deeply ingrained sense of respectability and it may be that his knowledge was weighing on his mind. Ormer is one who could quickly become unbalanced, I believe

214

his father was highly temperamental and finally committed suicide and I can see vestiges of this inherence in Rudie.

As the summer progressed I could see no signs of the situation easing, the problems solving themselves, as often happens with the passage of time. Indeed, the situation worsened considerably.

Annabel is not one to come rushing to me with her troubles, for all that I am her only confidant. It was only sometime after the event that I gathered, rather than was told specifically, that Annabel had screwed her courage to the sticking point and asked Rangward point blank to divorce her. The result was negative. I do not know what he said to Annabel, but afterwards she told me: " Richard will never let me go."

" He is a dog in the manger; what he does not want himself he does not want anyone else to have."

" But he says he does want me."

I believed her, but I could not find Richard's attitude reasonable; I failed to understand or sympathise with it.

" He said I have made my bed and I must lie in it." I could have said then that, so long as he did not lie in it too, Annabel might bear the situation but, Annabel being as she is, I refrained from such a remark.

I simply said: " There's something in that." And Annabel began to cry, presumably because I made no allowances for human folly.

If Annabel were a murderess, a fine motive was working itself up; I can see that now. But, however much I may now have been convinced that Richard had certain qualities necessary to a murderer, I could not build up a motive for murdering Annabel against him. Had I been able to do so, I would never have allowed Annabel to go to Portugal with him whilst the situation between them was so uncertain.

I was rather surprised, in fact, to hear that the holiday in Portugal was arranged. I wondered why Rangward wanted to go away with a woman who was longing to get away from him. I went so far as to suggest to Annabel that she simply leave Richard; but there was no doubt at all that the girl was terrified of him and I wondered whether he added wife-beating to his hobbies. Having spent a great deal of time thinking and wondering and coming to no constructive conclusion, I said good-bye to them, as they went off to Portugal, with the greatest misgivings.

After they had gone there was a considerable hiatus; I believe I had got myself worked up into a state of apprehension and their absence created an anti-climax. Tiddly Push, my lion-dog of Peking, and I had many a lonely walk in the park. Once the Welshman came up and spoke to me, asking me when we were expecting the Rangwards home. He seemed detached and unhappy, and I should have liked to tell him that I knew about him and his affairs; I should have liked him to tell me all about it himself. But he didn't and I don't blame him; who wants to pour out their innermost feelings to an elderly man wearing almost black glasses? I wanted to say: Don't dally; go to it, man, go in and seize your prey! In the olden days he could have snatched up the fair lady and ridden away with her on his charger to his fortified castle, but now he would probably be hauled up in a court of law, charged with " enticement " and fined a sum far above his means.

Six uneventful weeks passed. First Eddy Bolton and then Rudie and his Edna took their holidays. The day the Rangwards came back everything happened; to someone who leads as quiet a life as myself, it seems, looking back, like a day in a horror comic—all in crude hectic colours and not quite true.

It began with Tiddly Push. I must hasten to state that he has never suffered from worms, a degrading complaint of which I have always been determined my lion-dog shall not be a victim. Prevention, to coin a phrase, being better than cure, I put the poor chap through the lesser indignities of having a worm pill forced down him four times a year.

Tiddly Push, like myself, tolerates Miss Emms, but that is all. I should hate, repeat hate, Miss Emms to give me a worm pill and I do not intend that Tiddly Push should be subjected to something which I myself would not endure. It so happened that the time for him to have his worm pill came up whilst Rudie and Edna were away in Ostend. As I am particularly fussy about this, I mentioned it to Miss Emms, telling her that Rudie had better do it as soon as he got back and that she must not forget to starve Tiddly Push the previous day in preparation. Rudie returned late in the evening, but next morning he was up to see me, as usual. I told him that Tiddly Push had been starved and asked him to administer the pill at once. Rudie said he would buy one that morning, but I remembered that I had one to spare, which I had put in a small pill box and put away somewhere. I told him to go and look for it in the big bathroom cupboard where I keep all my medicines.

Presently he came back, evidently with a small tin

which contained a pill of sorts; he read out what was on the label: " *Toxicum, non sumendum,*" he stammered in atrocious Latin.

He nearly startled me out of my wits. I took the little box from him and felt it carefully, and then I remembered. It was a poor neurotic German-Jewish refugee who came to me the first year of the war, a nervous wreck, from whom I had wrested, almost by force, the capsule of cyanide of potassium with which he was threatening to do away with himself. It was in the same flat tin box and I had slipped it into the pocket of my waistcoat whilst I endeavoured to talk him into a reasonable frame of mind. (Incidentally, I wonder what became of the poor chap? Last thing I heard of him was that he was in the Isle of Man!) In the evening, alone in my consulting room and thinking over the patient's visit to me, I took out the little box and examined the capsule with some interest. I knew that cyanide of potassium in that particular form causes death within a few seconds, the symptoms being of the shortest possible duration. There was a small slip of paper, a little grubby and fingered, wrapped round the cotton-wool covering of the capsule and, having a few minutes to spare, I amused myself by translating the German. It was a quotation from the Psalms: " He giveth His beloved sleep." I thought again about the poor wretch who had written the words. It was clear that he had contemplated taking the poison many a time. I forget now what the man's history was, but I do remember that a number of his family had mysteriously vanished. We know now what, in all probability, became of them, but he could only guess and he was tortured with the agony of doubt. He had evidently been in possession of the capsule for some time and had over and over again withdrawn on the point of taking it. I think I was able to give him courage and hope.

These thoughts came to me when I had translated the line and, loath to destroy the evidence of that poignant consultation, I wrote, for safety, *Poison, not to be taken* in Latin on a small label which I stuck on the lid; then I slipped the tiny box into my waistcoat pocket and promptly forgot all about it.

Whether I took out the box with my money and keys when I undressed at night and my wife, finding it lying on my dressing-table the next day, put it away in the bathroom cupboard, or whether I myself, absent-mindedly put it there, I shall never know. There was an air raid shortly afterwards that made me exceedingly busy in the casualty department at hospital and I had no time to give a thought to the cyanide capsule.

" Don't you know what *Toxicum, non sumendum* means? " I asked Rudie. " I thought you knew a lot about medicine? "

Rudie took the tin from my hand and evidently studied the label.

" I didn't know it was in the bathroom cupboard! " I exclaimed. " It had better not go back there! " And I began to think hard where I could have put Tiddly Push's worm pill. In the excitement of running it to earth in one of my small bureau drawers, I forgot all about the little tin box; only after Rudie had gone I wondered where he had put it, reminding myself to ask him for it next time he came up.

If that little incident had been all you could call a happening that day, I would certainly not have allowed the sun to set on the fact that I had not been able to put my hand on the box after Rudie left my room. But there was a great deal more to the day than that, quite enough to

219

put all thoughts of a stray capsule of cyanide out of my mind, until it was forced into it.

The house was quiet without them and I was listening for their return. I could hardly conceal my pleasure when, not much more than fifteen minutes after they got home, Annabel came upstairs to see me. I could tell at once from her voice that something big had happened. I took care to close the door and make sure Miss Emms was not about, flapping her ears. I took Annabel's hand in mine. " Tell me," I said; " is everything going to be all right? "

" Oh, Mr. Toby! " She was excited and overwrought, and she burrowed her face into the crook of my arm; I didn't know whether she was laughing or crying.

" I'm going to have a baby! " she whispered.

I could hardly go into transports of delight over this news, which was the last thing I had expected; I thought young women knew what they were about these days.

" I'm glad you're pleased! " I said stiffly.

She did not bother to tell me who was the father of the child-to-be, taking it for granted that I knew as, indeed, if I knew Annabel as well as I think I do, I should have known at once. When I finally realised that the father must be Williams, I was relieved. It seemed a comparatively simple situation now.

But Annabel had not dared to tell him and now she had brought home this monstrous burden (sic!), and laid it on my shoulders. *I* was to tell Rangward.

I am no great shakes as a mediator and advocate and I did not at all fancy my mission. I did not say so, however. The situation was, at least, interesting and to one who fancies himself as a student of human nature, it should have had irresistible appeal.

Who am I to suffer from cold feet, having two artificial extremities? I think, in fact, that is what I was suffering from and in retrospect I can see that if I were scared at the idea of telling Rangward then it should not have been difficult to sympathise with Annabel.

" Why don't you simply go? Run away."

" But he knows where I live. He came to our house once when he first knew me. He's met Mum. He'd come down to Brixton and raze the place. He might bring a gun and shoot us both."

" Sh . . . sh! Don't talk rubbish! "

" You don't understand him. He is ruthless. He will have what he wants. He's a spoilt boy. His mother gave him everything, everything she could; she died of exhaustion, died trying to satisfy his extravagant needs."

" You've never told me that."

" There's never been any need to. But I'm telling you now, so you can understand how I'm feeling. He won't take no for an answer. ' I want,' he says, and so he must have! "

There was a pause, and then I said: " Do you know what he does for a living, Annabel? "

She obviously had no idea what I meant. She simply answered that he dealt in property and was a company director. I began to see that Annabel was right, surprisingly, in her appraisal of him. If Rangward was of humble origins, as I suspected, he had done amazingly well for himself. There must have been ruthless qualities in him to cause him to override difficulties in the way he had. I realised that her fear of him was a genuine thing and not simply hysteria.

221

What could I do with him?

The answer was clear, I had a weapon and a strong one. Knowledge, as I have said before and I say it again, because I suddenly saw how it was going to help us all, *knowledge is power.*

" Send Richard up to me," I said grimly.

" There's a dinner party on to-night. Anders Halvorsen and Charles Shefford are coming."

" Send him up before they come."

" *Send him.*" I think Annabel was smiling at the absurdity of the thought. " I think he'll come in any case. . . ."

About an hour before dinner he came up.

" What are you wearing, Rangward? " I asked. He told me he had changed for dinner as they had Shefford and Halvorsen coming, and that he had put on his red velvet smoking-jacket.

I asked him if he was tanned and he said, Yes, he had had all the sun anybody could want but that had not helped his sleeplessness. He had slept rather less well than at home. I murmured something about too much sun being bad for one and he told me about a new proprietary brand of sleeping tablet he had heard of but which he had been unable to obtain in Portugal. Had I heard of it and, if so, he supposed I hadn't got a few sample tablets for him to try? I had, in fact, received some literature and a sample of the tablets a few weeks past. My secretary, after reading the blurb, had put it away somewhere. But I had no intention of handing out anything to Rangward which could prove lethal, at this juncture. I was a little absent whilst he talked; I was wondering just how I was going to introduce the very tricky topic I had in mind.

At last I brought up the subject of Annabel, asking how she looked after her holiday and getting the answer for which I had hoped. She was blooming, he said.

So then I took a big breath and dived in head first. " Rangward," I said as pleasantly as I could, " are you, you of all people, guilty of shutting your eyes to a very invidious situation? "

I have no doubt he shot me a sharp look, I could almost feel it.

" I mean Annabel. I have no doubt at all you know how things are with her."

" I would rather not discuss this with you," he said in a curious voice. " You have never been personal before."

" I must be now," I said. " Someone must help you two people and it will have to be me. You both seem to me to be floundering about most unhappily."

" I'm perfectly happy," he said in a sharp tight voice.

" But Annabel isn't."

" It happens again and again," Rangward said in a complaining voice. " These girls want to marry, to have security, and then, when once they are married and secure they aren't prepared to keep their part of the bargain. They embarrass their friends by complaining about their situation."

I bowed my head in agreement, but added: " This is different."

" In what way is it different? " he asked angrily. " My attitude towards her hasn't changed at all. I am perfectly satisfied with the situation as it is."

I felt pretty restive because, of course, he had a case.

" You have to make allowances," I said sententiously, "for the fallibility of human nature." I plunged wildly on: " And now Annabel is going to suffer from the effect of her extra-marital infatuation. She is going to have a child."

There was a lengthy and ugly silence. I would have given a great deal to see his face. At one moment I had the uneasy feeling that he was standing over me with his fist poised, about to strike me on the head, but that was probably all imagination.

" She wants to leave you and go to—to her lover."

" I am sure she does," he answered unpleasantly.

" Then why not let her go? Why not divorce her and start again, there is no shortage of women? "

" What an incredible idea," he said, as though affronted. " She happens to be my property. I shall certainly not let her go."

" She can leave you if she wants, and there is no need for her to return. There is no law enforcing a woman to return to a man she does not want to go back to."

" She won't dare to leave me. I want her to stay with me and have her child. I will bring it up as *my* child."

I thought: For the love of Mike, why? But I said: " As one who lives off the immoral earnings of women it is no doubt an asset to have a wife and child. But is it in this case really worth the trouble and unhappiness involved? "

There was a very long pause, during which I could hear Rangward breathing heavily. " I see," he said. " Blackmail. People in my position are always open to it. I suppose I have been fortunate that I haven't come across it—much. But you, you are the last person I should have thought——"

" I'm exceedingly fond of Annabel," I said hastily, " and I won't make any bones about it: I will go to any lengths to see that she is happy. If you won't divorce her, or at least let her go peaceably, Rangward, I shall be forced to forward my information about certain properties in your possession to the right quarter." I hope I sounded a little more convincing than I felt; I had, in fact, no idea what the right quarter was, unless it was the aforesaid Committee on Homosexuality and Prostitution.

Tiddly Push was playing round, I could feel him passing and re-passing my feet. I bent down and tickled him behind the ear.

" I am a man of peace," I said, " and I don't like to know people are unhappy, especially people of whom I am fond."

I was surprised to hear him answer in a reasonably normal voice: " You've got it all wrong, you know. Annabel is infatuated with this musician, it is a momentary thing. She isn't going to throw up the fleshpots to go slumming again. She was only too glad to get out of her slum; she fell into my arms like a ripe peach. As long as I can keep her in reasonable luxury, she'll stay, whatever she may say to the contrary."

It was the smooth, convincing Rangward I have always known.

" And don't forget," he added, " that, if you ruin me, you ruin her. We sink or swim together. You had better think that over."

" It's your opinion against mine," I said feebly; " but I have warned you, Rangward. I mean what I say! "

" You are a vicious, two-faced, treacherous old devil! " he snarled suddenly. I heard him walk across the room and open the door. Then I heard his voice on the landing. " Get out of the light! " I heard him snap, presumably to Tiddly Push. He left the door open and a minute or so

225

later Tiddly Push came back into my room and jumped on to my knee.

Two and a half hours later he was dead and Annabel was crying bitterly.

Four people had had access to my cyanide capsule. First Miss Emms, Rudie Ormer and later, Annabel and Rangward himself.

Now, in a case of murder, there is no point in allowing the mind to rove about, wildly and disjointedly, flitting from possible suspect to possible suspect. There are three points which must be borne in mind: (1) *The suspect must have an interest in the immediate death of the victim.* That cut out Miss Emms, Rudie Ormer and certainly Rangward himself. (2) *The suspect must have the opportunity of administering the poison.* That cut out Miss Emms and Rudie, leaving Annabel and Rangward himself. (3) *The conduct of the suspects both immediately before and immediately after, and for some little time after the death.* Miss Emms's conduct had been in no way different from usual, nor was Rudie Ormer's. Annabel's conduct I knew all about and Rangward—he was in no mood for suicide.

Annabel was the only one who emerged from that small test. Her behaviour *before* was compatible with the act, and so was her behaviour *afterwards*; her tears might well have been reaction, and it was just the sort of reaction a girl of her nature might have.

I reminded myself of the short pithy maxim that has been used by counsel for the defence at a trial for murder by poisoning; a person without any homicidal tendencies whatever can, *if driven beyond endurance*, bring himself to administer the poison *given the opportunity*.

Neither Halvorsen nor Shefford, however much they

226

might have desired Rangward's death, and I have no reason to suppose they desired it at all, had access to my capsule and it would be carrying coincidence to the point of absurdity to imagine that either of them should ply Rangward with cyanide at the precise moment that my capsule was missing. I thought the situation down, peeling off irrelevancies like segments of an onion, till I got down to the least common denominator.

It looked to me very much as though Annabel had done it and if I, who loved her and knew she hadn't, might think that perhaps she had, what were the police going to think?

I am a blind man who has, since I was blinded, prided myself upon my sight. But after Rangward's frightful end I felt doubly blind. It was not until the eventful day of the funeral that my inner sight began to come back to me.

The fight between Annabel's two idiotic admirers was unnecessary and only complicated things. I was angry about it. Such childishness belongs to the early nineteenth century, not to to-day. Still, if it had not been for the fight, I doubt if Mrs. Dicky Rangward (as she called herself) would ever have reached me. Nobody would have dreamed of sending the wretched woman up to me. As it was, she arrived at the most unfortunate moment and to sweep her up to my room was the best I could do.

Whether I should attribute the fund of information I received from her to my erstwhile famous bedside manner or to the half-bottle of Perrier Jouet I opened for her is a moot point. Whichever it was, she came over in a big way. She shot off her mouth, as Rudie might say, and filled in a big gap in my reckonings.

It all came out, but back to front, as it were. She started at the end and we worked our way fruitfully back to the beginning; it was none the less perfectly clear for that.

There is no need for me, however, to recount the story in that manner. I can start quite comfortably from the beginning. Rangward, as I have long suspected, was the boy born with ambition under circumstances which were not conducive to success. His mother, there seemed to be no question of a father, doted on her only child. She wanted everything of the best for him and filled him up with the idea that only the best was good enough for him. Unfortunately she was in no position to provide even the second best. She carried on a small dressmaking business in a suburb not ten miles west of London. Her boy went to the local school where he did well, subsequently going on to a grammar school. It was the commission in the R.A.F. that really gave him big ideas. He emerged from the war determined to make money somehow and the easiest way of doing so seemed to be to marry money; which he did. He married a woman some eleven years older than himself, the daughter of a prosperous deceased grocer. With her money he bought himself some property; there is no doubt at all Richard Rangward had great ability and organising powers. He showed prescience and good judgment and from the very first he began to make money.

His wife must have had her share of avarice. She could not explain just how the brothel business started. I gather it evolved, one opportunity giving rise to another, it grew like a snowball and proved itself to be more profitable than the buying and selling of real estate, though that was doing quite well too. Once or twice the woman made some sort of attempt to retract. " I knew what we were doing was wrong," she said; " but, if we hadn't done it, some-body else would! Our backing out of the business wasn't going to make the women go straight, was it? " Such is the form of reasoning that blurs the line between right and wrong.

There had to be personal supervision, Richard and she were agreed on that point. A company was formed with herself, Rangward and the solicitor Pethod, who plays a small but deadly part in the final reckoning. She possessed a third of the shares but worked on a salary basis. " It was the greatest mistake I ever made," she said, " letting myself get talked into that. I gave up my position as his wife and took the job of housekeeper, that's what it amounts to, my dear! He didn't want me as his wife any longer, he'd made use of me, got all he wanted, used my capital and was sick and tired of me. But I wasn't having any divorce. Being his lawful wife was the only thing I had left and I was going to stick to that whatever happened. I showed as much common sense over that as I was bloody silly over the salary business."

" But what was the point? "

" I had a hold over him, see? "

Yes, I saw. I saw everything.

I saw the rancour and the bitterness. I saw Rangward forging ahead, rising out of his class and skilfully shedding that which he did not desire to rise with him. He did not want the loyalty and affection of the wife who had helped him to start, he no longer needed her money and he did not intend to drag her along after him, a social stigma. He established her in the position to which she was suited, he had business dealings with her, but that was as far as it went. He told her that if she insisted on remaining his

229

wife, he would have nothing to do with her socially. He intended to live his own life. And he did.

The elderly secretary in charge of the office of Southern Star Estates, Ltd., had instructions not to give anyone Rangward's private address and, except through the office, his wife was unable to get in touch with him. Having made a success of being a wealthy young-man-about-town, Rangward turned his thoughts to the setting-up of an establishment, complete with wife. It is surprising to me that he was not more ambitious socially. He might have " married " a divorced woman of title, he might have tried his luck amongst the monied débutantes. He did not fly very high when he chose Anne Brown. Perhaps there was a streak of social uncertainty about him somewhere and with her he felt safer.

Taking everything into consideration the establishment in the ground floor maisonette of my house in Park Row was a great achievement for the poor dressmaker's bastard son.

The worm, or rather the wife, had been writhing under these various injustices for some years, and now the time had come for it to turn. And turn it did, to some effect. She told him that she was having to work too hard for a woman of her age, she no longer desired to be mistress-in-charge of Oliver Lodge, or any of the other houses. She wanted to retire. Unfortunately for her, her demands were excessive; she over-estimated Rangward's financial position, she asked for too much. She wanted a large capital sum which was to cover the building of a small bungalow at Peacehaven for herself, and the purchase of an annuity. Rangward was not prepared to give it to her, nor did he want to lose her invaluable services at Oliver Lodge. The argument went on, to and fro, over the months. Whenever Rangward came to Oliver Lodge to collect his rents, there was a row with his wife. Then the inevitable pressure was brought to bear; either he give her all she asked or she would " expose " him, as she called it. Expose him as a bigamist, living on the immoral earnings of women.

Her continued existence thus became a potential danger to Rangward; to such a man as he the thought of being exposed as a fraud and a criminal was unendurable, his eminent respectability was as important to him as his life and certainly more important than her life.

" And I haven't been too well," the poor woman went on. " I've been worried to death, thinking I've got a growth. I've been under the doctor and I've been to the X-ray department at St. Mary's and had a thorough overhaul. They say they can't see anything wrong. But I don't know. You're a doctor, aren't you, sir? How can you account for me being so off colour if it isn't *something*?"

I asked her for a few details of her indisposition. I didn't need more than half a dozen answers before the whole thing was as clear as daylight. I began to get excited. My hunch had been right. I wasn't losing my grip. After all these years I could still trust my instinct!

He had, of course, been experimenting. His own sleep-lessness had given rise to ideas about the putting to sleep of someone whose presence was a menace to his whole way of life. He was uncertain of himself, though. He wanted to find out before he plunged wildly into murder. He had tried this and that, tentatively and in small doses, knowing that small indispositions on the part of the victim always come in useful in the final reckonings, that is, before the death certificate is issued.

It was not Annabel's death he had been planning, but

231

that of his wife. He had intended to kill her by administering, somehow, an overdose of sleeping-tablets. He would have arranged it to look like a suicide of the kind that takes place almost weekly in London. " She suspected that she had a serious illness and was unable to face the prospects." The coroner would return a verdict of " Suicide whilst of unsound mind," and tender his sympathies to the dead woman's husband.

How he would obtain the tablets was easy. It would simply be an extension of his own experiments in sedatives. I have no doubt he intended to give her the fatal dose in tea or coffee or possibly port. The action time would be important; if it acted quickly he would see her to bed leaving the necessary evidence before he departed from Oliver Lodge.

This was where I came in. It was clearly impossible to discuss the merits and demerits of sedatives with the family doctor. Rangward and I were on such terms that we could easily have had long cosy discussions on the subject, I being only too pleased to air my useless knowledge. Having obtained all the preliminary information from me, and possibly a sample of the tablets with which he could experiment, he could then ask his doctor for a prescription for himself without giving rise to the least suspicion.

And, too, my blindness came in useful because I could not read the papers and it would be very unlikely that my secretary would pick out one small paragraph about an obscure woman called Rangward who had died of an overdose of sleeping tablets somewhere in S.W.

I hope that none of the pleasure I was feeling at my own sagacity showed in my face. Here, I thought, is one of the many undetected crimes that the police know to exist. One of the many perfect murders.

The only thing was—it hadn't taken place. Rangward had died instead.

There was nothing more I needed from Mrs. Dick Rangward. But she wanted sympathy and understanding and a little kindness. I had quite a time with her but, when she left, I think she was comforted. She thanked me. " I'm so glad I came," she explained pathetically. " I've never seen Dicky's home that he thought so much of. And that poor girl! Bigamously married! " She clicked her tongue sympathetically. " Isn't it a shame! He was a bad lot, was Dicky, Mr. Totterdell, but you couldn't help but be fond of him."

I nodded. " I see what you mean, Mrs. Rangward."

" And that Pethod," she said, compressing her lips, " he's as hard as nails. He says the estate isn't going to be worth half what he had hoped. I'll be out on the streets before I'm through."

I managed to say good-bye fairly gracefully before she wept on my shoulder. I left Tiddly Push to see her off at the front door and, as I went back to my sitting-room, I'm afraid I was still feeling inordinately pleased with myself.

Pethod, the unknown, strikes me as being a particularly vile sort of villain. He never appears, but sits in some musty office quietly exuding evil, like the small octopus bleeding its foul waves of ink. I think he had more influence on Rangward than we shall guess, backing him up in his nefarious undertakings but taking good care of himself at the same time. Having none of the practical worries of the business, he kept his eyes fixed on the accounts pertaining thereto. It would not surprise me at

233

all to hear that he had been quietly cheating Rangward all the time and that, if it is true that Rangward's estate amounts to considerably less than was anticipated, it is the direct result of his partner's fiddling.

The interview with the dead man's " widow " had been put off, out of consideration for her feelings, until the day after the funeral. I did not want Annabel to go to the solicitor's office alone and I offered to go with her more than once. Each time she refused and I wish now that I had insisted. A blind man is better than nobody when a woman like Annabel is faced with a Pethod.

I can see Pethod smacking his loathsome lips at the thought of having the lovely young " wife " of his late partner bewildered and at a loss, delivered into his clutches.

With what poorly concealed delight he told her that Rangward had married her bigamously, had a wife in existence and had made no provisions for Annabel.

After a suitable pause he offered her the alternative, incredible though it may seem, of life with him. He had, of course, summed Annabel up quite incorrectly; no doubt he had certain preconceived ideas about the type of woman she was. But for all his evil, the man was an incredible fool, or was he? The woman who was Rangward's bigamous " wife " might have been quite pleased to transfer her favours to Pethod. He wasn't reckoning on Annabel—Annabel the monogamous, Annabel the altogether simple, Annabel the beloved of Clement Williams. I can see only too clearly the finger of the monster Pethod in Rangward's post-mortem letter to Annabel. I feel sure the letter was written as the outcome of a conversation he had with Pethod on the subject of the disposal of his property in the event of his meeting with

234

an accident. Pethod was not one to take any risks about money, things must be put straight. Rangward's shares in the company were to go to his wife. " And what," Pethod would ask, " are you going to do about the woman with whom you are living? " Rangward knew what he was going to do. He was going to put his legal wife out of harm's way, her interest in the company would revert to him when she died.

If, by some unfortunate accident, he were to die before his legal wife things were going to be sticky. " Far better," I can hear Pethod advising, " make a clean breast of it in a letter she'll only get if anything happens to you. Tell the woman you married her bigamously. It can't do you any harm, old boy. You'll be dead and out of it all. And as for her . . ." Then, possibly Rangward gave Pethod an inkling of how things were. Annabel, he must have known, had a lover, if not several. " Then why be squeamish, old boy? " I hear the voice of friend Pethod. " Write and tell her straight. She owes you nothing. Can't understand how you let a woman do the dirty on you like that. Why do you sit down under it? " " Because it happens to suit me," I can hear Rangward return abruptly. And so it did. But the conversation was not without its effect, it stuck. And hence the letter, with the sting in the tail. The sting that was going to hurt Annabel immeasurably.

And so Pethod, I can almost see the expression on his face, handed over Rangward's letter and watched, with anticipatory pleasure, Annabel's reactions. I think the tears stumped him. He did not like what he could not understand, and he did not understand Annabel's tears. She was a complete mystery to him, an unknown quantity. It was more than likely, he would think as he watched her

235

weep, that what the papers were implying was true, *she* poisoned Rangward. Oh, yes, Mr. Pethod had had his doubts, but now he was in no two minds about it. He could hardly wait for her to dry her tears before he bundled her out into the street. Then he looked out the copy of the posthumously-received letter which he had taken the trouble to preserve. He got an office boy to take it round to Scotland Yard in a taxi-cab so that no time should be wasted. Let them make what they can of it, Mr. Pethod no doubt told himself, it is my duty to help them in the course and interests of justice.

But even as scorpions exist for a purpose, so did Mr. Pethod; he had a purpose and has played his unpleasant part in the working out of God's will.

And now the tumult and the shouting has died, the Baron and the police departed and Tiddly Push and I are alone in my room which, a short time ago, was like Clapham Junction station.

It is very quiet now, Tiddly Push is sitting on the arm of my chair, being the nearest he can get to me as my knee is occupied by my writing-pad with the raised lines.

With my mind's eye I have been looking round my room; I hope Rudie and Edna, between them, will keep it as clean as Miss Emms has done. I hope they will keep the furniture polished and my books dust free. My old brocade curtains will have to go sometime; beyond ordinary shabbiness they are becoming threadbare. My two Dutch paintings will need cleaning this spring; they have not been done for ten years and, I think, they have a grape-bloom over their glowing colours; I don't like pictures to look unloved even if I can't see them. Then there is my little market scene attributed to Chardin. I had thought of giving it to Annabel for a wedding-present but on second thoughts I think she would appreciate a cheque more; she can buy a pram with it. And perhaps the top of the fender should have a new red leather cover.

Yes, Tiddly Push, my lion-dog, you'll look very fine and black and imperial, lying on the new red leather. . . .

I suppose the Baron looked upon me as *in loco parentis* to Annabel as there would seem to be no other reason for his wanting to see me. I am glad, on the whole, that Eddy brought him up to me because I felt the young man was sorely bewildered and needed to have things explained to him as far as one was able. He started off by telling me he had made a " full confession." The situation would now be dealt with by his ambassador but in the meantime he felt he should cease to see Annabel or have anything more to do with her.

" You mean you have got over your infatuation? "

He admitted, with some reluctance, that he had.

" I'm glad," I told him. " You see, you haven't really been in love with Annabel, you have been in love with something you thought she was."

But he did not agree with that. He said that he had not thought it possible that a man could love a woman as much as he had loved Annabel.

" And yet," I pointed out, " quite suddenly you don't love her any more, which proves, my dear Baron, that you were in love with a wraith, a ghost, something which did not exist."

Still he did not agree. So I told him about Annabel.

" She's not a *femme fatale* at all," I explained, " she's a

237

man's woman but not, unfortunately for you, your woman. All she now wants is to sit dandling her baby on her knee; modern women don't *dandle* their babies but she will; possibly jigging him in time to the piece her husband is playing on the violin; she will sit for hours, proudly, dreamily, smiling at her two menfolk."

It was clearly unfair to indulge my warped sense of humour at the poor fellow's expense. I tried to be a little more in keeping with his mood of blank despair.

" She's one in a thousand, and the man who finds her is the luckiest man in the world, the man, that is, who finds her and awakens her love. In this case, my poor Baron, it is a violinist called Clement Williams from Wales, a man with deepset Celtic eyes (*I think*) and ears that ' hear a sound so fine there's nothing left 'twixt it and silence.' They will marry and live happily ever after. That is," I added hurriedly, " provided we find the answer to the present problem, *who killed Rangward!* "

I gave the poor chap a whisky, he seemed quite " un-houseled, disappointed, unannealed."

" It is a pity," I said, " that your fine gesture of ' confession ' should, to put it crudely, be a flop. Another time, perhaps my dear young man, another time. . . ."

He shuddered, I could feel it two yards away.

And then the telephone rang. It was an irate father, Shefford the elder, and was he irate! He began by saying that he understood I was " in charge of affairs at Number 51," which there was no point in denying. " I want you to know," he shouted, " that my son Charles made a foolish and altogether false ' confession ' to the police last night immediately after being brought home in a semi-conscious condition. I understand that you are a qualified surgeon and physician, that you witnessed the fight and that you will possibly be called upon to give evidence at the forthcoming inquest? "

I said that a great deal had to take place before the inquest was resumed.

" Well, you know what I mean," the loud voice said irritably.

I asked him not to shout, I told him a few facts and then, not mincing my words, I told him that his son was a fool, that he had hung around Mrs. Rangward without the least encouragement from her for the past five years, that he had had an infatuation for her which he clearly enjoyed, otherwise he would have given it up long ago as hopeless. Now, I went on, that his son had made this perfectly insane confession, the best thing he could do would be to get him certified.

Oddly enough the old man gave a bark of laughter. He was not angry any longer; indeed, he seemed pleased and thanked me for my forthrightness.

" We see eye to eye, Doctor—er—Mr. Totterdell."

Did we, I wonder? I thought of something that might help the worried father. " Tell him," I said, " in confidence, of course, that Annabel is expecting a child by a man she has been in love with since before ever she met Charles. That may clear things up a bit."

The old man even chuckled with pleasure. " I'll do that," he said. " I'll write to Pendlehead straightaway and tell him. It may send him up on the rebound into the arms of that extremely pretty nurse he's got with him down there."

" That's right! " Obviously the only thing that worried the old man was the future heir, I felt pretty sure he wouldn't have much more anxiety on that score.

239

" Very many thanks. You're a man of common sense, if I may venture to say so Mr.—er—Doctor——"

" Mister will do," I murmured as I rang off.

" So you see," I turned towards the Baron, " just how foolish the police are going to find your ' confession.' "

It was then that my room began to fill up. People came into it one by one as they do at the finale of a musical comedy, crowding in and standing self-consciously, waiting for the final applause. What they actually did was to watch, with growing astonishment, the playing-out of the final scene.

The next arrival was Clement Williams himself; I introduced him to the battered Baron with some pleasure. " We were just talking about you," I said. " Do you remember, Baron? Before the telephone rang."

" I remember," the Baron said, with an ominous rolling of the R's. I felt he was looking Williams up and down in his " herrenfolk " manner; he made no attempt to take his departure.

Miss Emms had returned from her mysterious mission and had met Williams outside the house. It seems that Williams made a habit of standing outside the house, from time to time, for reasons best known to himself. Possibly he imagined that by doing so he was keeping a grip on the situation, I don't know. Williams knew Miss Emms well by sight and he had not been able to resist asking her where Annabel was and how things were. Miss Emms asked him who he was and he had told her that he was hoping to marry Mrs. Rangward just as soon as he was able. Miss Emms on her side had been unable to resist telling him in return that she was afraid it would not be long before Mrs. Rangward was arrested for murder. How she must have enjoyed it!

Miss Emms thinks that she is suffering over all this, but she isn't. She's enjoying every minute of it and when she is old and infirm she will look back with *nostalgic* pleasure on the only thing that ever happened to her.

Her manner, I noticed, had suddenly become unbearable. I said, very sharply: " Miss Emms, what is the matter? "

She had found something which she called in her absurd who-done-it language " a vital clue." She had taken it to the police and it was only a matter of time, she said, before an arrest was made.

" In that case," I said, " you had better tell us what ' vital clue ' you have found."

" Very well," she said tautly, " I will. You remember, one day last week, you were looking in the bathroom cupboard for something? "

" I do."

" A small flattish oblong tin, about an inch wide and an inch and a half long, you said it was. And it contained, you said, Tiddly Push's spare worm pill. Isn't it rather a funny thing that a tin which should contain a pill which you are going to give the dog should have a label on the lid with *Poison, not to be taken* written in Latin on it? "

" I didn't know you understood Latin, Miss Emms," I croaked.

" I don't, but I was a V.A.D. in the First World War and I certainly know the meaning of those three words." There was a short silence. " I found the empty, *empty* tin under the chest-of-drawers on our landing, just outside, this evening."

" And so? "

" Thrown there by the murderer after *they* had taken the capsule of cyanide out of it."

" Very clever, Miss Emms. Your powers of deduction are highly developed, and I liked your ambiguous pronoun. By they, of course, you mean Mrs. Rangward."

Silence.

" But you have always thought her so *nice*, Miss Emms! " I was, however, thinking rapidly.

The making-up of my mind seemed, to me, incredibly noisy; I was deafened by it, but I have no doubt the silence in the room was uninterrupted. I walked over to the telephone and dialled Whi 1212 (I am quite a skilful dialler by touch) and, whilst I held the receiver to my ear, waiting for an answer, I said: " I shall have to make a clean breast of it."

I said to Miss Emms: " You'd better get Edna to come up and make us all tea whilst we are waiting for the C.I.D."

Miss Emms did not like that, she said she was perfectly capable of making tea and I said that, as Edna would be taking over shortly, she might as well get used to her new surroundings. Miss Emms did not like that either. But, in any case, I wanted Edna and Rudie to be present at the final reckoning. I wanted everyone in the house to be there so that they would know the facts first hand and not from hearsay.

With a bad grace Miss Emms rang down on the house telephone for Rudie and Edna. Edna, they say, has a hard platinum blonde appearance, but for all that she is a good creature; she makes a fine mate for Rudie and so long as she keeps her old lag Bert reasonably in the background,

Rudie will be her devoted slave for life. I shall be glad to be rid of Miss Emms and the feeling she gives me that I should be deeply grateful to her for something or other.

Edna made and served the tea in an awkward silence, I seemed to be the only one who was at ease. The Baron did not have tea but his glass of whisky was recharged. Presently more people arrived. " Who is here? " I asked. The inspector, the sergeant, and another inspector from Marylebone. " I have something to tell you all," I said. "I should like Mrs. Rangward and Eddy here too, please."

When Annabel arrived, I could feel she had been through it. I led her to my own chair and I stood with my back to the fire. I believe Clement Williams came across the room and stood by Annabel. Putting out my hand, I felt for Tiddly Push, he was sitting along the arm of my chair.

" At present," I explained, " I don't want to see the police alone. We're all in this together and I think it only fair that I should tell everybody what I have to say about the cyanide capsule that, I believe, killed Mr. Rangward."

In the pause that followed I heard Miss Emms frantically whispering: " What's he going to say? What is he going to say next? " And then she ran forward and put her hands on mine. " Don't say anything," she hissed. " Wait! Promise you'll wait! " I was too astonished to do anything but pause. " Inspector, he's going to take the blame. You must tell him. . . . Please . . . now." Then she came back to me and I felt her hands pressing mine like the cold claws of a bird. " You can't do it, I won't let you! Now, Inspector, please . . ." And, whilst the inspector spoke, Miss Emms kept a tight grip of my hands.

" It seems, Mr. Totterdell, that your housekeeper has

243

found the small metal pill box which she believes contained the capsule, under the chest-of-drawers on your landing. It was empty. The remains of the glass capsule, you will remember, were found ground almost to powder on the carpet of the dining-room, beside the corpse. Have you any knowledge how the capsule got there and how the tin got where it was found? "

I was too surprised to reply at once. I was sorting out my thoughts.

So Miss Emms was not taken in by my search last week for the box containing Tiddly Push's worm pill. And for the last few hours she had believed that I poisoned Rangward; full of righteous indignation she took her find to the police but when she thought I was on the verge of confessing she tried to stop me. Was it the memory of my dear wife that came suddenly between Miss Emms and this sense of righteousness?

" Mr. Totterdell, is this the tin which contained the capsule? "

" I cannot see, Inspector."

" Miss Emms here," the inspector said approvingly, " took the precaution of picking up the tin in a silk handkerchief in which she very wisely brought it to us. Our fingerprint expert is not on duty at this time of night and to-morrow we intend to examine the tin thoroughly. In the meantime it has had a quick preliminary examination. As it happens, this tin is an excellent medium for fingerprints but it has been so much fingered as almost to seem sticky. There are certain curious marks other than those of fingers on the metal. We have, however, found, superimposed upon all the old marks, one almost complete print."

Miss Emms let go of my hands. The inspector was

evidently arranging the handkerchief and the tin on the wine-table beside my chair. He took my hand. " Now, Mr. Totterdell, please, I have covered the tin with the handkerchief, could you gently feel its outline and tell me if that is the receptacle in which the capsule has been kept? "

Yes, it was. I said: " And the capsule itself was wrapped in a tiny silk-stranded container over cotton-wool. There was also a scrap of paper with a verse from the Psalms written on it. It was written in a contempla-tive moment by a German patient of mine who had intended using it over a long period, I took the capsule away from him and to amuse myself in an idle moment I translated the verse into English. Is that scrap of paper inside? "

" It is empty."

" Eddy," I called, " was there a fire in the Rangwards' living-room on the night Mr. Rangward died? "

" Yes, sir. A log and coal fire, sir."

"Then the silk cover and the scrap of paper were thrown into the fire and burnt."

" Mr. Totterdell," the inspector said sternly, " did you give the capsule to Mr. Rangward? "

" No, Inspector."

" Did you give the capsule to Mrs. Rangward? "

" No."

" Then how . . . here, you little rascal . . here . . . catch him somebody! "

I heard Miss Emms exclaim: " Well, I never! " Suddenly everybody was vociferous, there was quite a clamour. I knew what was going on; Tiddly Push would have been eyeing his plaything where it lay on the silk handkerchief on the table a foot or so away from him.

At a moment when the inspector's attention was averted, he grabbed it and jumped down from the arm of my chair. He was showing us, bless him, how it had all happened. In a moment everybody but myself and Annabel had followed him out on to the landing.

I bent over her, feeling her hands. " It's going to be all right," I whispered.

Everyone was crowding back into my room. The inspector said: " Miss Emms declares your dog has been using the little tin as a plaything for some days. She says he was carrying it about in his mouth as he often carries a ping-pong ball and she did not take the trouble to look carefully to see what, exactly, he had got hold of."

" Then you are not in any doubt, Inspector, that my dog gave the poison to Mr. Rangward? "

" I wouldn't put it quite like that. He might have dropped it in Mr. Rangward's path. But why on earth should Mr. Rangward take the capsule out and, later on, dose himself with it? "

" I think I can explain that to your complete satisfaction, Inspector. Within an hour or so of his return from Portugal Mr. Rangward came upstairs for the express purpose of getting some new form of sleep-inducing drug out of me. It was a failing of his, Inspector; he could not sleep and he was ready to try anything and everything under the sun to give him some sort of respite from his insomnia. All of us present can endorse that. Have you ever suffered from insomnia? No? Well, it can become an obsession. His own doctor was losing interest in the subject and he found that I, having little else to do, was willing to discuss his complaint with him almost tirelessly."

" Yes," the inspector agreed, " we have heard as much

246

from Dr. Trench himself. He thought Mr. Rangward fussed too much about himself."

" I believe he went so far as to call him a ' bally valetudinarian!' But this particular evening I was not prepared to play ball. I was not inclined to hand over any samples of sleeping-tablets and I said so a trifle sharply. Mr. Rangward lost his temper and called me ' a vicious, two-faced, treacherous old devil.' Rather an overstatement, perhaps, but he was overwrought, he had hardly slept at all for the past week, I believe. As he left my room I heard him on the landing snap: ' Get out of the light ' to Tiddly Push. I have no doubt whatever that he gave Tiddly Push a minor kick and that my dog dropped what he was carrying in his mouth at Rangward's feet. Rangward could never resist a pill box, he opened it and took out the capsule. ' *He giveth his beloved sleep.*' He had no doubt at all that I had been keeping it for him, ready to give him on his return, and after our few words, I had withheld it. And as for the Latin; he was a self-made man, Inspector, and one who had never made a study of the humanities. He had no knowledge at all of Latin. *Toxicum, non sumendum* would be Greek to him."

" So Mr. Rangward took the capsule away with him and, after dinner, he took it believing it to be a sleeping draught? "

" Exactly. *Death by misadventure*, I'm afraid."

I could almost hear Rudie and Eddy summing up: " Just one of those things."

I said: " It is very sad indeed but these things can, and do, happen, taking into account the quirks in people's natures, the tricks of action or behaviour. If you find an otherwise perfectly normal boy hanged, his parents may tell you that he had a habit of ' tying himself up *for fun.*'

Well, it's the same sort of thing with Rangward, he took pills *for fun*. Inexplicable, but there you are. I blame myself for retaining the capsule for all these years and for not keeping control over it when it turned up."

There was a long pause, I think the inspector looked round at us all, possibly with a grim smile on his lips.

"It is a fanciful reconstruction, Mr. Totterdell, but stranger accidents have happened. I should be inclined to investigate the matter a good deal further were it not for two pieces of evidence corroborating your theory. Two pieces of pretty conclusive evidence, the only kind, I may say, that goes down in a coroner's court, or any other court, for that matter."

"And they are?"

"Fingerprints, my dear sir. You can't go wrong there. The most complete fingerprint is on the inside of the lid."

"Yes?"

"It is that of Mr. Rangward. The rest are very blurred and, as I say, the outside of the whole object is sticky, but as far as we can tell from the preliminary examination there is no doubt about its being the dead man's imprint. If we may, we shall take the prints of everybody in the house, as a check-up. Mrs. Rangward has allowed us to take her prints and, as far as we can tell from the hasty examination, they do not appear on the tin."

"How could they? She never touched it. You will find my marks and Rudie Ormer's."

"And the dog's teeth marks. That is my second piece of conclusive evidence," the inspector added, with some satisfaction. "But fingerprints always have the last word."

Miss Emms put in: "Would you believe it, that dog was keeping the tin under the chest-of-drawers on the

248

landing when he wasn't playing with it. Otherwise I'd have found it when I cleaned the room."

"Ah, that," I said, "is the dog in him, for, after all, he has some dog-like qualities for all he is the beloved of Buddha. Dogs always like to creep off in a cloak-and-dagger manner, to hide their bones from ravenous human beings. Tiddly Push, a town-dweller, had no favourite bush under which to bury his bone, he did the next best thing, he hid it under the chest-of-drawers, bringing it out when he felt like having a frolic with it."

I could feel the lessening tension, the atmosphere seemed almost gay. "Would you like a drink, Inspector?"

"Not on duty, thank you, sir. I must get back to my office and get all this properly worked out with my staff. Dear me, sir, I'm glad we've had this little show-down. It has saved the Force a lot of manpower and trouble and the country quite a bit of money."

Much more, I thought, than he imagined.

"It's a great relief to us, I can tell you, when what looks like a first-degree murder turns out to be a misadventure."

He was preparing to go out but he paused, I could feel his piercing look. "There isn't much you miss, is there?"

Was there a slight edge to his question?

"But I assure you, I'm quite blind, Inspector." It cost me something, but I knew it had to be done. I swept off my glasses and looked straight at where I guessed his face to be. "You see, I wear these black spectacles because I can't stand the sight of myself with two glass eyes!"

THE END